About the author

Frank Wingate lived in Hong Kong from 1978 to 2000. He witnessed the vast economic and social changes that engulfed China and metamorphosed the territory, and experienced the final handover to Chinese sovereignty. Arriving as a teacher, he became a freelance journalist, before founding his own communications business. After returning to the UK he continued in the commercial sector, while finding time to write books. He now lives in Kingston upon Thames, UK, and teaches economics part-time. Retaining a strong affection for Hong Kong, he hopes it can emerge safely from the profound challenges it faces.

IN THE HARSH LIGHT OF THE MORNING

Frank Wingate

IN THE HARSH LIGHT OF THE MORNING

Vanguard Press

VANGUARD PAPERBACK

© Copyright 2021
Frank Wingate

A CIP catalogue record for this title is
available from the British Library.

ISBN 978 1 784659 48 6

*Vanguard Press is an imprint of
Pegasus Elliot MacKenzie Publishers Ltd.*
www.pegasuspublishers.com

First Published in 2021

**Vanguard Press
Sheraton House Castle Park
Cambridge England**

Printed & Bound in Great Britain

Dedication

For my brother and sisters: Geoff, Sue and Sally.

Chapter One
Choices

His time was running out. The clock was ticking and his watch showed a quarter to five. Christ, he thought. Typical of that bastard to send this back late in the day. He stared hard again at the report on his computer screen, screwing his eyes as though that helped him find the words he needed to amend the text. After typing laboriously for a few minutes, he leaned back in his office chair, hands behind his head, expressing his frustration with loud sighs.

"You all right, Jack?" came a sympathetic voice from behind the anonymous office divider. "Sounds like you're having a heart attack." It was Nancy, his efficient and protective secretary, without whom he would never have lasted so long in this dystopian organisation.

"Yeah, yeah, I'm OK," he shouted back. "Just trying to finish off this stuff for the boss. I reckon the ol' monster sends it down late deliberately, just to torture me a little more on a Friday night." Nancy stood up and leaned over the divide and, facing him, put a finger to her lips in a sign of caution.

"I know," he said. "Anyway, you head off, I haven't anything else for you. I've just got a deadline on this and then I'm away too."

"OK!" she replied happily, "I will then. By the way, don't forget you've got the executive meeting on Monday at nine thirty."

The message wasn't lost on him. He had struggled in late a few times recently, usually with a hangover, and Nancy had always managed to cover for him with false excuses involving imaginary breakfast meetings and traffic jams. He appreciated her loyalty and protective instincts but was well aware of their limits.

"Me and Mal and the kids are away to the islands for the weekend. What are you up to?" she continued.

His heart sank a little as if someone was leaning their fist heavily against his chest. He envied her bright, contented manner so much that he intensely disliked it sometimes. He envied her established family life, yet disdained it at the same time. And, above all, he really didn't have anything planned for the weekend.

"Oh, I expect I'll go and get miserably drunk somewhere or lock myself in my flat and read some depressing Russian novel," he said, with a degree of seriousness.

"You poor old thing," Nancy said mockingly. "'Bout time you found yourself a good woman. You're still half decent to look at."

"Well, thanks for that!" he replied. "Easier said than done, I haven't failed in that through lack of trying."

As she walked briskly away down the office, he watched her, assessing her thin legs and hips, while thinking that she was an attractive woman, who nevertheless stirred little sexual interest in him. After she disappeared into the lift lobby, he pulled himself from his reverie, yanked his chair forward, screwed up his eyes again and tapped resentfully at the keyboard.

Just after five, his concentration was broken again by the appearance of Hal, his American colleague, who shattered the office silence with his booming baritone.

"Hiya, buddy, what's up? How come you're hanging around? Time for a beer, ain't it? Coming up the club?"

"Yeah, maybe... probably. Just gotta sort out this crap for the director and I'll follow on."

"Being ornery again, is he?"

"The usual, you know, demanding redrafts up to the last minute, but never telling me what he wants."

"Does he ever know what he wants?" laughed Hal. "We'll shoot the shit later, anyway, don't bust your balls, buddy. See ya."

I wish I had his casual self-confidence, thought Jack, inwardly laughing at Hal's breeziness. He always liked his phrase "Shoot the shit". Hal seemed to drift through his demanding job in the ministry as he sailed through life with unreasonable optimism and superficial bonhomie, which charmed even the hard-bitten director and serious-minded bureaucrats who worked alongside both of them. He had a buxom, garrulous American wife and four indulged, loud children. But none of this fazed the amiable Texan, who took it all in his stride.

Jack enjoyed him even though he considered him lightweight. He was generous and an easy conversationalist. Some of his tales of his war reporting experiences became tedious through repetition, but he sympathised with Jack's challenges at work and was a useful ally in the unavoidable office politics that complicated an already pressurised role.

It was a disappointment, this job. He had joined the Ministry with great enthusiasm and hope. After a series of unsatisfying roles in journalism and advertising, he had finally found a research position in which he could apply his economic knowledge and writing skills. But he was unfamiliar with the corporate hierarchies and had somehow alienated the director, for whom he had to provide briefings and speeches. The responsibility often made his life miserable.

He regarded himself as collegiate and supportive, but the director had rebuffed any attempt at dialogue beyond rasping out orders and work requests, which were hard to interpret. At first, he had tried to reason, asking for briefing discussions to help shape assignments, but the curt response had been that he was being paid to produce the work and not to waste the director's time.

The result was an endless series of drafts and re-writes, which never seemed to please the humourless man upstairs. Jack had come to dislike him acutely and the job itself became a trial. But there was no way to improve the situation. He found every meeting with the director an unpleasant ordeal, and the worst thing was that he knew he feared him — the man's sarcastic tongue and razor-sharp intellect gave no room for dissent or discussion, and he used the power of his executive status with blunt force. The awareness of his own vulnerability made Jack resentful and angry. He felt trapped in the role. He began to hate it. But he needed the money and the status gave him permanence in the city. So, he worked less effectively in a futile gesture of resistance. This only intensified his dissatisfaction, for he was proud of his education and skills, and knew he was, once again, not employing them fully. Constant criticism also made him begin to doubt his own abilities, despite the supportive words of colleagues like Hal.

He tapped on, correcting the minutiae of statistics and phrasing, trying to anticipate the director's idiosyncrasies.

A year had passed since he joined the Ministry. It had seemed a positive step forward in what had been an erratic and sometimes directionless career path. Somehow, he never quite achieved what he wanted, partly through bad luck and partly through his own lack of concentrated effort. Not that he was lazy, but intelligent enough to get by with just sufficient effort and too fond of enjoyment. Throughout his twenties this was comfortably justified as making the most of his youthful independence and putting "life" before work. He was a dreamer of the kind that exaggerates his own creative abilities and uses the self-delusion that he was destined for greater things as a smokescreen for half-hearted application to the daily disciplines of routine work.

He had thrived at university — a good provincial one in the UK. Relishing the late night, meandering academic and political student debate, he was popular and well-regarded. He dabbled — but only dabbled — in active student politics, finding the discussion more palatable than the practice.

But the distractions had been too many and the late nights too often occupied with frivolous socialising in cosy bars rather than focused study at a lamplit desk, with the inevitable result that he achieved a modest degree, when he should have gained a first-class result. This he knew. He was confident in his own ability.

There followed a number of jobs, none of which satisfied his intellectual or social pretensions. He was not particularly unhappy, working dutifully if unenthusiastically and generally engaging well with colleagues. He kept the faith that he was meant for greater achievements and this comforted him.

Writing for a local newspaper taught him a number of valuable skills — such as how to report accurately, how to file copy, how to type and edit text, and how to bluff your way into people's confidence so that you could obtain a killer quote that would illuminate your incisive article. The problem was the material. With the great affairs of state, and the turbulent currents of world diplomacy beckoning for his insightful analysis, he found himself reporting on a punch-up outside a local pub, or dispute involving pensioners and the building of a greenhouse. Well, good training, yes, he had told himself, but not motivating and certainly not lucrative. Living on the pitiful salary the local rag paid its junior reporters, he quickly came to appreciate the social limitations of poverty and the embarrassment of not being able to match your peers in status and activity. This made him more materialistic and ambitious for financial security. It was not the best of times to be working for a local newspaper, for the digital age had dawned, and advertising support was seeping away. Though many local papers still played a key role for democracy, keeping an eye on local politicians and digging up dirt when required, they were slowly withering, like plants deprived of moisture. Inevitably, Jack was made redundant just as he completed his training.

With a shrug of his shoulders, he looked forward and considered two options. One was to head straight for London. The big smoke. Take a punt on finding a decent job there, maybe on a national, or a think tank. Lots going on there. Plenty of opportunity. It was a matter of being dynamic and grabbing life by the balls. Or, take a new route. Forget journalism. It was a dying craft anyway. He took the easier option, deciding that staying where he lived offered the comfortable choice and familiar network of friends. He looked at business, where rewards were greater, and calculated that his economics degree would surely be valued there. It was. Within a couple of months, he had secured a position in a major company, working in marketing. Wearing a smart suit, shirt and tie for the first time in his adult life, he swaggered into the company offices on day one, confident that he would soon prove himself a star in this, after all, rather mundane role, which wouldn't test his intelligence too greatly.

At first, it was enjoyable — undemanding of critical thought, but requiring nervous energy, to deal with the long hours and deadlines. He found it refreshing and fun, and he did earn a better salary. Colleagues proved to be sociable and accepted him quickly into their circles. But within a year, the novelty had begun to wear off and he started to resent the increasing demands of management for targets and monthly results, which he considered unrealistic. Devising marketing strategies to sell canned food brands and frozen products soon became mechanical, while his relationship with his managers became increasingly fractious.

When he spoke his mind at the regular departmental meetings, criticising broader company policy on economic grounds, colleagues and superiors alike looked at him in dismay, because challenges to company policy were heretical, and, indeed pointless. Thought of as eccentric, and nicknamed "the professor" by his workmates, he was nevertheless regarded with mounting suspicion by the hierarchy. Matters came to a head when he disagreed with a formal appraisal and the argument turned into a shouting match with the manager concerned. Within a few weeks he was made redundant. There were no legal grounds for the decision, but he knew it would be too costly in time and money to mount any legal battle. Consequently, he slunk off, sullen and feeling underappreciated, bearing a resentment against the corporation. At least they gave him some redundancy money and a reference, to keep him quiet.

A year then passed in a kind of limbo. Determined to write, he started a novel, living off the redundancy money, driving taxis, and taking part-time labouring jobs. In many ways, it was a satisfying existence, demanding little responsibility, apart from increasing family concerns relating to his parents, and meeting his romantic idea of the bohemian artist, heroically sacrificing material encumbrances for the sake of his art.

However, the novel stalled at chapter three, several drafts having been torn up and rewritten. He had enough money to live on but saved nothing. Further drafts petered out along with his creative self-confidence. As the redundancy money began to run out, he had to take a hard look at his prospects, his modest bachelor flat, his lack of a steady girlfriend and his age, now heading towards thirty. In response, and beginning to feel slightly desperate, he began to search for vacancies in London, firing off applications for many types of jobs in marketing, media and economic fields.

Finally, his luck changed and a leading advertising agency, based in the West End, offered him an interview. Summoning his utmost charm, and carefully researching the company and its clients, he performed well, and was taken on. With minimal effort — he owned few possessions anyway — he moved to London.

Jack's mobile rang and he saw, with some discomfort, it was his younger brother, Doug. He noticed it was already after five thirty. With a gasp of exasperation, he answered the call.

"Yeah, Doug, hi, everything OK? Can't talk long. In the middle of a mini-crisis."

"Nothing new there then," said Doug. "Listen, just wanted to know if you're coming tonight. You said you would. We need all the bodies we can muster, you know."

"Yeah, I know, I know. I want to come, but a bit stuck in the office here for a while," he exaggerated, already building up the excuse he knew he would very likely use to avoid joining his brother's political group meeting.

"Well, you said you would. Anyway, we're on at seven. It's important and we need some balanced argument. The nutters here want to whip up the students and they're always plotting something daft. Try to make it, eh? And don't forget to call Mum tomorrow, it's her birthday!"

"I know. And I'll do my best to make the meeting," Jack said, trying to overcome his reluctance at the idea of going. "Depends on this damned report I'm stuck on," he added, summoning the foundations of the excuse.

"Must go, Doug, got a ton to do, hope to see you later. Take care and don't do anything stupid." He signed off with relief but concerned that Doug was becoming embroiled in the gathering political strife affecting the city. There was a major student demonstration building up at the university and rumours of a heavy police presence in the area.

He liked and admired his younger brother, who was gifted intellectually, politically committed and full of energy. But he was also wary of Doug's fervent views and suspicious of his self-righteousness. His self-belief wearied Jack. In London, he had seen quite a lot of Doug, who was at university there, and even shared some political activity together, but he had always stayed clear of Doug's more hard-line friends, whom he found humourless and one-dimensional.

Instead, he had settled into his new job, with renewed determination to succeed, and was soon enjoying the social attractions of London. Above all, he had met Prudence, who worked for a client company.

Tall, elegant and slim, with natural blonde hair, she was, in Jack's eyes, too good to be true. Doug always said she was the trophy wife that Jack was supposed to meet at the end of his successful career when he was discarding his first wife, but that he got it the wrong way round.

Oxford-educated and career-minded, Prudence was a reserved person, who blushed easily and seemed too naïve for the brash world of business promotion. She was much in demand from male admirers, but strangely insecure in her good looks and mistrustful of the motives of men showing an interest in her. Sexually lacking confidence, she gave the impression to some admirers that she was simply acting "cool" and affecting an air of aloofness, when all she wanted from them was a lack of pretention and directness.

For Pru, as she was known, Jack possessed the qualities that reassured her. He was kind and relaxed and amused her. His affected bohemian ambitions were interesting and charming, and he provided the comfort that she needed. When scrubbed up he was also good looking. Soon after meeting they were dating regularly and after two years had married, much to the delight of Jack's parents, who thought her very classy, but not to Pru's parents, who considered Jack pleasant enough, but lacking the kind of social ambition they thought appropriate for their daughter's future happiness.

They were content for the first year, flourishing in their respective careers, and enjoying a circle of friends and London's cultural scene — theatre and cinema in particular. They shared the same general interests and values, but not the particulars. Politically, she inherited her parents' soft conservatism and was patronising about his soft socialism — yet the differences were rarely aired. Pru was idolised by Jack's parents, and yet he always suspected she tolerated rather than warmed to them, though she played the part well.

His parents were, for Jack, a source of constant worry. It was a blot on the couple's lives in London, for he was concerned for his mother's health and the deterioration of her relationship with his father, for which Doug too, suffered.

Surprisingly, for the newlyweds, their sex life quickly waned. Although they were affectionate and caring, and physically attracted, the act itself became mechanical, and for Pru, something of a duty rather than a pleasure. This perturbed Jack, for, although Pru never denied him intimacy, he sensed her discomfort and lack of authentic satisfaction and this undermined his own confidence.

It was then, with a sense of relief for him, that his company provided an escape route. His advertising agency was looking for someone to join their new Far East operation, which had been set up with a view to cashing in on the newly liberalising economies in the area. He jumped at the chance. Here was an opportunity to travel and work overseas, something which had always appealed to his romantic side. It also meant he could escape family concerns and get away from the creeping routine of corporate life in London. What's more, he thought the move could inject new energy into his marriage, which he felt was too easily slipping into banality. Pru wasn't so enthused. Quietly successful in her own career, she saw no reason to interrupt its development and was more inclined to think about having a family and moving out of central London to the suburbs.

Jack persisted, however, and finally persuaded her to agree. Perhaps a fresh start was good for them and there was no reason she couldn't have a child out there, she reasoned. Consequently, he accepted the role, they packed and left within a month, his excitement mounting and her trepidation growing.

Within a year of moving there, they had separated. Jack revelled in the bustling, freewheeling business environment of the city and the alcohol-fuelled social life that accompanied it. Pru, however, felt alienated and uncomfortable, although she landed a high-powered job in the financial sector and buried herself in work. They drifted apart quickly, spending less and less time with each other. He spent more time with male friends, while she longed for home. Eventually, she found solace with a colleague, who offered her greater financial security, a more sophisticated alternative to Jack, and, above all, the prospect of family and home. They split up, and Pru moved in with her new partner.

Initially devastated, Jack reasoned himself out of grief. The marriage was lacking passion and authenticity, he convinced himself and they weren't really suited. Pru was a good woman, but inhibited and conservative, he told himself. Perhaps he was better off on his own. Anyway, there was a colourful and exotic social life to be enjoyed for a bachelor here. Nevertheless, it continued to irritate him that Pru's new partner could provide her with the material and emotional status that he couldn't equal.

In exploiting his new freedom, Jack socialised more, drank more and, whilst getting some superficial joy from it, felt increasingly lonely. His work suffered, and he found it difficult to maintain any kind of relationship with new girlfriends. After two years' carousing, however, he met Marion, an easy-going Eurasian woman, who coaxed him back into some orderliness in his life. They moved in together, and he left the agency for the Ministry, taking up a post which afforded him a much better salary and conditions.

At ten minutes before six, Jack's desk phone rang, interrupting his concentration on the report with a start. It was Daisy, the director's secretary.

"Hello, Jack," she said with a note of sympathy. "Have you finished the director's report yet? He needs to have it and wants to leave in about fifteen minutes.

Oh! And he told me to remind you to include the Dutch trade figures."

Shit, thought Jack.

"Yeah, fine, nearly finished, Daisy," he said impatiently. "You'll have it shortly."

Replacing the receiver, he spun round in his office chair and plucked a file from the shelf behind him. Hastily leafing through it, he found the right page with the trade figures he needed and began typing again, breathing heavily with the exertion, his head pounding with annoyance.

Six months after setting up home together, Marion had suddenly announced she was leaving him. She had come to realise, she explained, that she still loved her former boyfriend, with whom she had stayed in contact. She was very sorry and loved Jack too, but this domestic life was not for her and she would be returning to London. Her former boyfriend was a successful entrepreneur and very wealthy. Jack had met him and thought him a conceited, crass kind of a wheeler-dealer. How, he wondered, could this slightly seedy character be more attractive to the lovely Marion, than him? In his disappointment he could only gain some succour from the thought that he was intellectually superior to his rival. It was small comfort. He was beginning to think he was a failure when it came to enjoying a lasting relationship.

At six o'clock, he keyed in the last few corrections to the report, saved the file and then sent it to Daisy. He called her to confirm she had received it, then slumped back into his chair, with a mixture of relief and exhaustion. He stared at the ceiling for a moment, thinking life had been unkind lately and that he deserved some luck.

His desk phone rang again. This was probably Daisy telling him the director had already spotted an error in the report. Reluctantly, he lifted the receiver.

"Well, you poor old sod, still in the office! Having to do some work for a change. I thought you civil servants knocked off at five," the cheerful voice teased.

It was Les, Jack's good friend and squash partner. Immediately recovering from his thoughts, Jack took up the banter.

"Well, better than ripping off the public like some lawyers I know," he replied.

"Look, mate," carried on Les. "We're getting together with some of the gang at eight in the Indonesian, you know, the one down the waterfront, and would like to see you. That is, if you're not committing suicide this weekend."

Les's unforgiving Aussie humour was always a boost, preventing him from feeling sorry for himself. He and his wife, Valerie, had supported Jack through his break-up with Pru, whom they had very much liked, and his disappointment with Marion, whom they had always warned him about.

"Oh, great! That sounds fun. I'd like that. Thanks, Les," Jack said.

"OK, see you later, mate!" Les finished and rang off.

He would probably join them. He had a strong rapport with Les and Val and appreciated their support and good humour. As for some of "the gang" he was less impressed, but they were generally agreeable and amusing. Recently, he had been the single one among them, who were either married or with a steady partner, and this emphasised his solitude, so he often chose his bachelor set to socialise with instead. At least with the guys he could drink and flirt and whore with abandon.

Collecting up his scattered papers and replacing his files, he tidied up his desk and locked his briefcase, which he tucked into his filing cabinet. He had so much wanted to excel at this job and was fighting to retain his belief and enthusiasm. He knew he needed to keep his self-discipline in working the long hours and staying organised. There was no way he would be beaten or driven off, and the fact he had just finished an assignment on a Friday night, and was now free of cares, strengthened his resolve.

Guiltily, he turned over the immediate options in his mind. Doug had invited him to the planning meeting and had also reminded him of phoning home. His mother, who relied on him for infrequent words in her time of illness and despondency, needed a call. I'll shoot home after a couple of beers with Hal, call home, then meet the gang for a civilised meal. I can always join

Doug's diehards later; they'll probably debate the matter half the night anyway, he reasoned.

Striding to the lift lobby along the spacious, now darkening office, he glanced out of the window at the myriad neon lights of the city. From this twenty-eighth floor vantage point, he enjoyed a wide vista across the heart of this tantalising metropolis, with its ethnic complexities and international ambition, its glistening sophistication vying for attention side by side with its brash materialism and seedy, alluring night life. Captivated by its diversity and multi-faceted morality, he had plunged into society here, much to the dismay of his wife, who lost him to his search for hedonism and existentialist adventure.

As the lift doors opened, he received a jolt. Looking at him sternly was no other than the director himself, whom he had little option but to join. The thin-faced man peered at him, his blue eyes piercing Jack like lasers.

"I hope the report is error free for a change," said his boss. "Did you get the Dutch figures in? You know, you could be quite good if you got rid of these minor smudges in your work."

That was perhaps the closest he had ever heard the director come to praise him, and he felt his face flush, partly from embarrassment but partly from anger that he welcomed this patronising approval.

"Oh yes, all in there, Director, don't worry. Good luck with the presentation," he responded, his mouth dry with anxiety and deeply resenting his deference.

Finally, the lift hit ground floor, and as soon as the doors opened, the director strode off without so much as a farewell. Hope you're better at presenting than small talk, thought Jack.

He made his way to the main doors of the modern office block, wishing the security guards good night and stepped out into the darkness.

A wall of hot, humid air engulfed him, and its sweet sickly odours excited him, like the cheap perfume of a seductive hooker.

Chapter Two
Leaving

He woke up in discomfort, his head thick with the alcohol of the night before and his throat dry. His father was shaking him gently by the shoulder.

"Come on, lazy bones," he said. "Time you were up and look here, we've got a letter from the university. Aren't you going to open it?"

Jack propped himself up on one elbow and rubbed his eyes with the back of his hand. He cleared his throat, took the letter and tore it open. While his excited father sat on the edge of the bed, he read it slowly to himself, then announced in a flat tone. "I'm in, got the place for economics."

"Well, don't sound so pleased with yourself! Well done, son! Real proud of you. Now that's two of you off to university. Your grandad and grandma would have been so chuffed."

Bill Wilson leapt up off the bed, snatched the letter back from his bleary-eyed son and rushed out of the small bedroom.

"Lizzie!" he shouted to his wife as he ran outside to the landing and downstairs, "Lizzie, he's done it, he's got in! Not so daft as he looks," he chuckled.

Turning over and closing his eyes again, Jack pulled the bedcovers up over his head. He was pleased with the news. It was hard to get a place there, after all, and he hadn't worked that hard. But at the same time, he felt a rush of anxiety. This was a real commitment now. Did he really want to go to university? All that work and stress, clever classmates and essay writing. A new environment, greater challenges and expectations. Wasn't he just being coaxed along this path by teachers and family and peers? Life at home, with its cotton-wool comforts and easy habits, familiarity and sauna-level central heating, seemed very tempting right now.

He pulled the sheets tighter and imagined Eileen, the girl he fancied, who had been at the party the night before. He'd danced with her, kissed and hugged her and nearly persuaded her to let him in to her place as they said goodnight. Although he had admired her for a long time, he had never been so intimate. Now he had her number and determined to call her. Why couldn't life just settle at home and parties and going out with Eileen? But then he pulled himself together. No, no, this really was all too suffocating. He liked his family and home and had enjoyed school, but he had outgrown all this. He had matured intellectually, hadn't he? Time to move on, to break out from this suburban complacency and experience the world. Yes, and to help change it. His youthful swagger began to reassert itself.

"Come on, Jack," his father shouted up the stairs. "Get a move on, we want to celebrate!"

"Oh God," said Jack softly. He hauled himself up into a sitting position and swung his legs out of bed, feeling distinctly nauseous.

He looked around at the small bedroom where he had spent his teenage years. Its cheap wooden furniture, scratched desk, wardrobe and shelving, put up by his father. The posters of football teams, rock stars and revolutionary leaders. Two model plastic planes still dangled from threads in the corner. A Hurricane and a Messerschmitt 109 — he knew them well.

"Yeah," he spoke to himself again. "Time to get going."

This room, Jack's retreat, was part of a cramped three-bedroom semi-detached home, which was the pride of Bill Wilson. Nestling in an uninspiring, but safe and relatively traffic-free side road, in an undistinguished outer suburb of London, it was one of a row of fifty mock Tudor homes built in the 1930s. With their repetitious artificial wooden beams — in fact, planks tacked on to the facades — and their mock leaded bay windows, they were slightly comical, and typified lower middle-class pretention. At least, that's how Jack and, certainly, his younger brother, Doug, saw it. Rumour had it, they mischievously reminded their father, that the house five doors up had actually collapsed ten years after construction, owing to shoddy work, and had to be rebuilt.

None of this teenage superciliousness left a mark on Bill. For him, this house was the culmination of his life's work and stood for the status and recognition he had striven for. As a home it lacked nothing. Centrally heated and equipped with modern working kitchen gadgets, it boasted a sizeable colour TV, a cheap but impressive music system, which played LPs and tapes, and a large oak dining table that barely left room for the six large oak dinner chairs which surrounded it. At the front, a driveway for the car had been laid, and, in the back the thirty-yard-long narrow garden had enough space for a lawn, which Bill mowed regularly in the summer, and even a small vegetable patch which he tended skilfully, producing potatoes, carrots and lettuce.

For a boy who had a humble start in life and who had left school at fifteen, Bill sometimes mused with satisfaction that he had done all right. He had clawed free of poverty, built a professional career, was buying his own home — nearly paid for — and established a fine family. And now his second boy, following the eldest, Matthew, was also going to university. He felt pleased that his investment in time and money — and love — was bearing fruit.

"Ah, here he is, our great scholar," said Bill ironically, greeting Jack as he shuffled into the kitchen. "What a sight for sore eyes!"

His thick dark hair tumbling over his ears and still unshaven, Jack was dressed in a shapeless grey T-shirt and long denim shorts. He rubbed his eyes with his knuckles and yawned. Although Bill had always tried to inspire some military-style self-discipline into his sons' appearances, he had rarely been successful, but on this morning was in no mood to spoil the atmosphere.

"Come on, son, drink this and let's say congratulations on your good news and future success," chortled Bill, as he handed Jack a glass of cheap sparkling wine to complement the ones he and Elizabeth held.

"Dad! It's eleven in the morning and I've got a hangover," responded Jack pathetically, feeling slightly disgusted at the thought of any alcohol.

"Nonsense, lad, it's a special moment. Don't be a wimp. Any case, hair of the dog's good for you." With that, Bill said: "Cheers" and swallowed his glass in one draught. Jack's mother took a small sip from hers, after saying softly, "Well done, Jack."

The nineteen-year-old took a deep breath, pursed his lips, exhaled noisily, closed his eyes and downed the offering in a single movement. After a momentary gagging feeling, he felt the warming effect of the wine in his stomach and the spreading comfort as the alcohol took effect.

"That's the spirit!" exclaimed his father happily.

Some minutes later, as the three of them sat down at the breakfast table in the kitchen to eat, Jack experienced another wave of doubt about his ordained future.

"I hope I'm making the right decision doing economics," he mumbled. "There's a lot of maths in it."

"Oh, come on, don't start that nonsense again, we've been over this a hundred times," said Bill, irritated.

"It's common sense to do something useful these days," he continued. "At least with economics, you can go into business, or politics or accountancy, or something worthwhile — a proper profession — and earn a decent living. What on earth were you planning to do with English Literature, for God's sake? Be a great novelist, I suppose."

"Well, who knows," replied Jack, rising to the bait. "Money isn't everything, you know. Anyway, I certainly don't want to be an accountant. You are and you hate it."

The truth of this struck home, touching a raw nerve with Bill.

"That's not the point," he spluttered. "Of course money's not everything, but you need a decent home one day. You can't live on arty-farty ideals. They don't put bread on the table. You need to get a decent job and you stick at it."

"I've also got to get the grades," murmured Jack, feeling sorry for himself at the thought of the required effort.

"Well, you just make sure, sonny Jim, that you do get the grades, because you've a good opportunity here for a sound start in life and you don't want to throw it away because you're too lazy. Anyhow, your mother and me have put too much time and money into your education and we don't want that wasted," Bill shot back.

"Oh, that's nice, so I'm a financial investment then!" teased Jack, but with a smirk on his face as he knew he was winding up his father.

"Come on, you two, stop it now," interrupted Elizabeth. "Let's not spoil the day."

The two men were repeating a well-worn disagreement. Jack had originally wanted to study literature, partly because he found it easier, and partly because he thought about journalism or teaching as a career. And he did harbour private ambitions to be a writer, though he had no firm idea how this might come about. For his father, this was all too vague, and he had pushed Jack to apply for business studies or law. They had argued frequently, without rancour — for Jack avoided confrontation — over this issue. In the end Jack had compromised, particularly after Bill had threatened to withhold any funding support for university, but the settlement left him uncomfortable. A similar disagreement had clouded the departure of Jack's older brother, Matthew, who had left for university three years before. That had led to a serious breach in relations with his father, and these days they heard little from him, and he rarely appeared at home.

Although at times he imposed his will on his boys and his wife, Bill Wilson only did so because he was proud of his family and wanted the best for them. As a father he was kind and responsible, if not demonstrably affectionate. Never had he raised a hand to them, even when they frustrated him, and his voice only occasionally rose in anger.

Born into a large family in the East End of London, at the beginning of the war, he'd endured poverty in the early years, though in a supportive family. After his father was killed in the last year of hostilities, his mother struggled along with the help of Bill's older brothers. She too, overworked and careworn, had passed away the year Bill left school at fifteen. He went to live with an older brother and worked in a series of labouring and factory jobs.

At twenty, he joined the army — a decision, he always maintained — turned him into a man. The life suited him. He enjoyed the certainties of the service and found he compared favourably with his fellow conscripts. You could dispense with moral questions or life choices as a soldier, and instead feel a pride in defending your country and your mates. There was loyalty, comradeship, orderliness, self-respect, and occasional adrenalin-pumping danger. Even the boredom, of which there was plenty, was guiltless.

Working his way up, and proving his worth, Bill made it to sergeant. Serving in the Middle East and Ireland, he experienced combat and acquitted himself bravely. Well respected by his men and senior officers, he relished the clarity that hierarchy brought to existence. Life was simpler, purer and nobler. You accepted orders, even from the most chinless young wonder from Sandhurst, and implemented them to your best ability. And your men followed you. If not, there were consequences and procedures.

Everyone knew the ropes.

As he approached thirty, he made his plans to leave. He had already met and married Elizabeth and set about building a new career by training in accountancy. He had a good head for figures and a dogged perseverance that served him well, so by the time he packed up his uniform he was ready for the outside world. He eventually finished up at a local metal engineering company, where he had served the previous twelve years. It wasn't a job he enjoyed but tolerated, for the sake of the salary and respectability. As for the directors and senior managers of the company, he looked upon them with some disdain, while treating them with gruff courtesy. For their part they appreciated the precision and dependability that Bill brought to the financial role. Sometimes his blunt honesty with the accounts irked certain individuals, who would have preferred more flexible interpretations of the figures when it suited their objectives. However, they also recognised that Bill Wilson could keep a confidentiality and, furthermore, he knew enough about the business that he had to be treated with care.

Life after the army sometimes baffled Bill. Why, he would ponder, does everything have to be so complicated? He knew he wasn't perfect, and regretted the mistakes he'd made along the way, but, hell, he was basically a good and decent person. He did everything for his wife and boys — providing them with a decent home and a good education. He took care of them, drove them everywhere, and never sought much for himself. Yet as the years passed by, he found Elizabeth drifting away from him, their apparent closeness concealing a slow deadening of intimacy and a dulling of joy. And the boys — well, as they grew up, they seemed to deliberately oppose him. Not that they were delinquent or discourteous, but stubborn and opinionated. He couldn't understand them any more. They were critical sometimes, and whilst he encouraged their independence of thought, he felt they should take more notice of his advice and experience. Be a bit more compliant.

Jack was the easiest. A straightforward boy, good at sports, sociable, uncomplicated and not one to cause a fuss. He got along well with Jack. And Douglas, the youngest, bright, but hard-nosed and dogmatic. Where had he picked up those daft socialist ideas? He was a good lad, well-intentioned and kind-hearted, and protective of his mother. Bill respected Doug's toughness — would make a damn good junior officer, he sometimes thought — but not easy to manage. A bit too sure of himself. But at least he could communicate and argue with him.

Matthew was the strange one. Bill couldn't really relate with his eldest and never had felt close to him. Not that he was any trouble. A sensitive and dreamy child, who nevertheless prospered at school academically and socially, he lived largely in a world of his own, which was alien to Bill. Bookish and creative, he spent much of his time at home alone, reading, writing and drawing, inhabiting his own imagined society. Bill was never unkind or dismissive of him and dutifully enquired after his welfare and interests. Matthew always replied with a smile and a few words which signalled a recognition of his father's good intentions along with a clear message deflecting any further interest and guarding his privacy. There was a degree of resentment too, as Matthew was close to his mother, while excluding his father from any intimacy. It went back to the boy's very conception, unplanned and unwanted.

Bill and Elizabeth had married, after a short romance, a couple of years before Bill left the army. Smart, sure of himself and good-looking, he offered her the protection and security she needed. But the match was not approved of by her parents, who found the soldier too dominating and unrefined for their sensitive daughter. Her father, a concert musician, and mother, a teacher, had hoped that she would follow in her mother's footsteps, and were unimpressed by the thought that their daughter would be languishing in barracks life. She was a sensitive and cultured soul, who may find army society too rough at the edges. They expressed their doubts to their daughter and treated Bill with cool courtesy. But it was to no avail. Elizabeth was smitten by this masculine, no-nonsense and cheerful soldier, who compared favourably to the affected young men she normally met. None of this parental disapproval deflected Bill, who was planning his return to civilian life methodically and was quite happy with the thought of Elizabeth pursuing her own career. Then she fell pregnant.

This was disruptive to the clear plans that Bill had laid out and so he urged her to terminate. She tried this half-heartedly, using pills of uncertain origin, obtained by a friend. The result was a difficult, unhappy pregnancy and a baby born that was weak and sickly. From that moment on, she was consumed with guilt and became overprotective of the young child as it struggled through the early stages of life. Bill, whilst reconciled to the birth, and pleased to have a son, felt that she held him responsible for the baby's weakness and her discomfort. He detected in himself a quiet jealousy that this child had Elizabeth's full devotion, while he was held at a distance by both of them.

As the years went by, Matthew recovered from his fragile start in life and his relationship with his father was warm and respectful, yet somehow coloured by the unspoken guilt surrounding his beginning. Bill sometimes looked at his eldest quizzically, thinking, "Does he have some innate sense that I didn't want him?"

By the time he had reached sixteen, however, Matthew became more independent and began socialising in private ways that disturbed his parents. It wasn't that he was overtly delinquent, or staying away too long, or obviously doing anything illegal; it was the frequency and secrecy of his weekend evenings away that gave them cause for concern.

Typically, Elizabeth would stay up to wait for his return home, against Bill's advice.

"You really shouldn't wait up for me, Mum," was Matthew's standard comment on finding his mother sitting in the kitchen after midnight.

"Well, just worried you're OK, Mat."

"There's no need to fuss, Mum, really, just out with friends, hanging out."

"Where have you been? We didn't know where you were."

"Just hanging out, round a mate's house, nothing special."

"You can bring your friends around here, you know, whenever you like."

"I know, Mum, I know," he would say, and, kissing her lightly on the cheek, would quietly creep away down the hall and up the stairs to his bedroom.

Despite the mystery surrounding his social life, which even Jack and Doug knew little about, Matthew continued to study successfully, and when the time came to apply for university, he announced he wanted to do a degree in art and drama.

This did not please Bill, and for the first time his relationship with his eldest deteriorated into a frostiness that was worse than any confrontation, as it settled into a permanent condition rather than blowing away like a storm.

With his father insisting he choose something more practical, Matthew obstinately refused and despite being threatened with the withdrawal of parental support, shrugged his shoulders and smiled at his father with a smile that drove him to distraction.

"Dad, you just don't get it. You don't understand. If you don't want to pay anything, that's fine. I'll manage on the grant, or find a part-time job and work something out," he said, calmly, during one of their arguments about the matter.

"Well you're right, son, I don't bloody understand. You manage on peanuts then and you might learn a lesson!" was Bill's response to this frustrating self-assuredness.

The result of the rancour was an unhappy departure when Matthew finally left to take up his place at university. He had not changed his mind on his application, and Bill had, up till then, refused to agree any financial support. Both father and son were civil and managed an awkward hug on the day of leaving, while Elizabeth shed tears. His brothers embraced him warmly.

Three months later, Bill relented under the persuasion of his wife, and began to send Matthew his monthly funding, but the damage was done and the frost became permanent. To his mother's regret, Matthew rarely called home and when university holidays came, declared his intention to earn some money and travel, rather than returning.

Now it was Jack's turn and he determined not to undergo the same disagreements with his father. Although his heart was set on studying English and, hopefully, writing one day, he settled for economics, which was marginally acceptable to his father as a "useful" subject.

He continued to study fitfully the rest of that school year, applying himself sufficiently so that his natural academic ability, along with a sharp memory that served him well in exams, enabled him to reach the necessary grades to ensure him his preferred university place in the north of England.

But his self-doubts lingered. Not so much about the subject — economics was interesting and relevant, if sometimes too theoretical and mathematical for his liking — but about his own stamina to last a three-year degree. Truth was he didn't really enjoy studying.

One summer evening, the weeks ticking by until his first term would start, Jack lay on his bed, staring at the ceiling, which was the same gloomy dark blue as he had painted it three years before in a fit of adolescent creativity. It was a warm, humid evening, with the air hanging motionless and languid, and he had the window wide open. Outside, their suburban road was unusually free of traffic noise, silent, apart from the melodic singing of a proud blackbird artfully defending its patch.

He had been trying to read from one of the books on a reading list proposed by the university but found it hard to concentrate and now reclined on his back, hands behind his head, eyes closed — the book open and downward facing on his chest.

"A perfect moment of indolence," he was thinking to himself. "Just to be here, to enjoy existence pure and simple. Warm, well-fed, safe, unchallenged, solitary. There should be more times like this, when you're not pressured, unsure or worried. Just to feel the pleasure of that bird song — of the world — without the pressure to succeed or accomplish. It would be good to stop time for a while and cling on to this feeling of suspended animation."

There was a rap at his bedroom door and in came Doug, without waiting for a reply.

"Working hard, I see," teased his younger brother, throwing himself onto the bed beside Jack and shaking him from his reverie.

"Well, I was until rudely interrupted," he replied. "I was just contemplating Keynes' theory of the diminishing returns on investment actually, which I've just been reading about," he added, feigning intellectual gravity.

"Bullshit," shot back Doug. "You were half asleep, thinking about Eileen and, anyway, you better read some serious economics like Marx if you want to understand anything about the real world."

Jack laughed. "Oh yes, Mr Leftie, who hasn't been able to get past page three of Das Kapital. You better stick to Groucho rather than Karl."

"Bastard!" said Jack. "By the way, just came in to see if you wanna come down the Labour Club later on, we've got quiz night on."

"No, don't think so, got a few things to do," answered Jack.

After Doug had left, Jack picked up his book again and attempted to read on, but after a page or two further of reading and rereading, he flung the book onto the bedside table. He thought about his brother. He envied Doug's certainties. Doug was well-read and a committed party activist. He saw the world through a clear prism, enabling him to differentiate good from bad with a sharp clarity. He was convinced of the correctness and accuracy of his views. There was little room for self-doubt unless it involved unravelling an argument dialectically. Jack, on the other hand, though broadly sympathetic to his brother's political views, found the issues and people complex, and the debates less clear cut. He agonised over such matters and found it difficult to reach conclusions of his own.

A car with an ineffective exhaust roared noisily past in the street, chasing away the blackbird and scattering his thoughts.

Looking at his watch, he saw it was seven o'clock. Guys will be down the pub by now, he thought. Grabbing his faded denim jacket, he jumped up and went down the stairs. Before going out he poked his head into the kitchen.

"Bye, Mum, just going for a couple of pints with the lads," he said softly, so that Doug might not hear.

"What about dinner, love?" his mother responded.

"Just leave something for the oven, Mum, that'll be enough. Bye!" And he was out of the door.

Some weeks later, the four of them — Bill, Elizabeth, Doug and Jack — sat together in the kitchen, preparing for Jack's imminent departure. He had been adamant he would go by train to the university and did not want his parents to drive him. As they ate their breakfast, conversation was sparse. Jack's optimistic anticipation was spiced with a degree of anxiety as his old doubts about his motives, or lack of them, troubled him. For Bill, however, this was a moment of satisfaction — to see his second son head off for a bright future, and a world of education that he had made possible through his hard work and parenting. Elizabeth, on the other hand, was suffering, as another son left home, never really to come back, at least not to enjoy the closeness of dependence and shelter that motherhood provided. Soon, she imagined, Doug too, would leave and she would be left with Bill. Bill, whom she respected and relied on, but whose dominance suffocated her.

"Expect you'll be partying away next week then, in freshers' week, enjoying the booze and the wild chicks on offer," chirped up Doug, aiming to lighten the general mood.

"Very funny, I expect I'll be networking and making new friends, and joining the football club, and the economics society," said Jack with mock earnestness. "But certainly not the Marxist-Trotskyite Far Left discussion group," he added.

"No, didn't think so, more like the Jane Austen society for you then," countered his brother.

"Well," interrupted their father, "whatever you join, make sure you fit some work into it too and make the most of your time. Shall we get going then?"

"Take care, love, eat properly, won't you, and don't drink too much," said Elizabeth as Jack pulled on his jacket and slung his heavy rucksack over his shoulder.

"Don't worry, Mum, I like good food too much to go without."

After saying his goodbyes to Doug and a tearful mother, Jack loaded his large suitcase and rucksack into the boot and got in the car for the drive to the local station. Father and son sat silently for most of the way, each lost in his own thoughts.

"I'll miss you, Jack," said Bill unexpectedly. "Do your best, won't you? Have some fun too."

Surprised by his father's comments, Jack could only murmur an agreement and felt a sudden surge of sentiment for his family and home.

At the station forecourt, both men preferred a swift and unemotional farewell.

"Take care then," said Bill curtly.

"Thanks, Dad, and you will take care of Mum, won't you? I mean, you will look after her properly, won't you?"

Without waiting for an answer, he pulled the rucksack onto one shoulder, turned and strode off to the entrance, dragging his large suitcase clumsily and only pausing briefly to turn and wave. And with that he felt an enormous surge of relief and excitement. Finally, this was happening. He was getting away, and his misgivings dissipated like a summer morning's haze.

Bill turned and got back into the car. Before starting the engine, he sat, disquieted, for a few moments, pondering Jack's parting words.

"What did he mean by that?" he thought. "What did he know about anything?"

Chapter Three
Just Words

As soon as he walked through the doors of the club, Jack's mood lightened. The frustrations of work and its irritating demands dissolved in anticipation of amusing and sympathetic company and a weekend without responsibility stretching out before him.

The dingy lights of the Headline Club contrasted undemandingly with the glowering neon glare of the city centre, and its air-conditioned smokiness offered relief from the oppressive humidity of the outside world. His favourite retreat after work, the club was both relaxing and entertaining, its expectations limited to engagement in conversation, an appreciation of wit and an interest in politics, current affairs, and — above all — a heavy dose of social gossip.

Journalists, aspiring politicians, lawyers, PR practitioners and hopeful musicians and artists gathered in the gloom, particularly at the weekend, in order to vent their frustrations with the world, articulate their ambitions and exhibit their vanities. Intercourse was fuelled by a steady consumption of alcohol, successfully loosening tongues, as well as consciences and confidentialities. Thus was "the Club" a hunting ground favoured by hacks wheedling for inside stories and leaks; business people promoting themselves and marketing men stalking potential clients.

Jack, fitting none of these categories, was searching only for distraction. He was not a hunter in this community, but was often hunted, as his role in the Department made him a source of interest to some.

He walked straight up to the bar, which stretched for twenty yards down the side of the ground floor establishment. Low, round rattan tables, surrounded by four or five wooden chairs were scattered around the spacious area, where a supply of typical bar food dishes and snacks were served. At one end of the room, opposite the swing doors at the entrance, was a low stage, where, during the week, occasional guests attempted to stoke the intellectual climate by pontificating on some topic of political or literary worth, and, where, at the weekend, as the evening air grew staler and thicker and blood raced quicker round the veins, aspiring local music bands would make their bid for fame and generally be tolerated as acceptable background noise.

Ordering a bottle of local beer from the Filipino bar tender, Jack, who was well known to the staff, greeted him.

"Hello, Larry, how are you doing? Usual busy night expected, I suppose?"

"Hi, Mr Wilson, you know, Friday night, everyone wants to let off some steam," replied Larry, who had worked there as long as Jack had been a member.

Balancing on a bar stool, Jack surveyed the scene, looking for anyone he knew.

Friday was the most crowded, loudest, heaviest drinking night, a billowing tide of debate and disputation, fallings out and emotional outpourings building up through the evening hours until it reached a crescendo between eleven and twelve midnight, after which the mood settled for the remaining three hours into increasingly morose fractiousness and weary resignation.

Already quite busy, with customers lining the bar and half the tables occupied, the place was filling up fast.

People were vacating desks and offices and eagerly heading for this oasis from the driven world of work.

He soon caught sight of Hal, sitting at a corner table. His colleague waved and summoned him over to join him and two others drinking beer. Jack accepted the invitation, recognising one of Hal's companions as a well-known journalist who frequently passed through the territory and reported on the volatile political situation in the region. Australian Charlie Burrows, a rugged character with pockmarked skin and a gnarled nose, battered from his rugby league-playing days, filed stories for the BBC and other leading TV stations, as well as respected newspapers. His success impressed

Jack, who would have loved to emulate him. With them sat a serious-looking Kwok Ming, who reported for one of the leading local Chinese papers. Jack knew Kwok quite well, and respected him as a principled and talented journalist, albeit stony and austere. He nodded a greeting to both men.

"Charlie, this is Jack who works at the department, looking after the research needs of our beloved chairman and director. Jack, you know Charlie?" said Hal.

"Yeah, hi, Charlie, we have talked on the phone, when you were chasing information on the border tension," answered Jack, feeling slightly intimidated by the presence of this uncompromising reporter.

"Jack," nodded Charlie, not remembering the phone call.

"How's your director bearing up under all the pressure?" he added, referring to the mounting political crisis between the federation and the territory's growing breakaway movement.

"Oh, you know, hedging his bets and saying as little as possible. The government here seeks a compromise, looking for more autonomy, not suppressing the democrats, but trying not to upset General Khan, so we're officially behind that," answered Jack, feeling self-conscious as he spouted the department line, knowing full well that the director was in direct communication with the federation and opposed to independence or further democracy of any kind.

"And what's your take on it, Jack," followed up Burrows, staring intently at Jack with a piercing look that made him uncomfortable.

"Well, I... mm... I hope the government here can cool things down and find a compromise. I have some sympathy with the independence movement. My brother's mixed up in it. But I'm worried about the federation overreacting and taking heavy-handed action," Jack said, hesitantly.

"Well, I'd get your brother out of there, sharpish," countered Burrows, "because that 'overreaction' might be happening sooner than you think."

"Charlie's just come back from some light-hearted chats with a few of the federation's heavies," interjected Hal, with a guffaw. "And they ain't feeling too happy, right, Charlie?"

"Let's just say that if the hotheads in the independence movement push it too far, the federation's so-called law and order squads, who are right now a stone's throw away over the border, might just be unleashed... and that won't be pretty."

"I think they would be very careful before coming in," added Kwok, whose paper was known to back the independence movement, "because the international outcry would be great... that would damage the federation's attempts to improve their international image."

"Come on, mate," replied Burrows, becoming more animated. "Do you think him and his cronies give a stuff about international concern? They couldn't give a monkey's. How are the US or the Europeans able to affect the situation on the ground here? Anyway, they're more interested in trade with the federation's masses than this poke hole."

"You're wrong," said Kwok, reddening. "This poke hole — my home — is worth fighting for and we have support, real support, coming in."

"Oh, keep your hair on," answered the Australian, grinning and warming to a potential hot news story.

"Kwok, my friend, tell me more. You talking about finance... or even more?"

"Couldn't possibly say," Kwok said, regaining his composure and smiling enigmatically. "But enough to encourage the independents."

Jack listened with some concern, for if Kwok meant serious money or, more alarming, weapons of any kind, then the whole situation was more precarious and volatile than he realised. He thought about Doug. But no, he thought again, we were a long way from the political standoff leading to actual violence. The federation was capable of thuggery, even against its own citizens, but was this territory worth the trouble?

"Come on then, guys, let's have another beer, before world war three starts," Hal broke in, as he stood up and pushed his way to the bar.

"Are they really bringing their troops up to the border?" Jack anxiously asked Charlie.

"You better believe it," said the Australian. "If the government here can't put a damper on the protests and calls for independence, our friends over the border won't hesitate to intervene… in the national interest, you understand."

"I don't think they'd dare," Kwok said. "There would be such an uprising here if they try to suppress the people in their legitimate aims. People here have nothing to lose and they don't want to stay in the federation."

"I sure hope so, Kwok, but passion can't defeat rubber bullets and armed force," averred Burrows.

"Sometimes, they can… in the long run," insisted Kwok.

Lightening the seriousness, Burrows went on to tell anecdotes of his travels in the North, how he interviewed some of the federation leaders, with sometimes disturbing but sometimes farcical results. This entertained Jack and Hal, while Kwok listened dispassionately. After a while, he excused himself and left.

By now the place was filling up, and Jack began to look round restlessly. Though Burrows always intrigued him, he felt he was somehow on the receiving end of a lecture, rather than a partner in the conversation, and that Burrows assumed a patronising dominance over those who, like Jack, shared neither his calling nor status.

Having caught sight of a group of friends standing at the bar, across the room, he made his polite exit and moved over to join them.

"See you Monday, buddy," said Hal cheerfully as ever. "And don't take any shit from the director over the weekend!" referring to the boss's habit of contacting his staff at any time that suited him.

Jack noticed it was already seven o'clock and remembered his promise to join Doug's meeting and to see Les and friends for dinner. His intention of honouring those commitments was already weakening.

"Well, look here, it's Mr Wilson, commercial guru and government lackey," teased a large man with a tousled mop of dark hair in a loud voice, as Jack joined a group at the bar. Kevin Schmidt was dressed in an expensive well-cut dark suit and white shirt open at the neck down to the third button, which arrangement flaunted his hairy chest but thankfully concealed his ample stomach.

Successful barrister and man-about-town, Schmidt was highly intelligent, sharp-witted, entertaining and deliberately provocative. Rumour had it the South African was dangerous, and in former times had been involved in gun-running. Famed for getting into legal and social scrapes, from which he barely but regularly extricated himself, he was a fount of topical news and gossip. Jack found his company amusing — and informative — though after too many drinks he was liable to degenerate into the boorish.

With Schmidt were two attractive women and a business friend of his, all of whom were familiar to Jack. One of the women was Schmidt's Filipina wife, Marrietta, a vivacious heavy drinker, with a flashing smile and curvaceous figure. Jack found her sexually very alluring. The other was Anastasia Wong, also a lawyer, though not as prominent as Schmidt. Slim, with an angular face, she wore a severe, short hairstyle with girlish fringe. She was not desirable in a traditional way, but Jack found her challenging and would have liked to know her better. The male companion by her side, and, Jack presumed, her current lover, Julius Fong, was a gregarious banker, whose easy-going charm and considerable wealth Jack envied.

"Hello, Jackie boy, how are you, darling?" said Marrietta, putting an arm around his waist and kissing him on the cheek.

"Oh, for God's sake, put him down, you don't know where he's been," jested her husband. "I suppose you need a beer, young man," he offered.

"Thanks, Kevin, yeah, that would go down well, need something to brighten me up after a day's grind at the department and intense lectures from Mr Burrows."

"You poor sod," countered the lawyer. "Burrows been spreading his usual light and joy, has he?"

"Something like that," Jack replied.

"Well," came in Julius Fong, "don't scoff too much at Burrows' views. The money follows him and his reports count."

"Ah, bullshit, Julius. Money" — Schmidt made a sign of inverted commas with his fingers — "doesn't know its arse from its elbow. Money goes where the quickest short-term buck is to be made. Come on, investors are fickle, irrational and just follow the herd. They don't care who rules the roost as long as they get a return on their loot."

"Wish it was that simple, but in fact investors do analyse the situation. They want economic growth and a stable government. And, naturally, wise advice from experts like myself," argued Fong with a smug smile.

"Exactly what's wrong with the system," shot back Schmidt. "The blind leading the blind." He laughed loudly.

"What have you been up to, Jack," asked Anastasia. "Seen anything of Marion or is that a sore point?" She had been acquainted with Marion before Jack got to know her.

It was a very sore point, but Jack fought back the flush of embarrassment he felt, like swallowing back reflux, by brushing off the enquiry.

"I'm fine, thanks, busy... no, haven't seen Marion lately, that's history now. She's back with the old boyfriend and they set off for London."

"Shame," said Anastasia, with a throwaway tone that made the comment more poignant. "She was fun," and turned back to talk with Julius.

She was much more than fun to me, thought Jack, and he felt angry with himself for allowing the memories of their break-up to intrude on his present equilibrium. It wasn't just losing a lover and the intimacy that entailed, but his feeling of powerlessness and betrayal. How naïve had he been in not recognising the significance of her continued contact with the former boyfriend, despite hints from friends. How casual her announcement that:

"Although she loved Jack, she found him too serious and he was always thinking too much". Her other boyfriend was more easy-going. He should have seen it coming. There were times when he couldn't, didn't want to, keep up with Marion's hectic social life. The cocktail parties, dinner invitations and fancy-dress events (which he particularly despised) he suffered, but sometimes declined, leaving Marion to go on her own. Should have seen the danger there. It was the loss of status and self-esteem and the inability to deal with that loss which maddened Jack. He remembered how, in a fit of frustrated, childish anger, he had torn up every photo he could find of Marion. And how he had thrown the few remaining clothes she had left behind in the flat into the rubbish disposal chute. Then the ridiculous denials to Marion when she called to ask about her possessions and the refusal to meet with her. It was humiliating. Worse than that, the failure of another relationship in which he had invested long-term hopes, following the splitting up with Pru, seemed to typify his life — never quite reaching what he wanted. Never being in control. Never grasping success on his own terms. He felt his life had meandered into a kind of slurry, a warm but disagreeable state which offered no clear direction and hindered progress. It was like trying to run away in a bad dream when being chased by some demon, but at the same time sinking knee deep into glutinous mud, while being seduced by the safety of knowing it was a dream.

Before he could allow himself any further self-pitying thoughts, his mobile rang, jerking him back to the moment.

"'Scuse a moment," he said as has saw it was Doug, and moved over to a quieter corner of the bar area.

"Are you coming, then?" quizzed his brother in a waspish tone that already predicted a disappointing response. "The meeting's already started. We need as many here as possible. We're probably going down to join the sit-in later, which is really building up. Are you coming?"

"Well, maybe later. I'll join you later. I just need a break for a while," replied Jack.

"You're at the club, aren't you?" interrogated the younger brother. "I suppose you'll be there all night then boozing?"

"No, no," protested Jack. "Just having a couple of quick beers, then I'll grab a bite to eat and join you down at the university. Maybe nine or ten."

"OK, see you later." Doug signed off, resigned to the idea it was unlikely Jack would show up.

Back with the crowd at the bar, Jack found Schmidt holding court, regaling the company with tales of his last case. Like every bar room braggard the world over, with his expansive frame and baritone voice, he dominated the conversation and bludgeoned his audience into attention with his flow of words, invariably laced with humour and a hint of malice. Defending two incompetent Malay criminals, Schmidt outlined how they had kidnapped a Chinese businessman and demanded a ransom — not even a particularly large ransom — from his family. The family had, against instructions, gone straight to the police. They arranged a simple sting — getting the crooks to nominate a meeting place for the payment of ransom money — which led to their rapid arrest and release, unharmed, of the victim.

"These two dickheads were caught within twenty-four hours and didn't even have the nous to take any precautions in collecting their stash," Schmidt was explaining.

Jack meanwhile bought a round of drinks for everyone.

"Lucky I managed to keep the sentence down to ten years," the barrister boasted. "Though they were up for twenty or more. Fortunately, they didn't hurt the guy much, just roughed him up a little."

"Don't you feel strange sometimes, I mean, I know everyone deserves a defence and all in law, but don't you feel kind of false defending people who are obviously guilty and potentially very dangerous and possibly murderers," asked Jack provocatively.

Schmidt's answer, with its sliver of empathy and social consciousness, surprised Jack, who expected a more dismissive reply.

"Look," said Schmidt, "the poor bastards were nineteen and twenty years old. They've either been unemployed or working in shit jobs since leaving school. They see all this wealth around them and they get tempted. They act stupid and deserve everything they get, but someone's at least got to speak up for them."

As the conversation moved on and broke up, Jack edged closer to Anastasia, and tried to engage her in small talk. Polite, but keeping her distance, the chic lawyer fended off Jack's questions about her background and her relationship with Julius, but was interested in Jack's job and the political currents swirling around the territory.

After a while, he tired of the conversation, seeing that his attempts to flirt with her were getting nowhere. Another round of drinks.

"Don't worry, Jackie boy." He was approached again by the increasingly tipsy Marrietta, who took hold of his arm and beamed up at him.

"We'll find you a nice Filipina girl to look after you. I got plenty of relatives, you know."

Jack liked her. She was funny, genuine and generous, but although he always thought he'd like to bed her, he recoiled at the idea of her as a partner.

Her drinking bouts with Kevin usually ended in the two having embarrassing public rows during which she accused him of infidelity and neglect of her, while he accused her of drunkenness and flirtatiousness. These confrontations would end with Marrietta, after some theatrical weeping, lying asleep with her head on the bar or a table, while Kevin recalled some obscure ancestral connection with Germany and began to sing forgotten German sea shanties that his grandmother had supposedly taught him in the old country.

No, thought Jack, I couldn't deal with the drama.

The time had drifted by, swept along by conversation, the increasing vibrancy of the club atmosphere, stoked by humour, and by sexual desire and anger. Then Jack realised it was just past eight o'clock, the time he had agreed with his friend Les that they would meet for dinner.

"Right, I've got to go," he announced abruptly. "Meeting some friends for dinner. Might catch up with you later, probably still here, right?" he added, smiling.

"Could possibly be so," said the expansive barrister as Jack took his leave and said goodbye to the others.

Passing through the doorway, he bumped into an acquaintance who was looking distractedly at his mobile.

"Hi, Jack," said the man. Daniel Leung, who worked in the government communications department and intermittently had liaised with Jack on certain issues. "How's it going?"

"OK," said Jack. "Everything all right? You look a bit stressed out."

"Aw, just these flaming students making a fuss again. Wish they'd just get on with their studies. Means I've got to head back to the office again — so much for my Friday night out," he complained.

"Well, good luck with that — give me a call next week if we can help," he said as he pushed out into the black night.

Within a few moments a taxi came along and picked him up. He leaned back on the shiny plastic-covered seats and closed his eyes, suddenly feeling quite tired.

"Where going?" asked the Chinese driver. Jack told him the street name in Chinese, which prompted the driver to compliment him on his language skills. "Yes," thought Jack, that's a comment on most expats' inability to learn even how to pronounce the real names of local places.

During the twenty-minute drive, Jack dozed in and out of consciousness, remembering a vivid sequence of images — Burrows' gnarled face, Kwok's impassioned embarrassment, Schmidt's unconditional self-assurance, his brother's nagging voice. And when he opened his eyes briefly, he was once again dazzled by the garish, neon world of the packed evening streets of this teeming city, streaming past him, always fascinating, always exhausting, always taunting him and sucking him in.

At the restaurant, before joining the company, he splashed his face in cold water in the gents' toilet, took off his tie and straightened his collar.

"Ah, there he is at last, our lovelorn poet," said Val, as Jack approached to greet her with a hug and a kiss on both cheeks. He didn't mind the teasing from Val, who was too kind and well-meaning to mean anything by it.

"Come on, you old bugger," said Les Broughton, who'd been close friends since Jack arrived in the city, when they had met playing together at the squash club.

"I don't care about him being lovelorn, or a bleedin' poet, but he's late and it must be his round," added Les, extending a hand and giving Jack a strong intimate grip.

This Australian friend, who worked in a demanding but, for Jack, slightly mysterious role for a major textiles trading company, owned in the USA, always had a mischievous look in his eye and a story to tell. He and his wife were engaging and generous, loyal and frank.

Jack also greeted Bob Smyth and his wife Deirdre, as well as Marcus Chan and Josephine, his partner, the other participants at the table. This was relaxing company for Jack, especially Les and Val, who had always provided him with sympathy, as well as hard advice when it was needed. He wasn't so close to the Smyths, as Bob tended to have a loud and entrenched opinion on all matters, whether they ranged from squash club politics to international affairs. Deirdre, meanwhile, was pleasant but drab, probably drained of personality by her overbearing husband, thought Jack. Nevertheless, this ex-policeman and his wife were easy company and could be fun.

Marcus and Josephine were bright, cosmopolitan success stories. Both had an international education, spoke several languages and traversed the cultural divides of this city with ease. Successful in their respective careers — both flourished in the hothouse of local finance — they retained a freshness and lack of cynicism that Jack found optimistic. While he found them engaging, however, he never fully trusted Marcus. There was a hint of calculation and ulterior strategy about his socialising.

Their squash playing being the common bond between the men, the conversation predictably revolved around respective team performances and tactical nuances of the previous round of league games, but then, as the beers flowed and the dishes of spicy Indonesian food stimulated the tongue and the palate, it spun out into various subjects.

Les entertained them with anecdotes from his business life and observations of the eccentric characters he met on the international rag trade circuit. He was an amusing raconteur, casting a laconic eye over the subjects under discussion. Marcus, meanwhile, brought a more serious tone to the table, explaining his concerns over the fragility of the local stock and capital markets, as they were buffeted by the darkening politics of the region.

Jack listened with interest at first, but as the matters turned trivial, and gossip focused on common acquaintances, their marital difficulties and sexual peccadillos, his attention began to wander. He often experienced this feeling of detachment, of alienation, from this amiable but superficial society. These were good people, generally tolerant and generous-minded, but in sudden moments of doubt, he felt he hardly knew them and that they had no idea of his inner turmoil, and that he could not articulate that without feeling foolish.

"You still with us, mate?" said Les, bringing Jack back into full awareness of the moment. "Looks like you had a hard week. Have another beer, that'll sort you out."

"Yeah, you're right, was under the cosh a bit," said Jack. "Work's been pretty frantic, what with the goings-on with the federation."

That comment brought the conversation back to politics, which none of them particularly wanted to spend leisure time on. Apart from Les, who expressed a vague sympathy for the democrats, the others thought their attempts to break the city free from the grip of the federation was pointless.

Bob Smyth was particularly sarcastic about the students' protests.

"They deserve what they get, frankly," he said. "Typical dangerous idealists, rocking the boat and stirring up the authorities. It can only end in tears. There'll be a crackdown, and the only result will be a temporary shock to the economy and more loss of liberty for the rest of us."

"But you must admit," Jack countered lamely, "that many politicians here quietly support the protests. There's a good economic argument for the city going it alone, and the federation is becoming increasingly authoritarian — don't you support democracy?"

"Come on, Jack, who cares about democracy here. The politicians you're talking about are not interested in democracy. Like all politicians they're on the make and no different from that lot up north. It's money that counts here, not ideals."

Marcus agreed and spoke again about the damage being done to confidence in the money markets.

"The banks are very nervous about the independence movement and, believe me, they will pull capital outa here before you can say Jack Robinson," he added.

Well, thought Jack, while feeling too weary to make an argument of it, it's OK for us expats. We can get out if the going gets rough. We'll take care of our money, and our children are not the ones who will suffer oppression. He was irritated by the smug confidence of the Smyths and Marcus, and even more annoyed by his own inability to summon up rebuttals to their views, without sounding pious. Doug, he thought, would not sit quiet in these circumstances.

So it was, with his feelings soured by his own weakness, Jack settled up with the others and, with a degree of relief, made to take his leave.

As they left the restaurant, Les suggested a "couple" more drinks somewhere, as the night was young. After nine now, noted Jack. The Smyths and Marcus and Josephine headed off elsewhere, for which Jack was grateful, and he relaxed at the thought of some casual time with the Broughtons.

"Come on," encouraged Les. "Let's hit the Top Cocktail, it's just up the road."

Chapter Four
Courses of Action

It was not an inspiring place to hold a meeting, for its gloomy interior exuded a sense of depression rather than optimism — its atmosphere promoting apathy rather than activism. But for the generally young and hopeful disputants who gathered there regularly, it was their base, where they felt secure from observation and free to discuss their political and social ideas, in fact, any kind of ideas, which exercised them at the time.

Theirs was an informal discussion group, focused on intellectual pursuit, their themes centring on politics, but meandering regularly into economics and philosophy, as well as other topics such as the environment and women's rights. But of late, with unrest stirring in the territory and ominous clouds gathering on the northern horizon, they had felt the need for more practice than theory. They had been holding seminars on the importance of democracy, the rule of law and a free press, distributing leaflets criticising the growing authoritarianism of the federation and submitting the occasional opinion piece to local media outlets.

The flat where they met was the home of one of the leading lights of this serious-minded group. Part of a block not more than twenty years old, built by the university for staff and postgraduate students, it was a drab place. Though spacious and potentially a comfortable family home, its location next to a busy motorway intersection meant that a restricted style of living took place. Residents existed behind windows that were permanently shut to exclude the noxious traffic fumes and allow the air-conditioning to work at maximum effect to counter the debilitating humidity.

Partially closed plastic venetian blinds covered the panes, while a single strip neon bulb in the centre of the ceiling cast a pallid light over the lounge. The furnishing might be considered minimalist by some, but more accurately reflected the inhabitant's lack of interest in material comfort or aesthetic pleasure. Ill-shapen black PVC-covered sofas and chairs, standard issue from the university, lay against the wall or were strewn around the lounge, while various coloured cushions and blankets were flung over them in a careless attempt to brighten the place up. A plain wooden coffee table and sideboard, on which stood a radio and music system, complemented the seating and helped conceal the uncarpeted parquet flooring. Virtually covering one wall, however, was one feature which provided relief from the otherwise dour scene. A rickety but quaint bookcase was overflowing with books of all hues, shapes and sizes, indicating at a glance the owner's profession and breadth of reading. For the younger tutees and group members who visited here, this wall of knowledge was at once impressive and intimidating. How would they ever be able to equal this herculean reading task and ever approximate to the accumulation of wisdom and learning it implied? Only later would they come to understand the critical roles of selection, superficial absorption and forensic dabbling necessary for progress in the academic world, and that the library was status symbol as well as refuge.

Dick Brandon, politics tutor at the territory's leading university, was a natural leader. Intellectually acute, widely read and a formidable debater, he exercised a sway over the group, and as a teacher who encouraged free-flowing discussion, was widely respected for his fair-mindedness. Doug Wilson admired him, though Brandon unsettled him with his ideological certainty and unconditional self-confidence. Doug had always aspired to that kind of doubt-free political belief, but his conscience and honesty ensured that an element of self-questioning tempered his beliefs.

Since arriving in Asia two years before, Doug had worked at the university in the English Language Support department, assisting foreign speakers who wished to develop or brush up their English skills. Having achieved a degree in politics and international relations at home, he found the language work here unchallenging, but recognised its value to those students who needed it and he fulfilled his teaching obligations conscientiously. But his real interest was practical politics, for Doug was an organiser and an activist. At school, and then at university, he had been a committed foot soldier of the Labour Party, regularly attending the sometimes-tedious meetings, patiently delivering leaflets and diplomatically knocking on doors when elections required it. He was one of the few devotees who read all the minutes and argued steadfastly over the most tangential amendments when moved to do so.

He served as secretary and then treasurer for the party's university branch. During the nineties, while teaching civics and economics at the local comprehensive school, he rode on the wave of success the party enjoyed, as it hauled itself out the self-destructive infighting of the eighties and geared up for the exhilarating election victory of 1997. The early years of the New Labour government had promised so much; and for Doug, and many others, some of the damage of the opposition years was repaired. But disillusionment began to creep in and during the early years of the new millennium, Doug found himself increasingly frustrated with the cautious policies of the moderate leadership. The decisive parliamentary majorities were not being deployed in the cause. Economic, educational and industrial policies hardly diverged from the neo-liberal dogmas of their opponents and the opportunity to transform Britain's class-benighted society was being wasted. It was time for a change. Doug's personal life was similarly underachieving. He had broken up with his live-in partner after six years together. She finally rebelled against his lack of commitment and interest in having a family, and called the party "his other woman", before leaving him — quite suddenly. His older brother's colourful and enthusiastic tales of Asia, were, in contrast, beguiling and exotic.

Once landing in the territory, following encouragement from Jack, whom he was very fond of but found "lacking purpose", he quickly established himself in his teaching role and then sought a suitable political family. Early on he discovered the Politics Club, as they called themselves. Headed by Brandon and several other lecturers and tutors, the group meetings usually attracted twenty to thirty students and several "workers" — usually trade union representatives of the university's admin and support departments. In the early days of Doug's attendance, discussion centred around the prescribed university course topics in Politics, Economics and Philosophy, and the group had been little more than a talking shop. Brandon, however, had more visionary ideas, particularly as the political situation in this part of the world became increasingly unpredictable. He saw the group as a lobbying force which could influence debate and change in the territory. Promoting democracy — specifically social democracy — it should champion egalitarianism, one-man, one-vote elections, the free press and the independence of the judiciary. Doug sympathised with these views and became a supporter of Brandon, though harbouring scepticism about his ulterior aims.

On this particular evening, as the members gathered in the poorly lit apartment, it was clear that the mood was tense and troubled, on account of the student sit-in taking place on the campus.

Brandon stood up, confident and benign, his back to the bookcase. Tall and good-looking, he was an attractive figure, who exuded a kind of avuncular, common sense authority. With his well-trimmed beard and thick dark hair, swept back as if by an oncoming wind, his piercing dark eyes behind his black-rimmed glasses, he could have been a figure from a classic Russian novel.

"Well, evening, everyone; good to see such a turnout, but then, we live in interesting times!" Nervous laughter.

Some thirty people were crowded into the room, mostly students from the university, and several junior lecturers, like Doug. The majority of the students were local Chinese, but a handful of Filipino, Indian and Malays had joined the group. They lounged around the living room on the worn furniture, or sat on the floor, some of them sipping tea or beer that Brandon had provided.

"Over the last couple of years," Brandon continued, "we've had some great meetings, discussions and debates about the issues that motivate us, and should motivate us, for as social science students it is our responsibility to promote awareness of what's going on in the world and in our own society. It's our job to highlight the failings of government and propagate the values and principles that underpin fairer and more just societies."

"As well as studying hard and improving our own understanding, we want to add to collective knowledge, and that's why we research and discuss," he added.

"But, my friends, there comes a time when book-reading and the exchange of ideas is not enough. And I think that this time is upon us. The political situation in the territory and in relation to the federation has come to a head. This has been brewing for the past months and your classmates have finally taken action. The sit-in has been building up and tonight your friends and colleagues are flooding into the main union building to make their voices heard on behalf of democracy, fairness and independence. So the question is, my friends, what are we going to do about it? We, who are supposed to be the political thinkers, and opinion leaders, cannot sit idly by. Our question tonight then is how this group supports and participates in this movement, which is surely pivotal in the ongoing struggle against oppression and darkness from the North! What we need now is action; action, not words!"

Spontaneous and enthusiastic applause, along with cries of "Yeah, right" and "Let's go" and whoops of support greeted Brandon's stirring words. Doug shifted uneasily in his seat. Whilst he agreed in principle with the lecturer's sentiments, he was concerned at Brandon's whipping up of emotion and his influence over his raw recruits.

Having captured his small but devoted crowd, Brandon now moved on to his pre-conceived plans.

"I propose that we show real and meaningful solidarity with the students, by heading down there as soon as possible and taking a lead role in the movement. The student union reps and random leaders at the moment have only focused on the student demands over educational freedoms and fees issues and vaguest democracy issues, but we know this is bigger. This is about the students spearheading a genuine movement which will inspire the people into such mass protests and action that neither our timid, appeasing government here, nor the fascists up North, can ignore. This is a chance to join the real protesters who are looking for independence, for that's the only way to defend our way of life here!"

"Are you with me?" shouted Brandon. "Are you with me?" his arm held aloft with clenched fist.

"Yes! Yes!" chanted his audience, raising their arms in salute.

"Wait!" came a voice from the back. "Wait a moment! We shouldn't just rush into this. The situation is dangerous. It won't do the movement any good to inflame things. Stirring things up and shouting independence slogans will only encourage the hotheads and provoke the authorities."

K.K. Wong, a mature student, born and bred in the territory, stood erect and spoke in measured terms. Slightly thinning, clean shaven and dressed in neat slacks and open-necked white shirt, he looked more like a junior manager in a business office.

"We need to stay calm. I'm with you in supporting the sit-in. But we do that with our presence. Let the union leaders keep control, if they can. If the university authorities give way on the key issues, then we have won a victory. Better to build support in the people step by step before rushing into battle. Why don't we offer to act as negotiators? We don't want the situation to get out of hand. We can push the government here into a stronger position. They need international backing. They can't confront the powers of the North on their own."

"No, no, no!" came an excitable response from another quarter. "This is no time for compromising or bullshitting. Politicians' mealy-mouthed negotiations have got us nowhere. Who trusts the lot we have in power here anyway? They're just a bunch of capitalists. They make any deal with Khan. They've no interest in the people, only their own wallets."

Waving his hand in a chopping motion as if to reinforce the strength of his words, Jo Chan spoke with passion. Sometimes more passion than sense, thought

Doug. His heart's in the right place but he lets his emotion get the better of him.

"Dick's right. We have hundreds of pissed-off students down there in the campus. Half of them don't really know why they're there, but they are ripe for the right kind of leadership. This is a revolutionary moment. We strike against the authorities and defy the police. The people will come with us. The government have to listen and the momentum for independence will gather. If the police want a fight, give them a fight and the government will be the ones to suffer bad publicity," Chan argued, reddening in the face and spraying spittle over his nearest colleagues.

"Whoa, hold on," came back Dick Brandon. "Let's not start talking about fighting yet — we don't want to see anyone get hurt. What we need above all is solidarity. We're not talking anarchism. We are talking about a movement. We got to see that sit-in build to a thousand students. It's got to grow. Numbers are important, so the police can't shift us out. If they move in, the TV cameras will pick it up and it will look bad for them, not just here but the world over. We just have to sit tight and insist on our demands. We've got to insist on the release of the pro-independence leaders who have been detained. We've got to insist on direct talks with the government, as representatives of the young people and workers in this territory. And we've to insist on a referendum on the future of this place. We need clear aims and a clear strategy," argued Brandon, his voice authoritative and measured and his tone seductively reasonable.

"Nice words. And you're right, brother," came another, soft melodic voice that almost sang. Everyone turned to look at the speaker, a squat, muscular person, with long black hair, tied back with a bright red bandana. Rocky Ocampo, half Filipino, stroked his dark moustache. Rocky, whom everyone nicknamed Jesus, was a paradox. Normally, laid back, dope-smoking, kind and considerate in his personal life, he nevertheless possessed within his opaque character a streak of black hard-heartedness, which occasionally erupted to the surface in political debates and face-offs, and led him into fist fights and problems with the police.

"But I tell you something, brother. Jo's got it. You will need to fight in the end and you need to be ready. Because the police, man, will move in if you don't leave. And they will beat you. So, you need to defend yourselves. It's not a picnic, man, if you want your rights, man, you have to fight, I'm telling you. Take your motorbike helmets and your baseball bats, because that's what I'm doing."

Some cheered at this, but others shook their heads. Voices clamoured to be heard and eager hands raised, while individual arguments and disagreements added to the din.

Brandon tried to settle things again and cool the rising temperature.

"OK, OK, OK, I understand your passion. And I appreciate your bravery. But don't get carried away. The last thing we want to do is provoke the police and start any violence. And if they move on us, we give passive resistance. Think Gandhi. Think Martin Luther King. Jesus, aren't you the one who's supposed to turn the other cheek!"

He lightened the mood with his teasing comment, but Doug remained uneasy. Brandon was clearly working this group up into supporting him, and inciting a mood of resistance and defiance. Could he do this and yet restrain the very emotions he was stoking at the same time?

"I'd like to say something," said Doug, finally, struggling with his own ambiguous thoughts and disinclination to commit to the debate. But you can't sit on the side lines, he thought to himself. You have to take part, take sides.

"I'd like to speak," he repeated, moving close to where Brandon was standing.

The noise subsided. Doug was liked and respected in this crowd. He was a sympathetic and dedicated teacher. And his views, although never spectacular, were regarded as worthy.

"I know I'm an outsider — a foreigner here — and it's your fight. You, KK. You, Jo. Jesus and all of you. It's your future and your struggle. But I am here, with Dick and many others, and it's important for you to know we are with you and will work with you. And that's not just extra brains and extra muscle. It's about making this struggle international. For this brave territory will only make way against a much stronger opponent with the help of the outside world, whether that's moral support or diplomatic or, God forbid, military support. And we, I hope, the foreigners, are a symbol of that support and a link to that support."

This was met with some grunts of approval and scattered applause. Doug was pleased. He just found the words flowing out and enjoyed the feeling of affecting the debate, being the focus of attention and receiving a positive reaction.

"Yeah, man," shouted Jesus, "great, but what good's international backing tonight, and during the night and tomorrow morning when the cops come wading in."

"Maybe, they'll be a bit more careful when they know expat teachers and others are around as witnesses, and even to film what's going on," shot back Doug.

"I hope so, man. I sure hope so," said Jesus.

"When I was coming along here tonight," picked up Doug again, "I wasn't even sure about joining the sit-in. I wasn't sure what good it will do."

Some groans of disapproval came from the more excitable members, whose passions were not easily going to be cooled.

"But," Doug paused for effect, his finger pointing to the ceiling, "but I see the mood of this meeting and I'm not going to let my comrades down. Of course, I'm with you. I'm also with Dick and KK though. We need to be disciplined and think about organisation. This sit-in's got to have purpose. Big, clear messages that the students and others can get behind. That the public can understand. That's what we can give — some strategic leadership."

Brandon, standing next to Doug, applauded conspicuously and put his arm around Doug, which made the latter blush and feel patronised.

"Well said, Doug. Well said," Brandon declared to polite applause.

"Colleagues… comrades," he carried on, "I think we are agreed. Let's ready ourselves and we can head down to the campus together. Let's stick together and let's make a difference! Come on. Let's go!" he shouted to applause and cheers. The group stood up, some swigging the last of their drinks, others pulling on their jackets and hauling rucksacks onto their shoulders. With Brandon in the lead, they began to file out of the flat, exhilarated, leaving a scene of disorder — crumpled blankets, empty cups and bottles, full ash trays and carelessly arranged furniture. It was nine thirty, Doug noticed. No sign of Jack, of course. He didn't really expect anything else, but it would have been good to have him here, he thought, just for the company.

As the group trudged their way from the residential area of the campus towards the central plaza area, they were silent or talking quietly. Doug was experiencing mixed feelings. He knew in his heart that he wanted to be a part of this gesture on behalf of their small group. For him it was a moral imperative. You need to make a commitment, he told himself, as he had repeatedly, throughout his political career. You can't let the opposition win by default. On the other hand, he was concerned about the repercussions of his actions, not least on his position as a lecturer. He didn't know, if, by taking part in the sit-in, he would be spotted by the university authorities and reprimanded, fired even. And, he thought, he really didn't want to stay too long. He had things to do tomorrow. Hopefully, he could slip away at midnight.

As they approached, the raucous cacophony of public protest reached them in rising volume. They could hear the dissonant megaphone tones of strident speakers exhorting the protesters with slogans and stirring words — though undefined and raw. Then the answering rumble of the crowd roaring approval — like a primeval beast provoked in its lair. As the student union buildings came into view, Doug took a sharp intake of breath. This was much more serious than he had thought.

Several hundred students had been expected to participate in this action. The politically conscious, the mischievous, and the curious, perhaps, to make a nuisance of themselves for a day or so. But, by the time the group appeared on the scene, well over thousand were there, with banners and flags — spilling out from the front of the building onto the concourse — a sea of colour and throbbing vitality, of hope and youthful optimism.

Many banners carried slogans demanding justice, or democracy or independence — the messages were varied, while others waved the unofficial bright red flag of the territory. Many young men and women sported white head scarves around their brows, bearing Chinese or Romanic character expressing defiance. They looked like a peacetime army of Samurai. A heaving mass, they swirled in front of, around and over the broad steps leading up to the student centre, where a speaker was rallying the forces with passionate but barely audible words.

They had come to answer a call from their student leaders. Discontent had been brewing on the campus for some months. There had been diverse causes. Attempts to alter textbooks, particularly of history, in favour of a partisan federation viewpoint; gradual rises in tuition and accommodation fees; and the appointment of an unpopular director had stoked the flames. But the glowing embers had lain alive if unfanned for some time. The students were known to support the independence movement, which had been gathering strength since the takeover of power in the North by the militaristic party of General Khan three years before. Following the reluctant withdrawal of the Western imperial powers at the beginning of the 1960s, there had been great hopes for this part of the world. Although the federation was a clumsy, artificial construct, bequeathed by the former masters, bringing together Chinese, Malay and Indian ethnic groups in five interdependent states, it seemed to offer economic sense and a way to avoid racial rivalries that had dogged the region since time immemorial.

For the first decades an uneasy balance was maintained, as each component had a degree of autonomy, but worked within a federal structure, which centralised strategy for economic growth, development, defence and international affairs. Steadily, however, disparities emerged. From the beginning a limited form of constitutional democracy had been accepted throughout, but progress varied. In the dominant North, parliamentary experiments never took root and within ten years in was a one-party state. But even that was usurped eventually by the military, which, as ever with soldiers' coups, promised a cleansing of the corrupt political scene, and a rapid return to elections. That return never came about because foreign threats and internal strife demanded the imposition of strict law and order for reasons of security and stability. As the head of the army, Khan had consolidated his power, reducing the judiciary and media, through intimidation and bribery, into his tools of oppression. Opponents had been jailed or exiled. A cult of personality was emerging.

Such developments were looked upon with dismay from the other partners in the federation, who felt the ominous threat of the central power upon their own arrangements. None were perfect, but they had attempted degrees of democratic representation, albeit limited in some cases, and they had established freedoms before the law and freedom of expression.

In the territory itself, where a benign oligarchy had embedded itself into society since the creation of the federation, a stunted form of parliamentary democracy, with one party dominating, had been tolerated by a population more interested in growing wealth than political rights. The Prosperity Party had the backing of the territory's elite. It had controlling access to funding, the media — mostly owned by its members — business and capital. Not surprisingly, it had traditionally won power in the House of Delegates, whereas the minority parties, winning a few local contests, and being factionally divided, could be little more than an irritant. An irritant which successfully masked an unrepresentative system.

Within the Prosperity Party, views towards the North differed. Some advocated closer alliance with Khan and greater integration, to protect the territory from outside interference. But they were a minority. Others wanted a strengthening and reform of the federal system to retain the territory's qualified freedoms — a form of appeasement. Minority groups proposed a more radical solution — independence and a complete break with the federation. Only this path would ensure the territory's future integrity, they argued. Otherwise, it would be absorbed — annexed — into the North. The only problem was how to achieve it. General Khan would not give up the lucrative territory without a fight. It was too precious, as an international port and business centre, to be released. Too precious as one of the jewels in the federation. To lose it would be a national humiliation, and a personal insult to the strutting Khan, who, in his own eyes at least, personified the virility and power of the Federal State.

In this context, and in the shadow of the North, the movers for independence in the territory could be seen as equally heroic and foolhardy. Their only hope lay in the power of their convictions, which through devoutness and the type of belief which sustained early Christians in their age of martyrdom, would help convert the people to the cause, and attract the assistance of the outside world if politics gave way to war.

Most of the students in the masses Doug now surveyed were believers. Some understood the cause and its ramifications better than others. Some were motivated by less grand, university issues or personal frustrations. Whatever their issues, thought Doug, they are a brave and defiant lot, with all the naïve optimism of youth. And as his small entourage mingled in the crowd and was being warmly welcomed on all sides, the exhilaration created by a vocal mass movement stimulated him like a sudden warm summer breeze blowing over him. He drew on that as he sucked in a deep breath, in order to embolden himself.

Meanwhile, at a distance, outside the campus gates, in the darkness, hundreds of officers of the territory's police force were disembarking from trucks and assembling quietly in rows to await their orders.

Chapter Five
Encounters

It should have been cool in this bar. In spite of the air conditioning working at maximum output, exhaling streams of cold breath into the smoky atmosphere, it was not. The sheer mass of human bodyweight, dancing, flowing, gathering in clutches, dispersing and gathering again, and cut by individuals forcing their way through, saw to that.

The lights were dimmed, but the gloom was rhythmically violated by the swirling lighting over the dance area. Responding in kind, the music pummelled the ears with its base repetitions and shrill lyrics. A shock to the system, thought Jack, as he squeezed into the main bar area with Les and Val. The scene facing him was like a picture by Bruegel, he imagined, pleased at his artistic allusion. Except these weren't Flemish peasants, but the young, elite society of the territory, confident in their right to party extravagantly in this expensive, swanky location, which appealed to their unquestioned entitlement to privilege. A concoction of sophisticated perfume hung in the air, slightly sullied by a hint of body odour emanating from the frenetic activity on the dance floor.

"Blimey!" exclaimed Les, as they fought their way through the crowd to the bar. "Haven't seen it so packed as this for a while!"

"There's been a trade event on the last three days," explained Val. "So, probably a lot of visitors are letting their hair down after finishing."

"Sounds reasonable," said Jack, as he eased past a thick-set man turning away from the bar, clutching several glasses and a bottle of sparkling wine. "What do you want, you two?" he asked as he planted his elbows on the bar in a determined gesture to claim his place.

He watched the waiters carefully, partly because he wanted to catch their eye as quickly as possible when they had finished serving another customer, and partly because he was fascinated by their dexterity in providing all kinds of drinks with precision and speed, while collecting an abundant flow of payments. This place must be a goldmine, he thought, as receipt after receipt was ripped neatly from card machines and handed back to the purchasers.

Bars like the Top Cocktail were relatively new to the entertainment world of the territory. Unlike the rarefied clubs of the seriously rich, or the over-priced hotel bars, or the drab drinking holes and seedy clubs of the entertainment area, they were aimed at the territory's growing middle class, which had emerged educated and assertive in the sunshine of the post-colonial age. Here, the young professionals of all ethnicities represented in the territory met to unwind, drink, strut, gossip, flirt and pair off. Jack told himself he found it all superficial and posturing, and reminded himself he was now more mature and cultivated than the average customer. On the other hand, he enjoyed its anonymous gaiety. Here you could hide in the crowd or in the shadows and, unlike the Headline Club, needn't worry about your reputation, or politics, or intelligent conversation. Here there was no demand on your wit or repartee, beyond some innovative chat-up lines. Anyway, the music was too loud and nullified any attempts to hold a sensible conversation.

Finally, he caught the eye of one of the frenetic bartenders and ordered two beers and a white wine. He turned and handed drinks to Les and the three of them pushed their way to a corner, where, luckily, enough seats were just being vacated for them to squeeze into.

They sipped their drinks and chatted, leaning in, heads close together in order to hear through the ubiquitous pounding music. It mingled with the staccato conversations of increasingly inebriated young people, competing for attention and laughing in an exaggerated manner.

Val talked about her children and their progress at school. Jack listened attentively and commented appropriately. He liked Val. The woman was unpretentious, intelligent and warm-hearted. She asked about Jack's family, and he reported on his parents' problems and his concerns for his brother. Jack queried Les about his business activities, eliciting, as always, convoluted answers which left him none the wiser about Les's precise role in his multinational enterprise. It didn't really matter, for he wasn't that interested.

After a while, their battle against the wall of noise petered out and they sat together looking around, taking in the colour and chaos of the scene. Les bought another round. Then he jumped up and took Val's hand to lead her to the dance floor. "Come on, this is an old favourite of ours. Bit slower, ya know!" he said, with a wink to Jack.

Immediately Jack felt a piercing sense of loneliness. What am I doing here? he thought. I don't even particularly like the place. Here I am, on my own, holding polite conversations with decent people, when I don't feel decent myself. I feel frustrated and angry and I'm not sure what to do about it.

At that moment someone tapped him on the shoulder. He turned and found himself looking at an acquaintance called Justin Gaynor. Gaynor, slightly older than Jack, was, as always for a man about town, immaculately dressed in designer jeans, blue silk shirt and smart white denim jacket.

"Hi there, Mr Wilson," beamed Gaynor, holding out his hand. "How ya doing? Long time no see."

Jack shook his hand warmly, for Gaynor, whom he knew through his previous job, was invariably cheerful and amusing company. Not only that, but he was a successful entrepreneur, having started a fast-growing communications company since leaving their previous employer. Both had a professional interest in the other. After exchanging pleasantries, Gaynor wasted no time making his purpose clear.

"Look, Jack, if you're hanging around a while, I want to talk to you later about some business. Something that should interest you — if you see what I mean? Gotta meet someone right now, back within the hour. Catch you later?" Gaynor spoke the last words in a conspiratorial tone, bending over Jack and winking. Jack nodded, without knowing what he meant. Gaynor was certainly talented and sharp-minded, but prone, considered Jack, to dramatics and unnecessary embellishment. He didn't take him too seriously.

The Broughtons returned from the dance floor, holding hands, perspiring, red-faced and pleased with their efforts. Les bought another round, but as he conversed softly with his wife, Jack's gaze wandered over the scene in the popular bar.

One group, by the bar, attracted his attention. Businessmen, by the look of it. Older than the average age in the place, wearing dark suits, ties removed and white shirts open at the top. Sipping light beers. What intrigued him was the mixture. A couple were likely European, while two others were probably Japanese, Jack assumed from their looks and behaviour. He couldn't hear any conversation, but noticed their repetitive nodding of the head. There were also several Chinese men and women in the group. From the trade fair, he assumed. These were the people behind the statistics and reports he dealt with. Buying and selling what? Fashion garments? Foodstuffs? Jewellery? Or perhaps they were bankers. This small patch of land has come a long way in recent years, Jack repeated the promotional mantra. International trade and finance meeting here to do business these days. No wonder General Khan wants to keep it within his control.

On the dance floor the movements were becoming more confident, suggestive and seductive, as the music seemed to speed up and force itself into every cranny of the room and out into the night air. Chinese, Caucasian, Filipino, and other Asian youngsters, jostled for space as they sought to attract and impress each other. Jack watched a couple of slim Chinese girls, one in a dark mini skirt, the other in leather pants, gyrate demurely and impassively on the edge of the floor. It amused him to see several young guys being waved away regally as they attempted to inveigle themselves into the girls' space. Others followed the music vigorously, though not always very rhythmically, on their own, while some flung their partners around in a form of rock and roll. A few just hugged their sweethearts and shuffled pointlessly around in circles, looking longingly at each other.

It was a joyful scene — colourful, cosmopolitan and energetic. Jack started to relax and enjoy himself.

It was well after ten when the Broughtons stood up to leave. They had the kids to think about, explained Val. They offered Jack a share taxi ride home, but he decided to stay for "one for the road". His intentions were to remain and look for some female company.

After his friends had left, Jack felt a familiar feeling of freedom and independence. He was on his own now. No work to trouble him. No demanding company. Not even the mild distraction of sympathetic friends. He was able to do what he wanted. And here, the businessmen at the bar, the two Chinese girls, the other dancers, had no moral hold over him. They didn't know him. They didn't care about him. They didn't judge him.

Although experiencing a little drunkenness, it was the euphoric kind — engendering lightness and the illusion of control. Therefore, it was logical that the first thing was to celebrate his liberty and enhance the euphoria with another drink. He moved to a free seat at the bar, from which he ordered a beer and began to observe the dance floor from closer range.

His eye soon lighted on an attractive woman with shoulder-length fine blonde hair swirling as she danced with a couple of girlfriends. Petite — probably just over five feet tall — she had a pretty angular face with flashing blue eyes and a broad smile, which she wore without affectation. Slim but shapely, her legs complemented by a short tight black skirt, she sported a white office blouse, as though she had come straight from work. Quite a beauty, he thought to himself. As he watched her, she glanced at him a couple of times, the smile still showing her even white teeth. It was enough encouragement. He stepped onto the dance floor and asked if he might join them.

"Sure, why not?" she said, and spun around coquettishly. A confident dancer himself, Jack settled into the rhythm of the song and was soon moving in unison with her.

"I'm Jack," he offered, as the track ended and gave a short respite to the drowning noise. "What's your name?" "Georgia," she replied.

"Georgia from where?" he asked, aware of the unoriginality of his lines.

"Oh, from here, these days, for a while anyway," she answered teasingly.

"And originally?" he followed up, already feeling like he was clumsily walking through thick mud in his efforts to generate a conversation.

"The States… California," she replied brightly, spinning away from him again as the music picked up again.

After a couple more dances and stumbling conversation, he invited Georgia for a drink, an offer she accepted willingly, bidding her girlfriends to "hang around" for her.

He found out that she was twenty-four years old and spending six months in the territory with her mother's fashion company, as a form of work experience.

"So, what do you think about this place?" Jack asked her.

"Oh wow! It's kinda fun and interesting and all that, but I miss home. There's more space and freedom. Too crowded for me here."

"Yeah, can imagine," laughed Jack. "Lots of surfin', sunshine and smoking pot, I suppose," immediately regretting the banality of his words.

"No way, yuk," Georgia furrowed her brow and pouted. "I hate surfing and never smoke stuff. Too busy with school anyway."

"Ah!" This caught Jack by surprise. "What are you studying then?"

"I'm doing a Masters in Fashion Management. It's cool, Mum and Dad are paying me through. I'm lucky, I guess." She sipped at her vodka tonic. "What do you do?"

"Me? Just a boring paper pusher working in the Industry and Trade Ministry. I have to get, you know, reports and things ready for the bigwigs."

"I see, sounds fascinating," said the American, screwing up her face in irony.

Jack laughed. She really was quite charming and alluring. He was already daring to imagine he might stay with her this evening and even sleep with her.

After a while, she suggested they dance again and they rejoined her friends on the floor. The club remained packed and noisy. By eleven thirty Jack was beginning to feel tired. He pulled Georgia by the hand back to the bar.

"Fancy going on somewhere for a night cap?" he ventured. "Or a bite to eat?"

"Oh… well… thanks, but I'm out with the girls tonight," she answered, pulling a face of mock contrition.

"They're fine, aren't they?" Jack followed up, sensing she was interested and just needed some gentle persuasion. "Look, they're chatting up a couple of guys and can look after themselves."

Georgia looked at him with sympathetic but serious face, as if she were talking to a wayward child.

"We're having a good time here, aren't we? Look, you're a real nice guy, but I don't want to get involved here. I'm only here for a while."

"Well, I wasn't necessarily thinking of getting involved, you know. More like just enjoying ourselves and having some fun," Jack said lamely with a weak smile.

Her look changed as though someone had presented her with grave news.

"If you're looking for a quick screw, Jack, I'm sorry, you've got the wrong girl." She looked away.

"No, no, don't get me wrong. I just thought… you know… we were getting along OK. Wasn't assuming anything. You're taking this the wrong way. Don't be so… so oversensitive." He struggled to find the words, feeling increasingly irritated at his own inability to handle the situation.

She read his mood and felt uncomfortable.

"Look, sorry, but I don't do one-night stands, OK? I've got a guy back in the States, all right?"

"Yeah, of course. Understand. No problem," Jack said, pretending indifference but thinking that further conversation was pointless.

"Well, shall we at least have one more drink? Let me get you one," she offered.

"No, I don't think so. Thanks anyway. I think your mates are waiting for you," he said sourly, looking away.

"Fine. Well, take it easy, stop being so wired and… try chilling, Jack," she said, looking at him sympathetically.

"Don't patronise me with your smart-arse phrases," he snapped back.

Surprised by his petulant tone, she hesitated for a moment, then said airily: "You know what… I don't need this shit. Fuck you!" She turned and strode off jauntily, her blonde hair flowing over her shoulders.

He watched her return to the dance floor, his annoyance turning into a kind of black humour at his own ineptitude. On reaching her friends, she was clearly explaining to them what a jerk Jack was, pointing back in his direction. As he swivelled around in his chair to avoid their looks and face the bar, he found himself laughing out loud, which attracted the attention of his neighbouring drinkers, causing him to stop.

What a fool, he thought. What a fool to lose my cool. What a fool to chase an attractive girl like that in such a clumsy way. It was laughable. Pathetic. Should act my age. But what the hell!

He ordered another beer. One for the road.

Then, quite suddenly, he froze, as time itself hesitated for a split second.

Across the other side of the seating area, he saw Marion. And what was worse, she was clearly watching him and was aware he had seen her. As their eyes engaged, she smiled and waved, like an old friend that hadn't been seen for a few days. As if their relationship was devoid of any passion or hurt. That smile and wave was neutralising the past, as if cleansing it of the feelings of which it was constructed and had made it both glorious and dark.

Shit, what's she doing here? he thought, as he smiled wanly and waved back half-heartedly.

Marion stood up and started towards him, working her way between the crowded tables. Moving with athletic elegance, she was striking in a bright red, figure-hugging short dress and turned many heads as she passed through the crowd. Her neat fringe framed her fine features, as she smiled in apology to those she disturbed.

Jack struggled with his emotions. On the one hand, he was pleased to see her, to enjoy once more her expressive face and long dark hair, her energy and sparkle. On the other hand, he resented her reappearance, reminding him of the disappointment and frustration of their breaking up. He felt his pulse quicken and his cheeks burn. Determined to be distantly polite, he sucked in a deep breath as she approached.

"Hiya, Jack, nice to see you. How are you?" she asked in a serious tone, and kissed him lightly on the cheek.

"Bloody awful," he replied with theatrical self-pity. "Drunk and depressed, as always."

"Yes, you poor old thing, I did see you suffering," she said, indicating with a nod towards the dance floor.

Jack smiled. "Oh, she's just a friend from work," he lied, not knowing why.

"Anyway," he asked her, "what the hell are you doing here? I thought you were settled with lover boy in London."

"Over here for the trade fair. Just for a few days. Buying garments, mid-range stuff. Got a new job in London. Buying for a new online operation, the future direction, you know, very innovative and tomorrow's world," she said, waving her hand in a grand gesture.

"How are you, really? How's the Ministry? Have you settled in now? Has it got better?" she continued, looking at Jack earnestly.

"Ah well, you know… it's OK. The boss is as much a pain in the ass as ever. I guess I'll stick it out till the end of the year and then decide what to do," Jack replied.

He felt uncomfortable. It seemed artificial having these polite, superficial exchanges with a former lover. But there was no point in going over the same old issues which had riven their relationship. He could talk of his resentment and express his anger and jealousy, but these feelings had no relevance now, which made them all the more excruciating.

"Do you miss me then?" he suddenly blurted out, trying to make it sound light-hearted.

She wasn't fooled by the tone and answered with a straight face, returning with the very seriousness he was aiming to avoid.

"'Course I do. But, Jack, you know it wasn't working. I had to get out of it, for your sake and mine. We're still friends, aren't we?" Her question was sincere enough, but Jack's first thought was retaliation.

"Friends? Oh yes! Just like we always were, apparently," he answered. "Because you were still in contact with lover boy, weren't you?"

"Ah look, I'm not going down that path again, OK? If you wanna turn over the old arguments, then enjoy yourself and wallow in your self-pity. I'm not interested. And by the way, David is a decent guy and he doesn't wind me up like you do." She turned her face away.

"Anyway, it'll probably please you no end to know that right now I'm not with him and that it didn't turn out how I expected." She kept facing away, and Jack suspected there were tears in her eyes.

He felt sympathy for this woman he had so adored but, at the same time, schadenfreude that her relationship was in difficulties. He even experienced a momentary shiver of optimism that he could get her back. But no, that wasn't going to happen.

"Sorry, Marion, really. Wasn't aware, didn't mean to hurt you. Sorry to hear that. What… er… what happened?" He touched her arm gently, so she turned to face him. Her eyes glistened but she was not going to cry.

"Oh, it's complicated. His work… his obsession with work. His family… London. Lots of things really. I had high hopes but it wasn't what I expected. Quite honestly, I was glad to get away, to come here for a few days. Clear the head. It's been fun being back," she explained, attempting a brighter tone but sounding the sadder for it.

"You didn't call me," he said, plaintively.

"No, and you know why," she replied.

"We had a good thing going there, Marion. Why did you stay in contact with David, anyway? It wasn't like you to be so deceptive. You didn't give us long enough," he said.

"I'm sorry. I just wasn't sure. I felt you wanted different things. You were so… so lost in your thoughts sometimes. So detached. So cold. I felt sometimes you didn't even like me being around," she replied.

"Oh no. That was never the case. Marion, I adored you. I do adore you. I was just fucked up about work and whether to stay here and where I was going," he explained.

"And that, Jack, was the problem. You were so restless. To be honest, you were hard work sometimes and I just needed someone a bit less complicated. Look, you're a lovely guy, but you need to take yourself less seriously. Chill out more," she said, taking hold of his hand.

"Funny, you're the second person to say that to me tonight," he smiled.

"When are you going back?" he added.

"Tuesday," she said.

"Fancy a drink on Monday night?" he ventured.

"No, can't. Have a business meeting and dinner with clients. But how about lunch? Would be nice to catch up in a quieter place. Maybe lunch is better," she suggested.

"Oh, and if you don't mind, you can bring along those few bits and pieces I left behind, especially my trainers," she added.

"Yeah, of course, yeah, I'll have a look," he replied sheepishly.

They agreed Marion would call him to confirm the agreed lunch date and venue. With a shy smile she kissed him on the cheek, like an elder sister, saying: "Well, I better re-join the others. Take care of yourself, Jack. And don't drink too much." She wagged a finger at him and took her leave. He yearned for her.

He watched her return across the room, until she disappeared behind the crowds of customers. He had felt aroused by her presence and happy at the thought of seeing her on Monday. Even though it was only for lunch. Who knows though?

Feeling less sorry for himself and slightly sobered, Jack determined to go home. He swallowed the last of his beer. Seeing Marion unexpectedly had confused him. Having convinced himself that being single again was not such a bad thing and that the relationship with her was doomed, and that she was not a trustworthy or particularly good person, he now found himself missing her again and experiencing the feelings he had before in her presence. He remembered how he first met her, at a party, and was entranced by her vivacity and unselfconscious physicality. She knew she was desirable and enjoyed the attention she attracted without needing to be coquettish. Their love making had been instinctive and affectionate, without artifice or complication. The memories came back and disturbed him. Without thinking, he ordered another beer, as if to quench them.

Suddenly, he thought of Doug. Looking at his watch, he noted it was approaching midnight and gave his brother a call to check on his whereabouts. He considered going to join him at the demonstration. Better late than never. But Doug didn't pick up. Never mind, perhaps I'll go take a look to show support, he reasoned.

On the way out he turned into the gents' toilet to relieve himself. As he turned to the basins afterwards to wash his hands, he bumped into someone leaning over the basin surfaces. It was Justin Gaynor, preparing to inhale a line of cocaine. Gaynor, without standing up, turned his head sideways.

"Ah, Mr Wilson. There you are. I was on my way back to find you. Wanna try a line? Good stuff. Nice and light," said Gaynor.

Why not, thought Jack. He had sampled cocaine a few times in the past and found its effects mild and without side effects. He was curious and accepted the offer, leaning over and sniffing up the white powder through the plastic straw Gaynor gave him.

After an embarrassing coughing fit, he felt quite clear-headed.

"Thanks, Justin. Haven't had that for a while. Can I get you a drink?" Jack recalled their previous conversation and wanted to know if Gaynor really had anything worth hearing on the business front.

"Sure, that'd be fun," came back Gaynor. "But not here. This place is too crowded with yuppies. Too loud. Let's go down the Old Ship. More action there. More tarts, you know." He pulled a face like an old uncle giving a nephew a laddish tip that the parents shouldn't know about.

"The Old Ship?" Jack grinned. "God, haven't been there for a while. Is it safe these days?" he asked mockingly, remembering the reputation of the drinking establishment. In colonial days gone by, it had been the haunt of visiting seamen and soldiers, and was in consequence the home of prostitutes, conmen and late-night revellers. Once the scene of frequent brawls, it had in recent years cleaned up its act, but never shaken off its image entirely as a last-ditch stopover for the flotsam and jetsam of the local night scene, most of whom generally washed up at midnight or after.

"Jack, my boy, you're safe with me," bragged Gaynor. "Let's go and sample the delights and I can tell you about my brilliant plans."

They passed out into the night, Gaynor holding on to Jack's arm, supporting him as if he were his girlfriend. They headed down the street, still full of cars and drinkers, a street bright with the vulgar neon glare of numerous small cafes, noodle shops and stores.

Jack's phone in his jacket pocket rang several times, but he didn't notice it in the midst of the noisy street traffic and Gaynor's inebriated rambling.

Chapter Six
Fading Away

"The important thing to remember about Shakespeare," said the earnest middle-aged man with the neatly close-shaven beard and dark-rimmed glasses, "is that he was very much a man of his time and yet, of course, he was, indeed a writer for all ages, dealing with the eternal themes of love, revenge, violence, betrayal, forgiveness, and so on, whose relevance touches us today with equal force."

"Well, he can't really be both... can he? I mean, it's not really logical, is it? We can say he was man of his time or he wasn't. Seems to me he transcended his time and became great because he could, sort of, see beyond his time," commented one of the students.

Taking off his glasses and rubbing his eyes with his forefinger and thumb, the tutor then looked towards the ceiling and sighed, as if appealing for some spiritual energy to strengthen him in the endless task of educating the enthusiastic but often dim-witted students who attended his Shakespeare seminars.

"Well, Jenkins, we have to separate the talented and commercially-minded playwright who represented the zeitgeist of the times; who could stimulate, inspire and amuse the unruly Elizabethan audiences of his day, with topical stories and fantasies, and yet, at the same time," he paused for effect, now cleaning his glasses with his handkerchief, "and yet, at the same time, become a literary giant, whose astonishing language, insight into human nature and wit, can entertain and move us all these years later. In other words, his genius is exactly in achieving that legacy. Do you see that?" he concluded with a measure of insistent pity in his voice.

Jenkins nodded resentfully in agreement, recognising that further debate was probably uncalled for and would likely irritate his tutor and the other students. The workshop was nearing its end and they were keen to finish.

"Anyway, we'll call it a day for now," said the tutor. "Before next week I want you to read 'The Tempest' and produce for us a presentation. The theme will be: 'Did Shakespeare mean Prospero to be portrayed as a magnanimous, wise and forgiving statesman, or a malignant, conniving colonial bully. OK with that? Any questions? Good, then see you next week!" The tutor nodded, collected together his worksheets, put them neatly into his battered briefcase and marched briskly out.

Matthew Wilson sat for a few moments, scribbling notes on the coming assignment, while the other students shuffled out, chatting noisily

"Come on, Mat, fancy a drink?" asked Jenkins. "Let's go to the union bar."

"OK, sure!" replied Matthew dreamily. He was still thinking about the workshop and the tutor's various messages and felt irritated. All very predictable and well-rehearsed, he thought. The role-playing and readings they had done were all conducted by the tutor with a pre-determined format and outcome. He felt let down. He had hoped for more creative challenges when he came to this university. Now, approaching the end of his first year, he felt some disillusionment with his chosen course.

"Mat, come on, we're going," shouted Jenkins.

"Yeah, yeah, on my way," answered Matthew.

Ten minutes later the group of six or so students settled into a corner seat of the half-empty students' union bar. It was a cavernous place, with high ceilings and bare concrete finishing. Brutalist, some called it. It was not built for comfort, or quiet reflection, but rather for the essential function of socialising, drinking and debating matters serious, sporting and frivolous in large numbers. At least the drinks were relatively inexpensive, and it was entirely unpretentious, to the point of scruffy neglect. This day, at the late afternoon hour, it was populated by a few groups of tired patrons, who, having completed their week's formal studies, were settling down to reviewing the challenges of the week and planning remedial activities for the weekend ahead.

"He's an arrogant bastard, isn't he, that Dr Williams," suddenly interjected Matthew, while the others were talking about the assignment he'd set. The others turned to him, surprised at the strength of this mild-mannered classmate's opinion.

They looked at a slim, pale young man, who appeared older than his peers. His long brown hair hung down over his ears and forehead, requiring him to frequently flick it away from his eyes with the back of his fingers. There was a seriousness in those eyes that some found intimidating when they were object of their fixed gaze. His intenseness gave him a force in debate that put those who disagreed with him on the defensive.

"He doesn't really listen, does he? Sort of a puts you down. Ol' Jenkins makes a reasonable point, and he just makes clear his boredom. Doesn't consider it or anything, just asserts a truth as he sees it," Matthew continued, clearly irked.

"Well, he did make a point about the difference between the writer being able to basically entertain Elizabethans and someone making timeless comments on human nature," said Penny, another of the tutees.

"Shakespeare was amazing after all, wasn't he?" she added.

"Oh, I dunno. I really think he's over rated," countered Matthew, warming to the discussion.

"All that Tudor propaganda in the histories — real ass licking stuff that — and those nonsensical and unrealistic plots in the totally unfunny comedies. The gratuitous blood-letting and violence of the tragedies. And the language — overblown hyperbolic verbiage.

Tolstoy saw through all that, you know. Its main value has been to keep generations of critics and academics like Williams in a job, scrutinising it with a magnifying glass. And we have to spend hours as kids learning to decipher it, and pretending we enjoy it, when the reality is, we don't really get it, and it doesn't relate to us! He might have been a man of his time, but definitely not of mine!" Matthew spoke quietly but with a conviction that silenced the others.

"Wow!" said Jenkins finally. "Heavy stuff, mate. Ought to get you delivering the workshop next time!" Everyone laughed, except Matthew.

"I know, I know, but you must admit, there's a kind of academic orthodoxy, where they have been studying these topics for years and can't afford to let go of their conclusions," he added.

"Maybe, but they're more experienced than us. They've read more, studied more and looked at this in detail. We have to live with that. It's hard to argue with them," said Penny, "when they know more than us."

"That's just the problem," answered Matthew. "There's insight and intuition and stuffing yourself with facts. It's not about the number of books you read. It's about understanding, about critiquing, about creative analysis. Are they really encouraging that? I don't think so. We might challenge their theories, after all. But when we do, they get all precious and patronising."

"Right, Professor Wilson, well said. And I've got a theory too. Theory of buying another round," said

Jenkins and his suggestion was greeted with cheers of approval. The conversation moved on to less demanding topics.

He had arrived at this red-brick university in the Midlands in 1987 full of optimism and a sense of new-found freedom. Matthew Wilson had not been unhappy at school and at home with his family, but he had felt confined. His teachers had been encouraging and his talents had been recognised at school, as he regularly scored top grades, particularly in the arts subjects.

"He has a way with words," said one staff member. "Matthew is too reserved, but has hidden depths," said another. "Wilson has potential if he applies himself," adjudged a third.

But he knew he had much more to offer. He felt himself driven by a creative spirit, that just needed the right environment to be unleashed.

His parents, whom he loved and respected, couldn't be expected to appreciate this. He knew they cared for him, and even though his father could be difficult, Matthew was aware of Bill's sense of duty of care, and never understood why he laboured under the idea that he didn't like him. His relationship with his mother, however, was simpler and loving. She left him alone. She had an intuitive understanding of his wish for privacy. But she no more empathised with his feelings than his father. Even in his teens, he felt he had outgrown home and family and longed for escape.

University life — resident on the campus along with other students and having the freedom to largely set his own schedule — was at first exhilarating. He launched himself energetically into his course work, attending lectures, even optional ones, seminars and workshops, punctually and with enthusiasm. He also enjoyed the company of his fellow students, although some of them seemed to him superficial — more interested in a social life centred on drinking to excess and dabbling in drugs.

Nevertheless, during the course of his first year, his eagerness to please had begun to pall, and his positivity dulled. His unease began with his grades, which, despite his efforts, normally failed to exceed the average. Contrary to his understanding of his schoolteachers' views of his ability, and his own innate belief in his talent, his tutors were not of the same view. This frustrated and disturbed him and, as a result, he began to challenge his mentors' assessment of his work.

His Creative Writing tutor, who was kindly and sympathetic, advised him to inject more discipline into his writing, for it lacked coherence, he told him.

"Don't try so hard to be unconventional or avant-garde," he had suggested. "You have some good ideas, but you don't put them into a framework that communicates them to others. And this is all about communication," he had said to Matthew.

To his colleagues, however, the same teacher had described his student's work as: "Unusual, but opaque. I really don't know what he's getting at half the time."

"Yes, interesting character, but a bit mixed up," the colleague had replied. "He's trying to fly before he can walk."

Matthew, however, was definitely keen on flying high. His impatience soon led him into questioning the validity of the course and the competence of his teachers. He was also beginning to find the company of his fellow students tiresome. By the end of his first year, he was openly critical of the effectiveness of the course and relieved when the summer break enabled him to neglect his studies and turn attention to his own reading.

He spent the summer weeks in the university town, organising a place to rent, with fellow students, working casually in a local bar/restaurant and reading and writing. Working on an idea for a play, he was finally able to start realising it on paper. It never really occurred to him to go home, though he did spend a long weekend with the family. During those few days, he didn't speak of his disquiet, giving the impression to his parents and brothers that everything was progressing smoothly at university. Given his reserved nature, none of them observed any discomfort on his part.

As the months of his second year passed, however, his unease grew. The Art and Drama course demanded more active workshops and practical work in this part of the course, but that failed to reassure him. He felt he was failing, being unsure now whether it was his lack of ability or the deficiency of the course. Perhaps it was just unsuitable. As a result, he began to resent the lessons and started to skip them. At first, his absence was intermittent, and as long as he sent in the required excuses and submitted assignments, it was not noticed much by the administration.

By the time the summer weeks came around, however, he had avoided so many teaching hours that he was embarrassed to return. He had fallen behind with assignments and sank into a paralysis of lethargy. The university pastoral authorities had noticed something amiss for a number of months, but merely assumed it was a case of illness. Now they questioned his classmates, who reluctantly covered for him, pleading ignorance as to his whereabouts. But then they sent a letter to his parents, asking to know of Matthew's intentions. Had he dropped out of the course? Was he safe and well?

At home the message was received with shock. Bill flipped between anger and worry. What was the matter with this boy? He had allowed him to go his own way. He had warned him about doing "arty-farty" courses, hadn't he? This was inevitable. At the same time, his paternal instinct, tinged with the guilt contaminating his feelings for his eldest son, provoked him into immediate action. He determined to go and seek Matthew out and bring him home. Jack was to go with him. Elizabeth was too upset and Jack had visited Matthew in his student home and knew the location. The two of them drove up to the university town.

But the visit was ineffective. Matthew appeared to them pale and listless, but not unwell. He was in full control of his reasoning and emotions — emotionless, rather. Calmly he declared his intention to drop out from university, for the "experiment" had been a failure and he had other plans now. No, he had no intention of returning home, as he intended to find work and stay where he was. He could pay his own way. Bill was alternatively insistent and pleading, citing his mother's anxiety as a reason for him to return, but to no avail. His bluster ran out of energy, leaving him deflated, while Jack could only keep asking his brother: "You sure you're OK?"

"Don't worry," was Matthew's stock response. "I'll be fine." He had always said that to reassure his family. His father and brother returned home worried and baffled.

In the next few years, Matthew enjoyed life. To be exact, he enjoyed certain aspects of his life. He had no wish for the comfort of family domesticity, relishing the uncertainties of independence and avoidance of responsibility it allowed. For a year or so, he continued to live in his student-shared accommodation, eking out a living from part-time menial jobs — working as a shop assistant, call centre operative, and private tutor, among other things. At the same time, he wrote prodigiously, mainly plays, of an abstract and metaphysical nature, poetry and outlines of novels. He submitted material to publishers and publications but met with little success. Occasionally a publisher responded with an acknowledgement and even more infrequently with a comment of encouragement. One regarded the synopsis of a play Matthew was drafting as: "Interesting but too esoteric for a general audience". This lack of success, or understanding, as Matthew came to see it, frustrated him and cast a shadow over an otherwise carefree bohemian life style.

After a year or two, he joined up with an experimental street theatre. Moving away finally from the student community, he took a room in an old Victorian house, shared with other members of the troop, two men and two women. They won a few commissions from the local council, performing at schools and local further education colleges, as well as acting in town centres and shopping malls, where they collected cash from curious or bemused onlookers. Their educational pieces made fun of Shakespearian and Dickensian classics, ones that students would recognise, but made amenable through humour and satire. For the streets they played farce, but also what they intended as biting satire on the political establishment of the day. It was at times exhilarating, and dispiriting on others, but they made enough of an income to pay the rent and their living expenses. Matthew often wrote, or co-wrote, their pieces and played a full role in performances, always enthusiastically if not with great talent.

After nearly two years, however, his intimate group broke up. One couple, male and female, decided to marry and "settle down." They moved away, while the other man obtained a regular job in a repertory theatre company and the remaining woman decided to travel.

Matthew needed to find an alternative place to live and a means of paying for it. At the age of twenty-six he found a shared flat with a young professional man, called Joshua, or "Josh," as he was commonly known, and he applied for his first full-time job — at a marketing agency as a copywriter.

Although at heart he saw this step as a compromise, or a "sell-out", he nevertheless told himself that the role was a temporary expedient — a means to an end. He would continue with his creative work and keep an eye open for positions in the theatre and media world that better suited his ambition.

In practice, the role at the agency proved not only comfortable but pleasurable. The owner of the company, which was only a few years old, but growing successfully, discovered a unique talent in their new recruit, who proved adept at writing succinct, witty and persuasive copy for their diverse clientele. Though finding him odd and far too intellectual for his taste, the owner pampered him and soon raised his salary. It was an investment worth making. Colleagues also warmed to Matthew. He was, after all, non-competitive, polite and reserved, while contributing manifestly to the success of the business.

For the first time in his life, Matthew now found he had some spare money in his pocket. It offered the opportunity to explore avenues of social life that had been previously restricted by lack of purchasing power. Fashionable clothing had never before interested Mark, but he now discovered it as a means of expressing his individuality. Rejecting the standard big-name brand labels on principle, and steering away from any punk influences, he found his own discrete combinations, which could have been labelled "neo romantic", but which he just considered individual and subtle. He kept his hair long, but had it cut stylishly and subtly tinted, at a fashionable hairdresser's.

A regular income also meant he could socialise more. Until this time, he had always been private to the point of evasion. Even in his teenage years, his circle of real friends had been confined to two, a boy and a girl, and on those long evenings when he decamped from his parents' house, he was usually to be found with both of them, in the bedroom of one of them. Mostly, they sat, listened to music, and talked of books and music. Occasionally, when they had the opportunity, they smoked a joint. Sometimes they watched films, or, in the warmer months, went for long rambling walks.

At university he had been more convivial, at the beginning anyway, making an effort to find new friends and broaden his acquaintances, with whom he might share his ideas. Despite his popularity, however, he chose to become increasingly a loner, having found the company of most students juvenile and boorish.

Sexually, he was detached, even neutral. Though he often found friends, male and female, physically attractive, it was in an aesthetic way, rather than lustfully. His lack of drive didn't trouble him too much, as he reasoned it to be a result of his greater interest in people's character and moral standing. He did sleep with, and make love to, two women while at university, and he found the experience pleasantly intimate and even amusing, but not ecstatic or urgent. The women remained friends rather than lovers.

Now, with a regular and substantial income, and with the encouragement of his new flatmate and colleagues, his demeanour and his behaviour changed. Finding that he enjoyed company, he began to socialise more, joining colleagues at pub evenings or house parties. But Josh was the real catalyst.

His flatmate, self-assured, good-looking and always conservatively smart, took a liking to Matthew and very quickly confided in him that he was gay. This was not obvious, for Josh had decided for career reasons, and because of his natural modesty, not to advertise his homosexuality."

"What about you?" he asked Matthew one evening, soon after he had moved in. "You straight? You haven't mentioned any girlfriends."

"Me? Oh, straight, I think. I mean, I don't think I've got a strong sex drive either way. I find some women and men very attractive, like I'd want to paint them or something, or caress them, hug them maybe, but I don't have a great need to think about screwing them."

Josh laughed heartily.

"You're funny! Maybe you just haven't met the right kind of person — or people — that turn you on. You should come with me to one of my clubs sometime. Might open your eyes," he said.

"Maybe," Matthew replied, thinking it would be a new experience. "What kind of club, exactly?"

"Well, a night club, of course, a gay night club." Josh ironically emphasised the word gay, smiling at his flatmate's naivety, not sure whether it was real or confected.

"Sure, why not. Might be fun," he said unconvincingly.

Two weeks later he joined Josh on a Saturday night cruise, going to several clubs that Josh was familiar with.

Although they varied in quality, they had certain features in common. They were deep, dark, warm and comfortable, and Matthew, despite initial misgivings, soon felt at ease in their intimate surroundings, as though he had found some kind of secure refuge. As for the other clubbers, he enjoyed their sense of uninhibited fun and flamboyance, if not the exaggerated camp posturing of some of them.

The first partner he relented to was a shy, beautiful Chinese Malay man called Lim, whose soft-spoken intelligence and exotic — to Matthew — background, won him over. A student of languages, Lim was sophisticated and charming. He intrigued Matthew with his profound knowledge of literature, and critical insights, for he was widely read and an original thinker. He had also travelled widely in Asia and America, acquiring a worldliness that Matthew found fascinating. His full mouth, his light bronze skin, defined cheek bones and appealing brown eyes were erotic and sensuous for the boy from the Midlands of England. For Lim, Matthew was bright and challenging, but also delightfully innocent, both intellectually and sexually. When they became lovers, Matthew discovered a world of physical intensity and yearning that he had not previously experienced.

However, after three months of a passionate relationship, Lim suddenly declared he was leaving, to return home to Malaysia. His study visa was expiring, and he was to go back to his country, which frowned upon people like him.

Josh was dismissive when Matthew spoke of his love for Lim and distress at his leaving.

"I know it's hard. Your first boyfriend. But you'll get over it. Lim was no angel, you know." He tried to reason his friend out his misery.

"What do you mean," Matthew replied, annoyed. "You trying to tell me he was sleeping around or something?"

"Just saying. He was a nice guy, and very attractive and everything, but you weren't his first and won't be his last, so you gotta be realistic, see?" Josh reasoned.

"I trust you had safe sex," he added in a throwaway fashion.

"Of course," said Matthew seriously, the gravity of his tone smothering a stab of unease in his heart.

Over the following months he went less to the gay clubs, gradually retreating back into his former isolation. But this once tranquil zone was now blighted with an acute sense of loneliness, following the elation of falling in love.

Also, his health began to show alarming signs in the months that followed. Flus and colds that persisted. After a year he reluctantly went for an HIV test. He was positive. Fearing the stigma, he told no one, not Josh or his family, but continued to work intensely at the agency, suppressing his anxiety through overwork.

The call to Matthew's home was picked up by Bill.

"Mr Wilson?"

"Yes, that'll be me. Who's calling?"

"Mr Wilson… this is Josh, Matthew's flatmate."

"Yes, I've heard of you," said Bill.

"Mr Wilson… I'm… I have to… terrible news… I'm so sorry."

"What news? What's up then? Is Mat OK?" Bill Wilson was deeply alarmed and irritated by Josh's hesitancy.

"No, no, he's been in an accident... a traffic accident outside work. Mr Wilson... he didn't make it... I'm so sorry." Josh broke down.

Bill felt his whole body go limp. His arms hung down to his side, still holding the receiver. His first thought was "How do I break this to Lizzie?"

Then he fought hard to regain his self-control.

"What happened, lad?" he asked in a barely audible voice. "Tell me."

Josh explained that Matthew had been hit by a lorry, crossing the road near to his office, as he was leaving work. He passed that way every day. Medics had arrived quickly, but Matthew has died on the spot from fatal head injuries. He was twenty-six years old.

The unexpected news froze the family like an arctic blast. Jack and Doug were summoned home to console their mother, who was immobilised with grief. This child... we never looked after him well enough, she thought. We let him drift away.

Bill's anguish was on his wife's account, while Jack could hardly entertain the reality of the news. He had visited Matthew a couple of times in his post-university existence and found him calm and just as enigmatically content as ever. Doug's grief was more bitter than sorrowful. He railed against fate in general and against the random cruelty of chance.

A witness to the accident testified that Matthew seemed to be day dreaming and stepped onto the road without looking. Another thought the lorry had been going too fast. The shaken lorry driver swore that Matthew stepped out on purpose and turned to look at him before his vehicle struck him. But no one knew for sure why this had happened. The death was recorded as accidental.

On the day of the burial of Matthew's ashes at the cemetery close to the family home, Jack found himself staring round at a bleak scene. It seemed as if nature were deliberately denying the family any comfort as they huddled around the grave. The wind was unforgiving and, in sharp gusts, dragged winter's ragged leaves and scraps of litter across the graveyard.

Later, at a dismal wake in a local pub, in the company of a few close family friends, several of Matthew's old school friends and Josh, Jack read a short eulogy to his lost brother.

Having spoken of Matthew's kind and reserved nature, his talent for and desire to write real literature, and having tried to lighten the tone with remarks about his brother's uniqueness, he concluded with the words:

"Dear Matthew, we will all miss you so much. We didn't see enough of you in recent years and you went your own individual way. The greatest pity of your life being cut short is that you won't achieve the great dreams you had. We are so sorry we weren't there for you near the end. We are sorry as well, that, as your family, we didn't try hard enough to get to know you better."

Once the company departed, the family left together. Bill walked by Jack's side down the short car park walk. He put a hand on Jack's shoulder.

"Well done, son," he said. "That weren't easy. You said good words."

Then he added: "He was gay, weren't he? I mean, I don't mind, but he was strange. Do you think he did it on purpose?"

"I don't know, Dad. I really don't know," answered Jack and he turned his face away from his father to conceal the tears in his eyes.

Chapter Seven
Manoeuvres

Actions like this, thought Doug, as he sat in an overcrowded area of the students' union cafeteria, surveying the exhilarating disorder around him, have a thrilling, but terrible energy of their own. They carry you along as if you were a pleasure-seeker riding a surging current, enjoying the momentum and power. But then, without warning, they are just as likely to dash you against the rocks, or hurl you exhausted onto an empty beach like so much flotsam.

He cast his mind back to some of the protests and marches he had participated in back home. Generally, they had been good-natured, carnival-like affairs; but he had also experienced flashes of violence, when tempers had frayed, when militants provoked the opposition or the police, or when the police themselves reacted with disproportionate violence. He had experienced fist-fights, scuffles and arrests, suffered tear gas and seen missiles exchanged as in primitive warfare. This was something different, however, with larger, graver issues at stake, and more ominous undertones. He felt like he was sitting in the belly of a monster.

"How y're doing there, Doug? Fancy a beer, while there's any left?" asked Brandon, yanking the younger man from his daydreaming. "Rocky's scrounged a couple of six-packs from somewhere."

"Sure," replied Doug. "Sounds good."

As he sipped the warm beer from the can, he continued to look around the scene, forever morphing, as groups of students came and went, searching for a place to sit, meet with friends, or search for food. The place was packed full with bodies. Bodies sitting and lying on the floor, on the tables, under the tables, lounging on the uncomfortable plastic chairs. Everywhere there was excitable, loud conversation as groups discussed their cause and motives and the implications of the sit-in. Some groups sporadically broke into rhythmic clapping, rousing chants or songs, rising to a crescendo, then fading again into the general hubbub, like the chanting in a football stadium.

It was an untidy and chaotic scene, with the casually but colourfully clothed participants sprawling amongst the inevitable detritus of protest marches and mass actions — hastily fabricated wooden banners, and sheets, bearing various slogans and demands, discarded water bottles and plastic lunch boxes, tissues and toilet paper. Young and shining with optimism, the protesters were emboldened at defying authority and feeling part of a purposeful movement. Most were local Chinese, but there were also small groups of Malay and Indian youngsters, along with a scattering of Filipinos and

Europeans, usually visiting scholars at the university's well-regarded language departments.

"What do you reckon, Dick?" Doug asked his senior colleague. "It's got some good support. Lots of enthusiasm, but is it going anywhere? They're having a lot of fun, but are the student union people actually doing anything? Don't see much sign of leadership. Do we know what the university's response is? What are the police up to? I hear there's a good number of them forming up outside the main square entrance."

"Yeah, well, exactly, Doug," replied Brandon. "We need to do some thinking here, don't we?"

Chuckling at Doug's string of questions, the lecturer waved other members of the group around him. He sat on the edge of one of the fixed tables, with the younger men and women sitting around on the chairs or squatting on the floor, looking up at him, like eager acolytes awaiting the guru's words of wisdom.

"Look, everyone, we've come here to support. And, believe me, this is worth supporting. They reckon there are about two thousand of us here now, and they're still coming in over the back ways. They're all spread over the union rooms here, and over the lecture hall and classroom floors. My friends, this is big."

"Doug's just asked what leadership there is, and the answer is… not much, or at least not very positive. I saw Jonathon Yu about twenty minutes ago, and he tells me they're holding a mass meeting in the theatre hall at eleven. He says the director has sent word and

131

demanded an end to the sit-in before midnight. He's promised talks on the main issues. The student union looks like agreeing to this, but Yu's action group are demanding some solid promises on fees, the immediate withdrawal of the contentious textbooks and the scrapping of some of the disciplinary measures on political activity. So they can't agree and will debate next steps at eleven. We're gonna be there, of course, and push for a stronger line. Everyone OK with that?"

A high-profile figure in the student movement, Jonathon Yu had been something of a thorn in the side of the university authorities for some time, and his activism and charisma had been significant in pushing the more moderate union into calling for the sit-in in the first place.

"I think it's good to talk to the director's people." K.K. Wong, standing up, spoke over the chatter around him to respond to Brandon's words.

Ever the calming voice in the discussion group's robust debates, he urged caution.

"Of course, we go to the debate. But if the director's offer is genuine, we gain concessions, we claim victory, go home and go back to study. Win, win!"

But others jumped up to attack Wong's approach.

"No way!" one woman shouted emotionally. "You can't trust this director. If we leave without promises now, he'll trick us. We must go on. We must stay till we get what we want. As long as it takes."

This was greeted with cheers and clapping, and Wong, unable to press his point further, sat down, shaking his head in frustration.

"Well, OK," said Brandon, quietening the excitable conversations criss-crossing the animated group with a wave of his hand, palm up, as if he was blessing them.

"Well, OK," he repeated. "We definitely go to the meeting. But we're here to make a mark. Not just to listen and nod our heads. K.K.'s right. If we get concessions — in writing — then we win. Can't see it though. Can't see it. Alice is right," he went on, naming the woman who had spoken. "Do we trust the director? Really? I don't think so. Nothing he has done here, since arriving, makes us trust him. Cutting costs. Cutting staff. Disciplining staff and students who disagree with his right-wing bigotry. We go to the meeting. And we make a mark. That's why we've been studying and working and formulating our ideas."

He spoke like the experienced teacher he was in the seminar room — calm, dispassionate, logical and convincing. His words were greeted with cries of agreement and applause.

Some moments later, after their discussion came to an end, Brandon ushered Doug to one side, waving over Jo Chan and Alice Yau and a couple of the more articulate members of the group to join them.

"Listen, we've got to get organised for this meeting. We can't let it drift," Brandon said.

"The union guys are going to push for some kind of compromise, based on the promise of negotiation. But I've spoken to Jon Yu, and his Action Group aren't going to stomach that. They're going to go for solid concessions before anyone leaves this place. Concessions around fees, around the text books and disciplinary matters. But, more important, they want to insist on full student representation on the university council and joint committees to cover discipline and policy. I think we're all for that, right?"

The others nodded and murmured their agreement, except Jo Chan, who expressed disappointment.

"OK, that's fine, but what about our big issues? What about our democratic aims and our hopes for independence?" he said.

"A lot of these people came here with a passion. To change things. Not just for some boring joint committees."

"Dead right, Jo," countered Brandon. "Spot on. And that's where we make a difference. I've drawn up eight key demands... here." And he waved a piece of standard A4 paper.

"I cover the union points and Yu's points, but the big ones are the last two. Point seven: we, as representatives of the future generation of this territory, demand that the government immediately introduce full and free elections, based on the principle of one man, one vote." Brandon paused, shook the paper straight, looked at the others, then turned his eyes back down to the paper.

"And, point eight: we, as representatives of the future generation of this territory, demand that our government take immediate steps to withdraw this territory from membership of the Asian federation." He looked up again, seeking the approval of his companions. "These are demands we want to be taken to the government. To go out to the media. To reach the people! For this is much bigger than a dispute between students and the university. This is launching a wider political movement!"

"Great!" said Jo Chan, clenching his fist. "Great! Just what we need to make a difference."

"Exactly," followed Brandon. "And you, Jo, and you, Alice, are going to introduce this to the meeting and get a winning vote on these demands."

"Wow, I'm not sure… I mean… I've never spoken in front of a big crowd," Alice said, nervously.

"Well, I can't do it. That's for sure. As a foreigner, I'd be seen as a provocateur and it would damage the case. Same for Doug. No, you two will be fine. It's got to be locals. Don't worry, Alice. We've time enough to brief you. We'll talk it through with Jo here," explained Brandon.

"What do you think, Doug?"

Doug shrugged his shoulders.

"Well, I think they're demands worth making, but can't possibly be accepted by either the director or the government. It'll make a strong public point, but what happens when the police move in at midnight?" he responded cautiously.

"What can they do?" fired back Brandon. "There are over two thousand of us here, all fired up. They reckon there are about two hundred police outside the gates. If we just sit tight, passive resistance, and they have to carry us out protesting, one by one, it's gonna make a great show for the media."

"What media?" Jo asked.

"There's international media outside, beyond the police lines. But, more important, certainly some of the local press, and no doubt some foreign press, are in here among us, infiltrated in. They'll get pictures out, as well as words," Brandon claimed confidently.

Outside, the police had been standing down, resting before they might be called to action. The commanders had been told that they should not enter the university precincts until specifically ordered. Apart from a few stationed at the main gates leading into the expansive university square, to prevent additional students or press entering, the young officers lounged about, checking their equipment and relaxing. The authorities were concerned at the size of the demonstration, but felt confident that once the police moved in and made a gesture of removing or arresting a few students, the rest would quickly disperse.

In his office the director sat with his senior staff. Although irritated by the sit-in, and particularly by the demands for his removal, he felt confident that it would be resolved satisfactorily. A few token gestures towards negotiation would be enough the mollify the majority, he had said. And once the tired and frivolous ones began to drift away as the night wore on, the rest could be dealt with. Ringleaders could then be identified and arrested for breaching university rules and expelled where necessary. Once you remove the snake's head, he had said, you kill the serpent.

A midnight deadline would be sufficient to sober them up. Either they agree to it or the police move in and crack a few skulls. There was no way these upstart student leaders were going to challenge his authority and embarrass him in front of the government. His colleagues noted the director's apparent enjoyment of the dispute and his pleasure in furthering confrontation.

Just before eleven Doug made his way, with Brandon and some twenty others of the political group, towards the Great Hall, as it was called, where the mass meeting was to be held. As the university's grandest lecture room, this theatre-style facility was designed to comfortably accommodate some four hundred students. It was clear this night, that numbers would far exceed that total. As they pushed their way through a dense throng in the corridors leading to the hall, the group sensed a mood of expectancy mingled with anxiety. The raw power of the crowd, palpably energised by hope and its collective strength, needed harnessing with leadership and direction.

When they finally squeezed their way into the room, they found it packed to capacity. More than a thousand, they said later, had forced their way in. With the waving flags and banners, colour and noise, it was more like a pop concert or a jamboree. Doug's group stood in one of the narrow, stepped side aisles, jammed against the wall.

On the stage, two men and a woman sat on bar stools behind a standing lectern and microphone. The stage itself was bare, apart from a hastily hung large white sheet, some fifteen feet high. On it were scrawled in red, applied with a crude brush, a string of dynamic Chinese characters, under which read the slogan in English: "Students Fight for Rights". Bit vague, thought Doug, but at least a backdrop to proceedings.

First to stand and approach the lectern to speak was one of the men. With lank, long hair covering his ears, clean-shaven and wearing round steel-rimmed glasses, he looked like the studious scholar he was. As the newly elected president of the student union, Stephen Tam was well respected.

Behind him sat Ashok Sharma, the vice president, and Wong Mei Kuen, representing the women's group on the union council.

Tam, greeted with warm applause and cheers, raised both arms in thanks and to quieten the assembly. Eventually he began, speaking in Cantonese slowly and deliberately from prepared notes. His tone was serious but positive.

He thanked everyone for their support and enthusiasm and praised them for staying with the sit-in. Justifying the action, he recalled some of the events which had provoked it and condemned the directorate for failing to deal with grievances through discussion. The directorate had, he said, ignored the students and they had had no option but to protest in this way.

Their decision to call the sit-in had, however, been vindicated because the directorate was now talking, and he was pleased to say that real progress had been made in meeting their demands. It had been agreed that a joint committee of students and university staff would be set up to consider the key issues concerning the students. Along with this, the issues of fee capping, new text books and student discipline would be reviewed by this committee. Tam felt that the setting up of this committee represented a successful outcome to the sit-in, which had forced the director to back down. He was now seeking the support of this body to accept the director's offer, and once negotiations had begun, to call off the sit-in. Handing over to Sharma, he sat down. An uneasy muttering spread through the meeting and sporadic applause.

While Tam had been speaking, Jo Chan had been translating for Brandon and Doug.

"Thought so," said Brandon, as Tam concluded. "Total fucking sell-out. No demands on representation on the council and nothing political. It's up to you now, Jo, and you, Alice."

Sharma read out the four demands of the union and intended to put it to a vote, following questions, which he pointed out, had to be limited as time was now passing by and they were approaching the midnight deadline.

Dozens of hands shot up.

"Now! We've got to act now! Too late otherwise. Jo, go to Jonathon Yu. He's got a hundred people in here. Tell him to get moving." He thrust the A4 sheet into Jo's hand. Nodding, Joe set off, pushing his way through the throng.

Meanwhile, there was growing uproar. Sharma was trying to calm the situation, and pick out individuals for their questions, but too many were demanding a voice. Eventually, he succeeded in getting enough attention to hear what some of the questioners were saying. They wanted to know if the guarantees had been written — no, was the answer, but the director had given his word, face to face, with the three on the stage. What was the timetable? Were there guarantees there would be no disciplinary action against those prominent in the sit-in? No arrests? But the answers weren't satisfying the crowded hall.

"What's Jon Yu planning?" Doug asked Brandon.

"I reckon you'll see soon enough," Brandon replied. "We had a good chat earlier, and he's not going to put up with this nonsense."

A few minutes later Doug found out the answer to his question.

Jonathon Yu had pushed his way to the front and vaulted onto the stage, followed by a dozen or more of his followers. Ignoring the demands of Sharma and Tam that he give way, he marched up to the lectern and brushed aside Sharma, who, visibly intimidated, backed off before the sudden assault.

"Comrades," Yu shouted into the microphone, raising a clenched fist into the air. "Comrades. Friends. Fellow students. Fellow citizens. Enough of this bullshit." Cheers and applause. Continuing in Cantonese, in a strident tone, he berated the union representatives for their timidity — their lack of ambition, and their cowardice. Every scathing sentence he uttered was greeted by a louder chorus of approval than the one before.

"Yes," he continued, "yes, we want reforms to fees and books and committees. But we also want a meaningful reform — full student representation on the university council — and we want to see it written down before we leave here!" A great roar of approval as he stressed the last few words.

"And yes, as students we do want — and deserve — these reforms. But we have not given our time and energy and our nerves to this sit-in, just for a series of reforms to this university.

"No, my friends, just look around. Look at the banners. Look at your words, your real demands. I see the word 'Rights'. I see the word 'Democracy'. I see the word 'Freedom.' Comrades, my fellow citizens, we are here, giving our sweat, to something much greater, much more important. We are here as the future generation of our territory, our home. We are here to fight for real democracy, not the sham that's been put on us by self-interested oligarchs. We are here to fight for the right to build our own freedom. Freedom for this territory — to escape the shackles of that dark tyranny to the North. We are here to fight for independence from the federation. No less. No less. That's what we are demanding. And, comrades, we are not leaving here until our politicians agree to fight for that too! We have history on our side. And we are making our own history. Freedom now! No surrender! No surrender! No surrender!"

His audience followed each cadence with growing passion, bellowing their support until they reached a climax of noise that drowned out any further words from the speaker. Action group followers began orchestrating a repetitive chant of "No surrender! No surrender!" quickly taken up by the entire hall, until the noise seemed to make the building vibrate, as though repetitive rolls of thunder were bearing down upon it.

Yu paused for breath. The sweat glistened on his brow. He wiped his forehead with his neckerchief. His eyes blazed with intensity. The crowd was his. He felt invincible.

Then, calling for attention, he took a sheet of paper from his pocket and deliberately read out eight demands in English. They were the ones drafted by Brandon and delivered by Jo Chan. These demands, Yu declared, would be sent immediately to the directorate. Did the comrades agree with this? All but a few doubters raised their arms enthusiastically.

"Passed unanimously," said Yu victoriously.

Doug looked at Brandon. Both had followed Yu's impassioned words with Alice's help, though a detailed translation wasn't needed, such was the force of the message and its reception.

"So you had seen Yu about this?" Doug asked his older colleague.

"Sure. We planned this earlier. We both thought the union would back off any confrontation, so we had to do something.

"And now?" Doug said.

"Now we have a real protest. Now we force the authorities to pay attention and the world to take notice." He turned to look at Doug.

"Now we have a revolutionary act."

Many people left the hall, though some stayed to take advantage of the long benches to snatch some sleep. Others became very busy, including the discussion group members. In half an hour the director's ultimatum would take effect. It seemed impossible that he would accept all the demands and highly probable that the police would be moving in at midnight. Some of the protesters began organising food supplies, as anything in the union canteen had been consumed. Others began preparing material to barricade the impressive large double doors of the main union building, piling up filing cabinets, desks and chairs and assembling makeshift props ready to prevent their opening. A few, like Rocky, were preparing themselves for forceful resistance, gathering motor cycle helmets, baseball bats and batons made of chair legs, as well as makeshift shields of dustbin lids and the doors of cupboards. They passed around napkins, which, when soaked, might prove some defence against tear gas.

Doug looked upon the scene with concern. It was in a way comical to think this motley collection of sincere, but ill-organised battalions of inexperienced fighters could stand up to the disciplined, well-equipped forces of law and order.

Hopefully, he considered, it won't be necessary. Once the police come towards the union building, most will run away or let themselves be shepherded out. A lot of these youngsters treat it like a game.

Predictably, the director rejected the students' demands out of hand.

"Who do they think they are?" he had shouted in a rage, tearing the document in half.

"You tell your friends," he shouted threateningly to the nervous student courier who had delivered the demand note, "that enough is enough. These demands are unrealistic, ridiculous and insulting. They must leave the campus immediately. The police will enter at midnight, as announced. This is your last chance. That's it. No more negotiation. Go!"

Beyond the university boundary, outside in the street, the police detachments began to ready themselves. The company commander gave orders to his section leaders to equip themselves in riot control gear. He didn't expect much trouble. His orders were to clear the building and disperse the protesters. The sight of his disciplined ranks of helmeted officers, wielding batons and plastic shields, would be enough to scare off these pampered middle-class kids. His orders from Internal Security were clear enough — empty the student union and the university square of all protesters. Use minimum force, with no firearms employed, but drive them out and arrest anyone who resisted. He had tear gas available, and even a mobile water cannon, just in case.

It had also been stressed to the commander by the authorities that it was of the utmost importance that he keep all the gathering media — newspaper journalists, photographers and TV crews — at an effective distance from the operation. A distance from which they could not directly film or photograph the proceedings. To that end, his men had barricaded off the ends of the main road running past the university square main gate, as well as the many side streets leading to the area. He was confident that it appeared to be a no-go area for media. He was also uncomfortably aware that people had been spotted viewing the scene from higher windows or rooftops of neighbouring buildings. He also knew from his men who had infiltrated the ranks of the protesters that some journalists were already inside. Anyone taking photos or video should be grabbed and arrested, he had ordered his men, knowing full well that the recording of violence, should it erupt, would be damaging to the image of the police.

Finally, at exactly midnight, the order to advance came. Whistles blew and the policemen shuffled into position. They then threw open the huge wrought-iron university gates and marched in. On entering the square, they fanned out to form two lines across the square, directly opposite the neo-classical façade of the student union building at a distance of some hundred metres from the main door. They stood silently, most of them no older than the students they confronted.

No students remained in the square. Everyone had retreated behind the barricaded doors. The square was empty apart from the police, illuminated in ghostly fashion in the darkness by the yellowish light cast from the union's windows.

Like many others, Doug huddled against a first-floor window, looking down anxiously. His instinct was to slip out one of the back entrances and disappear into the complex of buildings at the back. Hadn't he done enough? He had shown support for the movement, after all. He had shown commitment. And the movement would soon melt away anyway. Nevertheless, his curiosity got the better of him and he stayed, transfixed by the scene below. He felt like an alien observer, as though he was, in some way, disembodied and detached, not only emotionally but physically.

It was now quiet inside the building. Everyone waited in expectation — some in a cold sweat, some in a cloak of moral resolve, and a few in the taut anticipation of danger and violence.

Doug could hear the ticking of the clock of the seminar room, into which he was packed. He thought of his brother, and, taking out his phone, tried to call him. But after several attempts, Jack did not answer, and he gave up. Looking back again through the window, he stood on tiptoe to get a view over the shoulders of those crowding in front of him. He saw the lines of police open to allow a senior officer through.

Commander Stephen Wong marched to within twenty metres of the main door. He stopped, looked over his shoulder, as if to re-assure himself his men were still in support and in full order, then turned again to look up to the first-floor windows. Seeing the crowds of pale faces leaning out or pressed against the glass, he slowly raised a megaphone to his lips.

Chapter Eight
Troublesome Liaisons

By the time Jack and Justin Gaynor reached the Old Ship, they were feeling pleased with themselves. Although tipsy and tired, they were enjoying the self-assuredness and false energy delivered by the drugs Gaynor had provided.

Throughout the fifteen-minute walk, Gaynor had held firmly onto Jack's arm, partly for balance, but also to demonstrate the strength of his new-found friendship for him — at this particular moment, anyway. He talked non-stop, mostly incoherently, about their former boss, and about the runaway success of his new business. Jack barely paid attention, instead taking in the humid air and being mesmerised by the dazzling street panorama which swirled past them as they walked along.

Pushing aside the heavy wooden door, they entered the contrasting sepulchre-like gloom of the pub, which at least offered respite for the senses.

Not much changed here then, thought Jack, as he screwed his eyes up in order to adjust to the darkness.

"Great, isn't it?" enthused Gaynor. "I love this place. I love it! The grime, the shabbiness, the seediness. My kind of place!" he laughed sardonically, as the two felt their way to a corner table. Jack was already getting used to the dismal lighting and saw that, indeed, very little had changed in the general layout and décor of the place.

Long and rectangular, with the entrance door at one short end, the place had a single bar which stretched down half of one longer side. At the end of the single room were the doors to the toilets and on the wall to one side, a battered dartboard and blackboard for scoring. Two TV screens were positioned high on the wall opposite the bar. Normally, they showed Chinese soap operas, or pop music channels, or sport. That night, Jack noticed, one wasn't working at all, while the other flickered, without sound, showing some kind of football match. No one cared what was on, as no one paid any attention.

In one corner sat a group of older Chinese men, noisily and joyfully playing cards, drinking beers and jasmine tea, slapping their cards on the table in triumph or despair. At another table was a group of young expats, boys and girls, downing shots, loudly conversing and laughing frequently with the exaggerated, unearned laughter generated by alcohol.

In contrast, several young Asian women sat quietly talking and smoking. Could be Chinese or Thai, thought Jack. Probably on the lookout for male company. Perhaps for money, perhaps not. In the semi darkness, neatly dressed, coiffured and heavily made up, with cigarette smoke curling around them, they appeared exotically attractive. At the bar stood a small group of loud European businessmen, dressed in regulation grey and black suits, white shirts open at the neck, ties having been dispensed with. Sipping whisky or brandy, and smoking ostentatiously large cigars, they spoke with exaggerated intimacy and seriousness, finding it difficult to pronounce their words clearly. It had been a long evening since the closing of the trade fair, but they were comfortable with the idea that their indulgence was an extension of their commercial activities of the day, and, if not directly profitable, was building the bonds of trust on which trade everywhere thrives.

Next to them, some lounging against the bar, was a group of four younger Chinese men. Sipping a clear spirit of indeterminate source, they spoke softly, yet animatedly, as though they were arguing over some trivial matter, such as a football result, or an unsuccessful betting tip. With their tight T-shirts and tattooed arms, they gave the impression of menace.

Serving them from the bar, a middle aged, overweight Chinese lady, whom everyone called Mamasan, as though she headed a bordello, maintained her unsmiling dignity at all times. Helping her, a younger Filipino man, Eddie, chattered eagerly with all customers, flashing his white teeth and giggling constantly as he poured drinks, polished the bar and occasionally cleared the tables.

Jack surveyed the scene fondly. He felt secure here and it brought back memories and sensations of earlier times when he had frequented the place more often. It had been an after-midnight destination for a comforting hot meal to counteract the effects of an evening's drinking. The rapidly prepared English breakfast, burgers, chips, Singapore noodles, fried rice and wonton soup made up a homely East-West menu providing fat, spice and carbohydrates to stimulate and stabilise the overworked metabolism. It helped counteract the debilitating effects of alcohol in preparation for the demands of the next day. Several times Jack had taken advantage of its twenty-four-hour service to grab a hurried breakfast in the first moments of dawn, before guiltily sloping home to snatch a couple of hours' sleep and then heading off for an unproductive day's work. Odours had not changed either. The lingering smell of burnt grease, seared soy sauce and garlic, along with a hint of urine, was familiar and distinct.

Despite its reputation for rowdiness, he had never felt threatened or endangered in this forlorn bar. Although he had witnessed a number of fist fights and drunken confrontations, he had quite enjoyed them as voyeur, staying safely in the background.

"What's yours then, Jackie boy?" said Gaynor, shaking Jack from his reminiscences. "I think we should spoil ourselves, don't you? Only bubbly will do in these classy surroundings!" he added, answering his own question. Off he went to the bar, loudly greeting Mamasan and Eddie and disturbing others as he ordered sparkling wine.

"Fine," said Jack, as Gaynor returned with the bottle and two glasses." Are we celebrating something then?"

"We certainly are, Jackie boy," replied his companion, who poured out two generous tumblers full, passed one to Jack and then leaned towards him conspiratorially. "Cheers," he offered, looking him directly in the eye, and adding, "Let's drink to the success of Prime PR, and, maybe, Mr Wilson's part in it!"

"Oh right, well, I'll drink to your success, Justin, well done. Where do I come into it?"

Jack was curious. There was no doubt Gaynor had built Prime PR quickly from scratch. A natural salesman, flamboyant and persuasive, he was also an original and ambitious thinker, a source of innovative ideas.

"Ah well, that's the point. We've done OK. I have fifty staff now in the office here and a very healthy cash flow. And the office up north is growing nicely. Very nicely. But, Jack, we've only scratched the surface. Small fry. But up there," he pointed his finger to the ceiling," up there are some fat fish to be caught, and…" he leaned again towards Jack, "and I'm about to hook a whale." At that he burst out laughing, swallowed the rest of his drink in one and began pouring another.

"You know, as well as me. Well better, 'cos you work in that fancy trade department. You know that some of those federation-based companies are huge, and growing. They want to go international. But they're not sure how to go about it. That's where Prime PR comes in. We are the face to the outside world. We show them how to communicate and promote themselves in the big ol' world out there… right? Get my drift?"

Jack was well aware of the rapid development of the business sector in the federation, and much of his work centred on the role the territory would play in collaborating with, and benefiting from, this development. He "got" Gaynor's "drift" very well, but also appreciated the political sensitivities caused by the federation's headlong rush into economic growth. It was growth underpinning a keen political and military appetite. It was that same expanding power and dark ambition which has caused disquiet in the territory and other federation associates, and given fuel to the independence movement.

"Sure, I know what you're getting at. We do work in this area. Can be touchy though. Better tread carefully there. You talking to anyone in particular?" Jack probed.

"Well, there's the thing, Jackie boy," Gaynor responded. "We're talking to someone very 'particular.' We're talking to a whale. And the whale is too fucking big to worry about sensitivities." He chuckled smugly.

"Well, who's that?" asked Jack.

Gaynor hesitated, affecting gravitas. Lowering his voice, and pausing for effect, he said: "You better keep this to yourself. Right? … It's KFIG."

Jack felt the blood rush to his face. KFIG! Knowledge First Industries Group. Perhaps the most influential corporation in the federation. Run by General Khan's cousin. Popularly known as Khan's Family Industries. Notorious for its commercial ruthlessness and willingness to resort to underhand tactics, including political blackmail, when it suited its aims. Not the sort of company regional competitors would like to stand up to, but lacking the reputation for honest dealing to operate effectively in the wider world.

"Wow! You are kidding me," said Jack when he had recovered from the shock. "Jesus, Justin, you're pushing the boat out there, my friend. Why are they talking to you? I mean, no offence, but aren't you biting off more than you can chew! There are plenty of international companies out there chasing that business."

KFIG. A diverse conglomerate, which had started manufacturing household products, then machine tools, then vehicles. It had subsequently expanded into military equipment and weapons and had prospered on the back of the general's patronage and the federation's increasing military might. As Jack was well aware, it now was developing its telecommunications capabilities, producing networks, mobile phones and even artificial intelligence. Its international ambition and potential was boundless, and for many, alarming.

Gaynor was enjoying Jack's discomfort.

"Relax, Jackie boy, relax. Ol' Justin's got it under control. No problemo."

He drank again and filled his own and Jack's glass.

"You see, it's all about contacts. Good ol' Kentucky Fried Group's (he grinned at his own joke) got a lousy reputation, right? Shady... bit dodgy, right? But they want to woo the big wide world now. So... they need good PR. It's reputation management, Jackie boy, and you know all about that. But they, being connected to the general an' all, they want low key stuff. Below the radar. Subtle, long-term strategies. So it stands to reason — a small company, discreet, quiet, modest is what's needed. That's us, you see. Prime PR. Local, modest, low key. We are all those things!" he laughed again at the irony of himself being modest and low key.

"Right, I can see that," commented Jack, impressed by Gaynor's chutzpah and blasé analysis of powers that seemed way out of his league.

"Do you remember that dishy Chinese girl, Lana Kong, that I knocked around with last year?" continued Gaynor.

"Well, she just happened — and I didn't know this for a while — to be related to one of the bigwigs in KFIG, her uncle or something. So, I gave her a job with Prime — she was quite a smart cookie too — and in return she got me a meeting with mister uncle director. And it took off from there. Meanwhile, she's buggered off to the States to study, but the magic was done!"

Gaynor opened the palms of his hands upwards, to indicate the finality of his case.

"Impressive, Justin. I've got to give it to you for balls," said Jack. "But, why are you telling me all this?"

"Oh, Jackie boy, keep up, please!" Gaynor said with mock frustration.

"You," he said, "you, Mr Wilson, are going to help me look after this whale!"

"Are you kidding me?" Jack shot back, wide-eyed and with alarm in his voice. "I don't know what to say. I don't think I'd know where to start, and I'm not sure I'd want to work for that lot."

Gaynor was amused.

"Now calm down. Have another drink." He poured another glass of the mediocre sparkling wine, emptying the bottle.

"You are exactly what they, and what I need. Nice, clean, well-mannered, pink-faced, articulate Englishman. Good economics degree from sound UK university. Broad knowledge of trade and investment situation in the region. You could be the honest face of KFIG. I can see you now, on the BBC, explaining how KFIG are going to contribute constructively to community development in the UK, and elsewhere, with their far-sighted infrastructure and philanthropic investments."

He mimicked a BBC tone.

"Listen, Jack. I got the big picture ideas. I got the bullshit. I got the sales. You got the brains. You have the economic stuff — the facts and figures, and the pretty face. I'll look after you — gettit? It's a good partnership, no?"

Gaynor finished with a flourish, downed his drink, exhaled an audible sigh of satisfaction and jumped up, with the intention of getting a second bottle from the bar.

Jack was bemused. With all the drink and all the ideas tumbling around in his brain, he found it hard to think straight. He looked over at the group of girls, who, having obviously been watching him and Gaynor, smiled at him then turned away. Making a conscious effort, he sought to make sense of Gaynor's words. Was this a sample of his fast-talking bravado, or was any substance behind the bluster?

"What d'ya think?" said Gaynor on returning to the table.

"I don't know," was the best Jack could come up with. "It's a lot to take in. But, I mean, I can't even speak Chinese. How could I service a company like that?"

"No problemo," said Gaynor, with a flourish. "That's all taken care of. They have all the language skills there to help."

"Listen, how much do you earn at that boring department place?" he added with a note of seriousness.

"Well, forty thousand a month. It's not bad," answered Jack.

Gaynor shook his head, feigning sympathy.

"Forty thousand? Forty thousand?" He mimicked incredulity.

"Jack, some of my juniors earn that now. I'm picking up five times that much already. If we land this whale, Jackie boy, you can name your own salary. What do you want? Hundred and fifty grand a month? Two hundred? Jack, these dudes have more money than sense, and they need help. Like you say, their image is rock bottom. So? We got nothing to lose. We're starting from the pits. It can only get better. And they will pay top dollar. What d'ya say? Come on, it's the chance of a lifetime!"

Feeling dizzy from the drink and from Gaynor's overpowering flow of words, Jack could only manage an unconvincing nod.

"Think about it, Jackie boy. Think about it over the weekend and we'll talk first thing next week, OK?"

"Yeah. I will. I will think about it. Sounds amazing, amazing," Jack managed in response.

"Great. Let's drink to that!" said Gaynor as he poured two more glasses and raised his to clink with Jack's.

Without saying anything further, he stood up and walked directly over to the three Asian women sitting at a nearby table. After a few words with them, he returned.

"Seems like the ladies would like to partake of a little bubbly and are minded to join us," he said, with a knowing look. "Might be our lucky night," he added.

Within minutes the three joined Jack and Gaynor, who fetched extra glasses and another bottle from the bar.

"Well, ladies," beamed Gaynor, raising his glass yet again in a toast to all. "Here's to us! I'm Justin and this is Mr Wilson! Cheers!"

He then busily engaged himself in flirting with two of the women, putting his arm immediately around the shoulders of one of them and talking effusively to both. The third one, meanwhile, sat more modestly by Jack's side, looking at him questioningly. Jack, for his part, had yet to utter a word, being partially paralysed by Gaynor's hyperactivity.

When he finally gathered his thoughts, he managed to ask her what her name was.

Chera. Her name was Chera. She came originally from Thailand. She had been in the territory for three years, working as a maid and a dancer.

"You? You English. Live in West District," she said, observing Jack intently.

"Yes, that's right, good guess," Jack replied.

"No guess," followed Chera. "I go with you. Here. One year before. Go with you. Your home. You no remember."

"Erm, yes. Chera. Yes. Was I drunk?" he asked feebly.

She smiled. "Yes. Very drunk. I take you home. You sleep. You give me taxi money. Nice man. Very nice."

Jack struggled to remember. Her name was vaguely familiar. He looked at her again, in the half dark. "Taxi money" was a euphemism that women like Chera used for payment for sex. But many weren't full-time prostitutes, just poor women, scratching a living as maids or dancers in clubs, who combined a limited social life, or sometimes illegal status, with the chance to earn some extra cash. After his marriage broke up, Jack had met a number of them, usually late in the night, in bars like the Old Ship, and some had gone home with him. He felt ashamed that he couldn't even remember meeting this attractive young woman.

"Oh yes, Chera, I remember now," he said. "You're very lovely, you know," he added, not really meaning it, but urged on by the first flickerings of the possibility of sex.

"Not lovely. Just poor Thai girl. What's your name?" she queried.

"Jamie," he lied, with no good reason, apart from the feeling his real self was detached from the whole scene. Meanwhile, the present self was manipulating the situation, as in a dream when you know it is a dream and you have no genuine fear or regret and you can play out the action, aware that you will emerge sometime later unscathed.

"Jamie," said Chera, moving closer to him and putting her hand on his arm. "You buy me dinner?"

"Of course," said Jack. "What do you want?" And he passed her the tattered plastic-coated menu.

Without glancing at it, she replied: "I like fish and chips."

"Fish and chips?" said Jack, grinning. "That's not very Thai. You sure you want fish and chips? It'll make you fat!" he tried to joke, noting she was very slim.

"I like fat," she laughed. "Chera too thin, no eat enough."

Thinking she probably didn't eat well, either because she couldn't afford to, or because staying thin and attractive was vital for survival in her world, he went to the bar and ordered her food.

As he was returning to the table, the main door swung open roughly and a group of a dozen or more well-built young Caucasian men came blundering in, laughing and talking rowdily, some obviously the worse for drink.

"Oh great," exclaimed Gaynor, as he leaned across the table to Jack. "Just what we need — a bunch of drunken jocks."

"They look like rugby players, judging from the shirts some are wearing," guessed Jack. "I bet they're on tour here or something. They're just out for a good time. Just ignore them. They'll be OK."

Jack's intuition seemed right. The gang of young sportsmen were boisterous, and crude, and they drank heavily, but kept to themselves.

Gaynor continued his flirting, while Jack engaged Chera in a stilted conversation. He was warming to the idea of inviting her home, and she did nothing to quell his rising hopes, but rather encouraged him with her inviting smiles and body language. Her food arrived, and she began to eat in a measured and concentrated way.

Twenty minutes after the noisy customers arrived, however, Jack noticed a deterioration in the general atmosphere.

Becoming gradually louder the more they drank, the noisy crowd seemed to occupy more space, dominating the place with their bulk and volume. Slipping out quietly, the older Chinese men abandoned their cards and departed, feeling their peace had been disturbed. In their own time the businessmen at the bar also made their way, staggering slightly, guffawing inanely and still puffing on their fat cigars.

At this point Gaynor also stood up.

Swaying slightly, he put his arms around his two female companions.

"Jackie boy," he drawled. "It's time to go home." Then lowering his voice, "I think the tone of this fine establishment has been lowered..." He signalled towards the bar with his thumb.

"You heading out too, with your young lady?"

"Yeah, pretty soon," replied Jack. "She's just finishing eating. Then we're done."

"OK, my friend, I wish you buenas noches, au revoir, arrivederci and gute nacht! We..." he emphasised the word, pointing at Jack, "will talk serious business early next week. Remember, Jackie boy, think big."

With that, Gaynor turned clumsily, and supported by the two women, who giggled continuously, he stumbled away and left the bar.

"Shall we go when you're finished?" Jack asked Chera, assuming she would go back with him. He thought momentarily of Marion and what she would think of this. But he consciously put any thought of guilt out of his mind, reasoning that it was her fault he was reduced to this.

"Yes, I like to," she said, cramming a large piece of battered fish into her mouth.

Quite suddenly, there were several loud crashes of splintered glass and drunken voices, hostile and angry. A dispute had flared up between the sports crowd and the Chinese boys. What had provoked this confrontation? No one would ever really remember or know. Someone had spilt someone else's drink? A clumsy step backwards and someone else's foot was trodden on? Had racial slurs followed demands for an apology declined? It didn't matter. Young men, fuelled by alcohol, late at night, some nursing unrequited disappointments or insults from the day. Ready to prove their virility — their warrior status. There could be no backing down from the challenge of a rival.

An exchange of cursing and insults led to a flurry of ultimatums, to pushing and shoving and to blows being struck.

And then, the Chinese boys, outnumbered and outmuscled, instinctively armed themselves, smashing beer bottles against the bar and wielding them like knives.

Mamasan screamed and shouted for them to stop in a high-pitched stream of Chinese invective.

"Stop! Stop! I call police!" she also shouted in English.

But it was too late. The thin veil of decency that separates civilised behaviour from violence was already ripped apart, unleashing the visceral urge to attack and defend by all means at hand. Two of the burlier rugby players leapt over the bar and bundled the hysterical Mamasan out of the back door.

Within moments a chaotic brawl was underway. The rugby boys picked up barstools and used them to keep their bottle-wielding assailants at bay. They threw other bottles at them and drove them back. One was hit on the forehead and collapsed like a rag doll onto the floor. Cornered and frightened, the outnumbered Chinese boys returned some of the missiles, but effectively could only hurl abuse and wave the jagged glass in defiance.

It lasted only a few minutes, and then the battle was over. Recognising the futility of further resistance, and the overwhelming odds against them, the defenders defiantly smashed their bottles onto the floor and made a futile dash for the front door, dragging their semi-conscious friend with them.

Caught and with their arms pinioned behind them, they were pushed and dragged to the door. To jeers, kicks and further blows, and while they continued to howl blood curdling cries of vengeance on their attackers, they were thrown ignominiously onto the street through the main door, which was ceremoniously slammed shut and bolted from the inside by the victors.

Celebrating like tribal savages, the victors congratulated each other on their success and returned to the bar to continue the revelry. A terrified Eddie was hauled up from behind the bar, where he had been hiding, and forcibly sat upon it. Meekly smiling, he acknowledged his best chance of surviving the ordeal unhurt was to humour the mob. He could do nothing as they pillaged the bar.

Two of them appointed themselves bar staff and liberally served their comrades whatever they requested.

A cowering Jack, who had at the onset of the confrontation shrunk back into a dark corner, hugged a terrified Chera close with the intention of protecting himself, as well as her, and watched the events with growing anxiety.

"Well, let's drink to seeing those little pricks off," he heard one of them shout. "Looks like we've got this bar to ourselves, mates. Might as well enjoy it! Come on, get 'em in!"

As the drinks flowed and the crowd celebrated their triumph, the minutes ticked by. After about a quarter of an hour, Jack decided that he and Chera should try to slip out, preferably without attracting any attention. He pulled the shaking Thai woman to her feet, and they crept out from the darkened corner towards the door.

"Well, look what we've got here!" exclaimed one of the drunks, as soon as he spotted Jack and Chera on their way. "Stowaways!"

Within a second, they were surrounded by the overexcited group, laughing and leering at them.

"It's OK, boys, we were just sitting out there. No problem. We didn't see anything. Just going now. Nice and peaceful," Jack remonstrated, holding up the palm of his hand and impressed at his own coolness.

"What?" said one of the yobs. "You're going and taking this lovely lady away from us. Doesn't she wanna party?"

He moved towards a terrified Chera, who held tightly onto Jack, and began stroking her hair.

"You don't wanna leave with this pansy, do ya, darlin'?" he said.

Like a small rodent cornered by a predator, Jack called on an instinctive reservoir of courage, stepped forward and with two hands shoved away the larger man, who, being drunk and taken by surprise, stumbled backwards and fell on his backside.

As the rest of his cronies roared with laughter, the bully pulled himself quickly up and, before Jack could defend himself, lashed out with a vengeful punch that caught Jack unawares full above the eye, dazing him and making him slump back onto one of the bar's shabby bench seats.

He thought he was going to pass out. The room swayed before him and he felt like throwing up. Putting a hand gingerly to his eyebrow, he wiped away a trickle of dark blood, dripping into the corner of his eye. He leaned forward, head in hands, breathing heavily. Chera knelt beside him, sobbing and dabbing at the wound with a tissue.

"Oh, for Christ's sake, Stevie, knock it off. Leave the poor bastard alone. It ain't worth any trouble for the tart and he ain't one o' them. Come on, let's get a couple of drinks before we clear out o' this shithole," said another of the gang, and they moved off back to the bar.

One returned with a bottle of cheap white wine and plonked it on the table next to Jack, who was desperately struggling to clear his head.

"Here you are, mate," said the ungenerous donor. "Have a drink on us. No hard feelings. Take no notice of Stevie, he's a dickhead."

Jack put his feet up on the plastic-covered bench seat and lay on his back. Gradually, the room stopped swaying, but his head pounded.

"Jamie, you OK? Jamie! Jamie, you OK? Don't die, Jamie!" repeated the distraught Chera, who continued to pat the cut above Jack's eye with a paper tissue.

"No, it's all right. I won't die. Don't worry," Jack said feebly, almost enjoying the martyrdom of the situation and Chera's devotion, and experiencing the moments as if in a dream.

After ten minutes of this reverie, however, his consciousness was rudely invaded by an aggressive banging at the pub's door, which made him sit up.

"Security!" a harsh voice proclaimed. "Open the door... now!"

The rowdy mob instantly fell silent.

"Oh shit!" reacted one of them. "Looks like we've got company. I think the party's over."

He swaggered over to the door.

"All right, all right, keep your hair on, we're opening up," he said nervously.

He turned the key and pulled back the bolt.

The door crashed open and with violent force a dozen or more heavily protected and armed police officers barged their way into the bar, their automatic weapons held at the ready and pointed at the drunken group.

The one who had opened the door was thrust back roughly by the troop, and when he protested, saying, "Come on, guys, bit over the top!" he was clubbed to the ground with a rifle butt.

Standing along the bar, the shocked and sobered rowdies automatically raised their hands. No one spoke and the silence was menacing.

A senior officer strolled in nonchalantly behind his officers. He looked contemptuously at the scruffy and defenceless sportsmen and surveyed the mess and damage they had caused.

"You lie on the floor, face down," he ordered, in a cold monotone. "Hands behind your back."

They obeyed without a murmur. Their hands were quickly bound by the officers. But they left them lying at first, while the senior officer barked at them,

"You people. You make me sick. You come here and behave like animals. Well. Criminal damage and assault. Very serious here. Enjoy our prison."

As his men hauled up the humbled revellers and hustled them out of the door, the officer turned to look at Jack and Chera.

Assuming they, along with a trembling Eddie, were victims of the vandals, he motioned indifferently to the door.

"Go. Go home. Don't come to these places. Bad places," he said, and then marched out.

Jack pulled himself to his feet, still feeling like throwing up, and, with Chera supporting him, walked to the door. Just before they went out, Jack heard a muttering behind him and turned to see the Mamasan.

As she surveyed the wreckage of her bar, strewn with broken bottles and glasses, damaged furniture, pools of blood and a ransacked bar, she put her hands to her head and the muttering turned into a wail. The lone TV flickered on, showing a news item of police movements around the university.

Outside in the street, Jack saw a large police bus, full with the culprits of the night. A large crowd had gathered to witness the excitement of the hijacking of the bar and the arrest of the foreign vandals, and they cheered as the bus pulled slowly away. As it passed close by, Jack, standing on the pavement, looked directly into the face of his assailant at one of the vehicle's windows. Looking bruised, covered in sweat and stressed, he grimaced ironically at Jack and stuck out his tongue.

Jack shook his head and turned to Chera to take her home. He would enjoy some female comfort after the aggression of the evening.

But she had gone. Chera had slipped silently away into the city night. Jamie too much trouble. Too much problem. He would never see her again.

Chapter Nine
The Unspoken

She never recovered from her son's death. Losing a child of any age is, for a parent, a life sentence of grief and recrimination. When the sadness is infected with guilt, it's like a parasite gnawing in the depths of your consciousness, reminding you that you... you were responsible, because of your failings as a parent. Then the pain becomes an incurable illness.

So it was with Elizabeth after Matthew's death. Grief accelerated the desiccation process, ageing her body and shrinking her mind's horizons. It was a devastating psychological blow at a time when she was already vulnerable, dealing with an empty house after the departure of Doug, her youngest, to university. The vacuum was internal and external, created by the absence of the demands of mothering three lively boys. Now, there was no one to chide in the morning rush, none of their clothes to wash and iron, no one to counsel about school or girlfriends, no one to tell to turn down the impossible music, no one to worry about coming home late. Just a stillness: a silence signifying that her role as mother was completed. Her purpose was over. What now?

There was Bill, of course. But he was largely independent. He often did the shopping, and sometimes cooked their meals. He preferred plain honest dishes — meat and two vegetables were his favourite. Chops were easy, mincemeat too. He made his own battered fish, though the batter tended to be too soft. Cooking had to be done quickly. It was functional, and lacked artistry. Although he did become quite adventurous, discovering, to Elizabeth's dismay, instant curry and pasta meals. He even ironed his own shirts. He was a caring and dutiful husband, increasingly concerned at his wife's condition, but unable to comprehend the depth of her loneliness. Why, he himself had been shocked and deeply hurt by Matthew's inexplicable death, but life goes on, he told himself. You had to grit your teeth and face down adversity. He had survived some harrowing experiences in his time, witnessing death and inhuman cruelty, but that had given him strength of character.

He gently tried to revive his forlorn wife, encouraging her to keep active, visit friends and relatives, take up part-time work or volunteering, to get her out of the house and re-engage with a social life that seemed to have paused. This met with some success, as Elizabeth took up a paid role for three mornings a week at a local day care centre, where she helped look after the elderly and infirm. She enjoyed the work, which in many ways was an extension of her mothering role, and she made new friends among the colleagues.

Nevertheless, it failed to lift the overall mist of lethargy which dampened her optimism and curtailed her pleasure in life.

Neither of them considered that her mental state required any medical attention or counselling, for both of them regarded this as a natural state of affairs following a family tragedy. In time it would resolve itself, as any period of mourning comes to an end. They rarely spoke of it, because Elizabeth found it embarrassing, viewing it as weakness on her part. Bill thought the best way to deal with this kind of difficulty was to find distraction and substitution, not resort to analysis, which would merely compound the problem. Better to brush it to one side, he thought, march on and ignore it. Like a bleak winter, it would eventually pass.

For the next years, the two bereaved parents accommodated themselves to a quieter, more withdrawn existence. Whilst affectionate with each other, they communicated less, spending time reading or watching television together in long periods of silence. There were no quarrels or unkind words, but the passive companionship was lapsing into dull tolerance of each other. Repetitive household chores took the place of family life. House proud, they both spent more time cleaning and polishing their home. With its fitted carpets, thick curtains and heavy furniture, it was a place of solid comfort, but overpowering. Cluttered with unnecessary side furniture, bric-a-brac and pictures on all walls, it threatened to smother everyone with its history.

Matters were made more complicated by Elizabeth's menopause, which proved to be complicated and uncomfortable. Irregular periods, with excessive bleeding and pain became a reason for medical attention, and, finally, a hysterectomy. This added to her feeling of obsolescence and undermined her self-confidence further. Though Bill was understanding and supportive, the operation resulted in Elizabeth losing interest in sex, and she never again left the spare room, where she lay recuperating.

For the next few years their lives took on an uneventful, yet not unpleasant, routine. Bill continued to work conscientiously, perhaps spending more time at his office than before, and enjoyed his weekly Tuesday night session at the pub with his friends, playing cribbage and darts. He was never excessive, drinking no more than three pints and returning home by ten o'clock. Meanwhile, Elizabeth worked at the day care centre, where she was appreciated for her kindness and patience, but rarely socialised with her colleagues.

They hardly ventured out together, except for the occasional visit to the cinema. In the past they had met with friends for dinner parties or outings, and even holidays, but these gatherings became too stressful for Elizabeth, who couldn't face questions about her wellbeing or about the boys.

Visits from Jack and Doug provided the highlights in their lives, breaking the colourless routine of their existence. On these occasions, Elizabeth's spirits would revive, and Bill, enjoying his sons' company in equal measure, would be heartened by her temporary re-invigoration. For the boys, though, the mood in the household at these times was deceptive. They knew from conversations with their father that all was not well with their mother, but it appeared no worse than a mild depression or loss of confidence. Jack assumed that his presence helped, in that he had the knack of cheering up his mother, but he never discussed the issue with her seriously and with Bill the matter was underplayed.

"How's Mum getting on, these days?" he would ask his father.

"Well, she's still a bit under the weather," Bill would reply. Or: "She's not quite herself, but hopefully she's on the mend," he would say. And this would be enough to deflect Jack from further probing, though doubts lingered in his mind.

Doug was more concerned and pressed his father actively.

"I'm worried about Mum," he confronted Bill on one occasion. "She's really not well, you know. Are we doing enough for her? I think she should be seeing a doctor, our GP, at the very least. I understand she needs time to get over Matthew, but that was three years ago, and I get the effect of the operation, but she's changed, Dad. She's lost her sparkle. She never wants to go out or do anything. She's no interest in friends and seems lost. I think this needs seeing to. It needs diagnosing. It's more than just feeling fed up. She's ill. Shouldn't we get her to the doctor, Dad? I think it's agoraphobia."

For Bill, however, Doug's analysis was bewildering and hinted at his own failings in taking care of his wife.

"She's been to see the quack," he countered his son defensively, as though Doug had been making an accusation of some kind.

"And he agrees it's just a natural depression, given the shock of Matthew and the time of her life — you know — a woman's difficult time."

"Yeah, it's called menopause, Dad," said Doug, impatient with his father's euphemisms and refusal to confront the situation.

"Well, I don't see the need for fancy consultants and pep pills or whatever," continued Bill, reddening.

"Your mother's had a hard time, but she'll come through. We'll get over this together, as family, like always, and I'm here to take care of her, you can be sure of that," he added.

"I know, Dad. I know you're here," said Doug, putting his hand on his father's shoulder, recognising the strain he bore and realising there was little point in pursuing his case.

For Bill the situation was frustrating, in that he felt powerless to help his wife. He was also sad, in that he felt the intimacy of their relationship gradually fading, like the late summer sun giving way to the creeping chill of evening.

His affection for his wife, along with his sense of duty and lack of imagination, kept him unswerving in his care for her. It was not any search for sympathy or consolation that was to undermine his loyalty, but, as he was to explain to himself later, "the chance of circumstances."

Marjorie Bonfield was a confident and immaculately turned-out woman, who had worked as a personal assistant to one of the senior managers at Bill's company for several years. She was attractive, if not beautiful, articulate and, as some regarded it, self-confident to the point of being overbearing. With her subtly dyed blonde hair swept back and held in place with discreet spray, her smart suits with their pencil skirts, and not-too-ostentatious high heels, on which she skilfully balanced her trim figure, she cut a fashionable figure.

For the men on the factory floor, and in the sales department, whose heads she frequently turned, she represented a dash of colour in the routine grey of the working day, greeting them with a smile and fending off any saucy greetings with confident ripostes of her own. Among the few female colleagues, she was also well respected if not universally popular, and grudgingly admired rather than envied.

Bill and her had a friendly professional relationship, always courteous and warm, but personal matters never intruded. Marjorie would occasionally ask after Elizabeth and the boys out of politeness, as the tragedy of losing Matthew was common knowledge, but they never spoke of intimate matters.

This was to change, quite unpredictably, one Friday evening, when the two found themselves sitting together in a local pub with colleagues during an after-work drinks gathering. After a while, most of the others had left for home, or graduated to the bar, leaving the two with some privacy. Bill, uncharacteristically, talked of his wife's suffering, and of his impotency in dealing with it. He even solicited Marjorie's sympathy, speaking of his feelings of alienation from his wife, at the same time aware that he was exaggerating. She was a sensitive listener and felt emboldened to unburden herself, talking of her troubled marriage. Her husband was often away on business, she complained, and took her part in the relationship for granted.

"Malcolm's a good man, all right," she said of her husband. "And successful in his business, but I hardly see him Monday to Friday."

"Don't get me wrong," she added with an unnatural laugh, "I'm quite capable of looking after myself. I've many friends, my fitness club and bridge night. Plenty to do. But since Gina's gone off to university, well, it does get lonesome sometimes, I have to admit."

The conversation, encouraged by a few drinks, brought them closer, revealing personal doubts and vulnerabilities, removing the normal inhibitions. For the first time, Bill looked at her with sexual interest. Her interest in him, her understanding of the problems he faced, made her attractive, desirable and within reach.

He gave her a lift home, which was on the way for him, and stopped outside, by which time it was dark.

"Thanks, Marjorie," he said, suddenly and instinctively holding her hand.

"Thanks for listening, you're a lovely woman," and he leaned forward to kiss her on the cheek. She turned her head and met the kiss with her lips. One long kiss, that revived memories of passions long since diluted.

"Sorry." He flustered immediately afterwards. "Sorry, love, I didn't mean to…"

"It's OK, Bill, it's OK," she interrupted. "Perhaps we just needed it. We're not bad people, are we? Just need some closeness sometimes."

She put her hand to his cheek.

"Thanks for the lift, and take care, won't you? I'll see you Monday in the office."

With that, she smiled, gathered her bag and got out of the car. He watched as she walked down the front path, turning to wave.

As he started the engine to drive off, he felt a flush of confusion — elation and desire, guilt and longing. He wanted this woman and knew it was wrong. He had never been unfaithful to Elizabeth — not emotionally anyway — but he felt the delicious temptation of defying convention.

The matter exercised him all weekend. Particularly attentive and cheerful with Elizabeth, he nevertheless thought of Marjorie constantly and what that simple kiss had meant. Nothing, of course, he told himself. Just nonsense. A flirtation after a few drinks. Happens all the time. A one-off.

On arriving at work the following Monday, half an hour early, as usual, and before doing any work, he penned a short note to Marjorie.

Dear Marjorie, it read. I'm so sorry for my behaviour on Friday. It was really out of order and I hope you forgive me. I trust things are back to normal and we are still friends. Bill.

The next time Marjorie dropped by his office to pick up some files, they greeted each other politely, and he handed her the note, marked "personal". She took it, smiled at him, nodded and left.

He felt relieved. The disturbing feelings could now be suppressed. But he also longed for a response, and by the afternoon he received one. It said simply:

Dear Bill, no problem. It was just lovely to talk and I hope we can do it again sometime. Marjorie.

Not only did this free Bill from any concerns that Marjorie was going to be "difficult", but suggested the tempting possibility of another meeting.

On seeing her a few days later outside the office, he invited her for an after-work drink — just the two of them — so they might talk through their feelings. Meeting on a Tuesday, when Bill had told Elizabeth he was working late, then going straight to meet his regular pals.

That evening, when he gave Marjorie a lift home, she invited him in. Her husband was away. They went to bed together and made love. Bill was as nervous, clumsy and passionate as an inexperienced teenager, but Marjorie found this endearing and flattering.

Immediately afterwards, Bill experienced a predictable wave of remorse. It was not the first time he had been unfaithful to his wife, but this time was different. He desired Marjorie and found her elegance seductive. This woman didn't need looking after. She was not demanding, but understanding and supportive. This made his guilt the more acute, as he compared her self-assuredness to his fragile wife.

For the next six months, the affair staggered on. They met furtively for lovemaking, usually once a week at Marjorie's house, once or twice at a hotel a suitable distance away. Bill would tell Elizabeth he was meeting friends or working late, and this, being normal, caused no suspicion. Marjorie was relaxed about the arrangement, to the point Bill feared she might be careless, whereas Bill fretted constantly that Elizabeth, or workmates, would find out. He struggled with himself constantly, knowing he could never leave his wife and that this "affair", while addictive, had no purpose. He made a point of being honest with Marjorie. Whilst he had "fallen in love" with her, he couldn't promise her a future, because he needed to look after w

Elizabeth, and the boys wouldn't understand if he were ever to desert their mother. Marjorie, rational as ever, commented that the boys might well be old enough to understand that some marriages didn't last and would be able to come to terms with it. But she was not putting any pressure on Bill, and, for her part, she felt her own marriage was as good as over.

From the outset, they enjoyed each other physically. Their sex was energetic and authentic, if perfunctory, given the necessity always for covert organisation. Conversation between them never developed. Beyond the standard reports on family and partners, they actually had little in common, apart from workplace gossip. How could more meaningful exchanges develop, when the obvious topic — the future of their partnership — was taboo?

In this suspended state their relationship may have drifted on longer. However, inevitably, they were unable to continue to conceal it. People at work noticed the changes in the way they dealt with each other. Some commented on the fact they often sat together when colleagues went for drinks and gave each other close attention. No one knew for certain how intimate they were, but rumours sprang up about their behaviour.

One workmate, with Bill's best interests in mind, mentioned casually to him over a pint that people were gossiping about him and Marjorie, and that he should at least be aware of that. Naturally, he didn't believe it himself, but thought Bill should know. At the time, Bill laughed it off as nonsense and "tittle tattle," but the comments unnerved him. His reputation as a reliable, trustworthy and honest financial officer could be under threat.

Such was his obsession with Marjorie, however, that even this possible danger to his reputation did not prevent him from seeing her.

That was until the day that Jack, while visiting home, by chance saw his father's car one evening outside a strange house, fifteen minutes away from where they lived. On his way back from seeing a friend in the area, he was walking home, when he recognised his father's blue Ford parked in the street. Puzzled, he looked around for a reason, but seeing none, continued on his way home.

Later that evening, at about ten, Bill arrived home, while Jack and Elizabeth were watching television together.

He gave Elizabeth a kiss on the forehead.

"Have a nice evening, love?" she said routinely. "Was the pub busy?"

"No," replied Bill. "Quiet tonight. Just nice to chat with the boys."

Jack greeted his father, then asked, in all innocence, "What were you doing in Churchill Avenue, Dad? Saw the car there."

Bill, at that moment in the kitchen, felt an onrush of panic. In that instant, he knew his deceit was unravelled.

Gathering his thoughts with the desperation of a criminal found out, he answered calmly. "Oh, that, yeah earlier, yeah, erm… just had to drop off some papers to a colleague. You know, work stuff. Urgent."

Jack thought it strange, as it had been around eight o'clock he had seen the car, a significant time after work, but having no reason to suspect anything other, accepted his father's explanation.

But Jack's comment perturbed Elizabeth.

"Who was that then, love? Pestering you after work now, are they?" she asked, with all the sincerity of someone hoping for affirmation.

"Just one of the directors, as usual, making a fuss when there isn't one," he continued, feeling sick at heart.

The problem was twofold. Elizabeth knew her husband well. She knew from the tone of his voice that he was uncomfortable. Her husband was unfailingly honest to the point of being undiplomatic. He didn't lie convincingly. Second, she knew Marjorie Bonfield lived in Churchill Avenue. And the faint echoes of rumour about her and Bill had already floated across to the day care centre, where she had overheard but ignored them.

Later, when Jack was sound asleep, she crept over to Bill's bedroom and sat on the end of the bed. She knew he was awake and listening.

"So, Bill, what's happening? Something going on between you and Marjorie? And don't lie, because you were with her tonight, weren't you?"

She spoke with quiet determination. Without rancour, but with the steel of a prosecutor with damning evidence.

Bill sat up and moved next to her. He tried to put his arm around her, but she pushed him away.

"Well?" she persisted.

"No, love, you've got it all wrong. I did drop round to Marjorie's, I did. But it was to pass some work papers on. She invited me in and we had a cup of tea, and, well, she's a nice but needy woman and kept going on about her husband and her marriage and all, and I, well, I just listened. She is a friend, after all. But, Lizzie, nothing happened."

"She means nothing to me in that sense. I love you. You, and the boys, you're my life. You're everything to me. Everything. I would never risk that." And he meant it in that he determined there and then to finish the relationship with Marjorie.

"Have you slept with her?" Elizabeth was not put off so easily.

"No, of course not." Bill's insistence was enough to give him away.

"Look, so I gave her a hug, you know, just for comfort and we did meet for drinks a couple of times, because she wanted to talk. But it was nothing. I'll never leave you." Bill's telling of half-truths strengthened the case against him.

Elizabeth felt desolate. Without saying a word, she went back to her bedroom, shut and locked the door, and, without tears, tried to sleep. Her boys were gone, and now her husband had broken the one certain chain of trust and security she had. She believed him. He wouldn't leave. But she also knew he had been unfaithful. Not a one-night stand on a business trip, but an intimate connection with another woman, whom she knew and could not match for glamour. This represented a fundamental change to their relationship. It could threaten total destruction, or settle back again to an apparent normality.

In the morning the three of them, parents and son, had breakfast together. Bill was getting ready for work, as usual, and Jack preparing to return home after his short visit. Elizabeth busied herself, frying bacon and toasting bread. She had puffy eyes and didn't speak. Nor did Bill, who hid behind his newspaper.

"Everything all right?" asked Jack jovially, concerned by the awkward silence.

"Just tired, dear. Had a bad night," explained his mother.

Jack recognised the signal and, sensing the coldness between his parents, didn't pursue the matter. Instead he chatted on about the potential difficulty of his train journey home and the likelihood of delays, given the state of the railways. This continued until Bill stood up and made his way out, stopping to give Elizabeth a peck on the cheek as he left for work, saying, "Won't be late tonight, love." She turned her face away as he kissed her and didn't reply.

When he had gone, Jack turned again to his mother.

"Everything OK, Mum? You seem upset. You and Dad had a row?"

"Everything's fine, dear," she lied, putting a comforting hand on her son's shoulder.

"Your dad's been a bit restless lately, that's all, but we sorted it out. In fact, he was just saying last night how much he loves us all and how he'd never leave us."

"Well, that's OK then!" said Jack with heavy irony in his voice, taken aback at the very thought his father would even consider leaving the family. He looked questioningly at his mother, who forced a weak smile and then turned again to her chores at the sink.

Jack's heart sank a little but he let the matter drop, and he never discussed it again with his mother.

As soon as he got to work, Bill painstakingly wrote another note to Marjorie. As the first he had written to her some six months before had initiated a love affair, so this one concluded it. In the note he explained how his feelings for Marjorie — he avoided the word love — had been genuine and that at no time did he consider the relationship as anything but serious. He had even considered leaving his family for her, but given his wife's frailties felt that she needed him more than Marjorie, and that his sense of duty meant he had to stop seeing her. He was very sad about this but hoped she would understand.

Having delivered the note furtively, along with a file, he felt a great relief. Now it was over, he did not have to deceive his wife any more. At the same time, he would miss the excitement of the secretive sex and Marjorie's admiration for him.

Much to his consternation, she didn't reply this time. He had expected — in fact, quietly hoped for — demands for a meeting, a showdown, or, at least, a full explanation, some reaction indicating the strength of her feeling. But none came.

Whenever he saw her, she was pleasant and polite, to the point of diffidence. It was as though nothing between them had occurred. The hard truth came upon him that she had managed the episode, and its ending, with equanimity and that he was the one left diminished and regretful. At work gatherings from then on, although greeting him warmly, like an old friend, she was careful to sit apart and avoid conversation. He found himself feeling impotent jealousy whenever he saw her talking to another man. He felt foolish. He was the one who had strong feelings.

At home he gave full attention to Elizabeth, compensating for his infidelity. The two returned to their routine, based on convenience, habit and need, though their relationship was inevitably damaged. As the individual threads of a precious cloth are torn and the entire fabric weakened, so the family bonds were injured by the betrayal of trust.

Jack talked about it to Doug. They concluded that the lack of warmth between their parents was almost certainly due to their father having had an affair. Doug was all for confronting him and finding out the truth, but Jack dissuaded him.

"There's no point in stirring things up," argued Jack.

"He's remorseful and is unlikely to do it again. In his own eyes, he let his discipline slip and you know how important that is to his self-respect. As for Mum, I don't think she has any options really. They will stick it out and take care of each other. They've been together a long time and rely on each other. There's nothing to be gained by reviving regrets and bitterness."

Doug demurred and silence fell over the question in the months that followed, like an uneasy truce, tolerated but inconclusive. Both sons continued to visit when they could, partly to give additional support and encouragement to their mother, and partly to enjoy those comforts of home that never change whatever age the children reach.

Although there was superficial harmony in the household, they admitted to each other a little sadness that their parents no longer seemed to share much tenderness. Affection was fading like a delicate blossom wilting before the onset of autumn.

Chapter Ten
The Triumph of Hope

"Attention! Attention! This is the commander of the police force. You are now in occupation of the university premises illegally. You must leave the buildings and the university grounds immediately. If you leave now, peacefully, you can go without interference or repercussions. If you refuse, and continue to occupy these buildings illegally, you will be forcibly removed. You will be forcibly removed and subject to prosecution. If you have not left after five minutes, I shall order my men to remove you and arrest anyone who resists. This is a final warning."

Shrill and distorted by the screech of feedback from the megaphone, the words pierced the still darkness enveloping the university square. Commander Wong lowered the speaker, wiped his lips with the back of his sleeve and looked at his watch.

They have exactly five minutes, he thought to himself, before I order the men in. They'll come out before then, he re-assured himself. No one wants anyone hurt.

Stephen Wong was forty-nine years old. A career police officer, he had risen through the ranks, proving himself a brave street cop and a capable administrator. Twice he had been shot at by criminals, once getting a bullet in the arm. For that action, resulting in the arrest of the gangsters, he had received the highest commendation for valour. He had also faced down angry mobs during the bout of political turmoil fifteen years earlier. Defying flailing fists, hurled bottles and even paving stones, he had not flinched. He did his duty resolutely.

But now, standing before the university central building, and confronting a bunch of unruly, idealistic kids, he felt uncomfortable. Why, his own son had studied at this place, graduating only three years ago. He had posed proudly, clutching his degree certificate, with him and his wife on those very steps leading up to the building's main portico, with its grand columns. Thank goodness he wasn't involved in this mess.

It shouldn't take long. His men were well prepared. With their smart dark blue uniforms, heavy-duty boots, high visibility yellow jackets and striking red berets — to distinguish them in any melee that might develop — they were disciplined and trained. The majority, in their mid-twenties, were not much older than the students. They might be inexperienced in crowd control, but, armed with round plastic riot shields and batons, they had no reason to be nervous. Standing in the evening humidity, most were perspiring heavily, the sweat running off their foreheads into their eyes. They were keen to get on with this.

Following the commander's ultimatum, there had been no response from the students, just a stifling silence, as if there was a collective catching of breath, or summoning of courage.

Then, just moments before Wong gave the order to advance on the building and clear it, the large double wooden doors swung open and a group of students, perhaps a hundred strong, came out silently and spread themselves along the portico at the top of the broad stairs. The police chief raised his hand to pause his men.

One of the students stepped forward and, without referring to any notes, shouted his defiance. It was Jonathon Yu.

"We are not going anywhere," he proclaimed. "We are students here. This is our university. A place of learning. Why are you here? You represent the oppressors. We are standing for freedom. Academic freedom and political freedom. You, citizens of this territory, should be standing with us. Come and join us. Come and join us to build a new future for this territory. You are our brothers. We want no confrontation."

Commander Wong, thrown off balance by the unexpected challenge, raised the loudspeaker to his lips once more.

"You are breaking the law by occupying these premises at this time," he said sternly. "You must leave now, or there will be consequences. I shall order my men to clear the building."

"We stay!" shouted Yu in response, and immediately the students behind him began chanting, "We stay! We stay! No surrender! No surrender!"

"All right, young man," said Wong to himself. "You asked for it."

He looked over his shoulder at his men, raised his arm again, brought it down in a sweeping motion, and shouted, "Advance!"

As the order rippled along the ranks of young policemen, they began to beat their shields with their batons, according to instruction, and to repeatedly bellow "Advance!" in unison. The rhythmic beating and chanting, designed to intimidate opponents, just as the Zulus, soon drowned out the student chorus.

As the two lines of officers marched steadily forward, they presented a threatening sight, but the student phalanx, rather than retreating, steadied itself at the top of the stairs. Then, quite suddenly, the doors were flung open wider. Charging out came a further stream of protesters, to reinforce those outside. These arrivals, however, more like shock troops, were prepared for confrontation, most of them wearing motor cycle or yellow construction helmets and goggles and carrying makeshift staves and shields. Wielding a variety of baseball bats, broom handles and metal poles, they thrust their way to the front to meet the advancing police line head on.

The clash of the two front lines was sudden and suffocating. Like ancient armies they collided, at first pressing upon one another, trying to push the other back and impose their will, with those behind lending weight to the unfortunates bearing the brunt of the impact.

This was a contest of strength, heaving and shoving, with both lines trying to outmuscle the other, neither side gaining an advantage. Amid a rising tumult of chants, screams of pain and fear, cries for help and exchange of insults and curses, the struggling and jostling became ever more forceful and violent.

The officers had been instructed to aim their baton blows at shoulders, arms and legs, rather than heads or torsos, but in the cramped condition of the front line, such niceties were soon forgotten. Having not been equipped with full riot gear, they wore no helmets and were getting the worst of the contest as an increasing number of blows from staves and batons were exchanged. Out of self-defence and frustration, they began to lash out and the more aggressive defenders responded in kind. Blood began to flow and a number of casualties on both sides were dragged hastily to the rear, suffering from cuts and abrasions.

After ten minutes of punishing stalemate, the student numbers on the portico began to dwindle, as those who were unarmed at the rear retreated through the main door back into the building. Using their superior training and co-ordination, the police slowly forced the student combatants back also. Several of the more violent students on the front line were grabbed by police snatch squads and dragged, struggling, back behind the police lines, to face detention and arrest.

Yard by yard, the remaining protesters were funnelled back inside. Somehow, resistance was strong enough to maintain an orderly retreat, and as soon as the last few students squeezed through the doors, they were slammed shut by collective power from inside. The police were unable to gain entry. Finally secured, the strong doors were locked and barricaded.

Surveying the scene with dismay, Commander Wong ordered his men back to the centre of the square to rest and regroup. No one had anticipated such determined resistance. The protesters had been expected to melt away, or just give up, at the first sign of resolute police action. Instead, he could count half a dozen injured officers, needing medical treatment, and many more bruised and shaken young constables.

He ordered them to stand down, recover their strength and prepare to go again. He would tell them now to equip themselves with riot gear. Discarding their cloth berets, they would take up dark blue helmets with visors and neck protectors, throw down their yellow high visibility jackets and collect padded flak jackets, begin donning shin guards and clipping pepper spray canisters to their belts. There would be no more softness or colour in their uniform or their attitude.

Back inside the student union building, the cafeteria area was heaving with activity. There were a number with cuts and bruises to their faces and arms, being tended to by others, praised for their bravery and feted like heroes. A stench of sweat and the remains of cooked food pervaded the place. Everyone, combatant or not, was weary, but the physical symptoms of creeping exhaustion were overcome by an adrenalin-powered energy, which electrified the atmosphere. Feelings of apprehension and concern gave way to sheer exhilaration. They had held out! They had kept the police out! They had demonstrated the will of the people against oppression.

What next? That was the question exercising every group, large and small, that gathered to review the events and give strength to one another. One thing was sure — no one was leaving.

Doug had watched proceedings in the square and on the portico from a first-floor window. Standing side by side with Brandon and Jo Chan, he had been frightened at the approach of the police lines and suffered from profound doubts about the whole protest. For a few moments his courage failed him, and he felt sick to his stomach at the thought of students being hurt, arrested and humiliated. He feared physical violence himself. He had a strong urge to turn and run, away and out through the back of the union building. Back to the comfort of his flat and his books. Back to normality.

But as the struggle below developed and he saw the students standing up for themselves, holding the police at bay and eventually causing them to withdraw, he found himself yelling encouragement and support. His strength of purpose returned, and he felt solidarity with those young people, who put their own security at risk for their chosen cause.

Once the great doors had been bolted and they had returned to the cafeteria downstairs, Doug joined Brandon and Jo Chan, with others, in seeking out Jonathon Yu.

They found him, at the centre of his devoted group of followers, sitting on a table in the corner of the place. Yu was bloodied, with the scarlet trophy stain of battle on his T-shirt, resulting from a cut above his right eye. He held a cloth full of ice to his wound. Covered in perspiration, he looked gaunt and pale and close to exhaustion. Contrary to his physical appearance, however, his spirit remained undimmed. There was a gleam of evangelical passion in his dark eyes as he spoke with infectious fervour to those around him.

He praised them for their bravery and resolve and pointed out the significance of their resistance. As long as they stayed firm, they would succeed, he assured them, and they would light a fire that would ignite a movement in the territory and beyond. A movement that the authorities could not quench. Make no mistake, they were the vanguard in a wider struggle for democracy and independence.

Fine words, thought Doug, He's very motivational and a born leader. He's giving them all strength and belief. But how long can we really hold on? The police will come back stronger. When do we negotiate?

Brandon approached Yu when he had finished his words of encouragement, shaking him firmly by the hand and asking if he was OK. The two of them sat to one side, joined by Doug, Jo Chan and a couple of Yu's supporters.

Both agreed that the protest should continue and that it was too early to negotiate. Yu thought it unlikely the police would try again before the next day, but then the game would be up.

"I don't think we can hold off a strong police action to get us out," Yu was saying. "We only just kept them out this time. It wasn't easy and they weren't even coming in heavy."

"Well, get your boys ready," responded Brandon. "It would be a great thing if we can stay in occupation until, say, lunch time tomorrow. By then, in the full glare of daylight and media attention, it will signal a humiliation for the director and his mates in government. The public will be fired up and the democrats in the government will be able to stand firm on the back of their support."

"We'll do our best," continued Yu, "but everyone will get tired as the night comes on. We must keep spirits up. Stephen Tam has been talking about stopping now and negotiating before anyone gets injured, but most people are taking no notice."

"It would be stupid to give up now — the effort will have been wasted and disappear as just another pointless student stunt. But if we can show the public and the press that we really are willing to make sacrifices for the sake of this territory, then we can achieve something," added Brandon.

"We have at least two local journalists with us here, who have recorded some of the action on their phones and they're filing it right now. Plenty of shots of police aggression and injuries to our people. It'll make the headlines tomorrow. Police brutality and brave students fighting for people's rights," he said.

Neither of them at that point were aware of developments outside.

Beyond the black wrought-iron university gates that led into the square, the long straight avenue running parallel to the exterior wall was clogged with police vehicles and personnel. Having sealed off the avenue at either end, two hundred yards from the gates, and blocked off the two streets that fed into the avenue, the police had succeeded in keeping the public and media at bay. To the rear of the campus, where limited access through a dense residential area was only possible by means of narrow lanes and alleyways, the police had, since midnight, also prevented anyone entering, though allowing and encouraging a few fearful protesters to exit the site.

Despite these precautions, news of the protest and the police action was spreading fast. Photos and video clips were being circulated by the infiltrated media and by individual students, who were calling their increasingly anxious parents with updates of the action.

Crowds were gathering at either end of the avenue — the concerned and the curious — trying to understand what was going on, shouting questions and angrily demanding answers from the uninformed police officers guarding the barriers.

Several TV crews had shown up, alerted to the story. Eagerly, they scanned the scene, looking for ways of circumventing the barriers, or spotting vantage points in trees, or nearby flats, from where they might get their scoop.

For the university director, minister of security and the conservative members of government, the standoff was escalating into a major embarrassment. The messages coming out from the protest demanding democracy and even independence from the federation might be juvenile and unrealistic. However, they were powerful propaganda for those who wanted change and could incite a discontented populace to wider action. Phone calls and emails between the director's office, the ministry for security, police headquarters and senior government ministers were rapidly exchanged. The situation had to be resolved quickly and firmly before it got out of hand. Authority needed to reassert itself and the protesters had to be taught a lesson.

Irritable discussions were distilled down to impatient orders, which were relayed along the chain of command through politicians, bureaucrats and police officers until they finally reached Commander Wong, whose shoulders now reluctantly bore the responsibility of achieving a decisive outcome.

He ordered his men to ready themselves for another attempt to clear the university complex. This time they would be prepared for resistance.

"Don't hold back this time, men. You have the equipment. If you meet violent resistance, you can use reasonable force to arrest any aggressors. Force them out; push them through the back or let them through your lines if they want to leave. We have gas if we need it. Good luck!"

There was no lining up in orderly fashion for this push. That gave too much warning. They were assigned in squads. The main group would rush the main door, with a battering ram, and force an entry. Meanwhile, other units would look to gain entry through the ground floor windows or by means of the alleyway that ran along the side of the union building.

At the loud blast of a whistle, they charged through the iron gates and hurled themselves towards their objectives, shouting encouragement to each other.

A leading group of twenty or more officers made straight for the main door. Four of them, in the lead, wielded a heavy metal battering ram, used in police actions against heavy warehouse or garage doors. Behind them, thirty yards in the rear, stood another hundred officers, ready to charge into the building once the defence had been breached. At the same time, units of some fifty officers made for the ground floor windows in the façade, with the aim of smashing their way in. Commander Wong had also sent a further troop to break into the building by means of the narrow alleyway that ran down its side, separating it from the administrative office block on the right side of the main square.

The orders were clear. Break into the building and force the students to leave, either peacefully through the square, or be driven out the rear exits. Any violent opposition was to be treated aggressively, with the use of pepper spray where necessary, and the perpetrators arrested and handcuffed. There would be no mistake this time.

Within the union building, the students were shocked into action by the sound of the new assault. Lookouts immediately screamed warnings of the impending police impact and, amid a cacophony of noise, generated by panic, bravado and encouraging chants, swarms of students made for the main door and ground floor windows to defend them. Buoyed by the success of the first engagement, they rushed in large numbers aiming to block any entrance through force of numbers.

Doug found himself, along with Brandon and Jo Chan, swept along in the passion and stream of bodies towards the main door. He found the crowd so dense in the hallway behind the doors that he was still forty or more yards behind the doors. He was aware that the defenders were this time better protected and armed.

Nearly everyone had some kind of headgear and most wore soaked scarves or rags around their faces. Pushing past him, amid a group of well-armed militants, came Rocky Ocampo, who sported a blood -stained bandana like a badge of honour and a large plaster on his upper cheek. His dark brown eyes burned with excitement.

"Hey, man!" he shouted above the general tumult. "You made it to the action, then? Good for you, man! Told you we'd need to fight. We'll take 'em, don't worry. We're ready. Take care of yourself," and he was gone, pushing his way towards the doors.

Overcome by the general frenzy, and feeling ill-equipped to deal with violence, Doug began to feel nauseous. He manoeuvred himself back until he could slip away from the crowd and dash along the corridor, back to the cafeteria. He found himself a cloth napkin, soaked it in cold water under a tap and wiped his face and neck. Feeling refreshed, he then tied it round his face. Realising he was now alone and separated from Brandon and his gang, he then made his way up the stairs to the first-floor corridor and along to the front, where he found tense crowds already densely huddled around the windows.

There was a shuddering crash and splintering sound, which seemed to make the whole facade of the building tremble, as the police battering ram collided with the stout wooden doors. Upstairs the windows rattled in their frames. There were loud cries of dismay and fear inside, but the doors held. Seconds later came the ear-splitting noise of shattered glass, as the police vanguards smashed the panes of the four ground floor windows.

This is it, thought Doug. We can't hold out against this. And people are going to get hurt. He turned away, wondering what to do.

Many of the militant students were, however, made of stronger mettle than the teacher from England. There were several hundred Rocky Ocampos and Jo Chans, street fighters, who didn't need the subtle dialectics of the likes of Brandon to inspire them to fight. For them it was visceral. It was their past and their future. The police were the enemy. They would hold out or they would go down fighting.

With another sickening crash, the battering ram was driven again into the main doors. Along the front of the building, the officers attempted to clamber through the broken windows. To their surprise, the resistance remained stubborn. Following the first confrontation, the protesters had strongly fortified the doors, nailing planks across the back, angling posts against them and piling desks and bookcases into a formidable barrier.

At the third heart-stopping thud, the doors, cracking and splitting under the pressure, were pushed open inches, but not enough for any of the assailants to enter. Meanwhile, the defenders at the windows, through which only two people at most could squeeze through, were able to prevent entry merely through force of numbers. Individual officers then began resorting to pepper spray, trying to drive the students back. Some, who couldn't avoid the noxious liquid, yelled with pain as their eyes and skin burned agonisingly, and were helped to the back by their comrades, to be washed down with water. But still they resisted, those wearing goggles or visors on helmets, holding up makeshift shields and umbrellas, beating back the attackers with poles as they tried to force an entry.

To the side of the union building, the attempt to outflank the defenders by driving down the connecting alley also floundered. Being barely two metres wide, the narrow passage was easy to block. A hastily erected, six-foot-high barricade of sandbags, furniture and even bicycles, was enough to prevent the police gaining access, as a barrage of paving stones and other projectiles prevented them from dismantling the obstacles.

All along the front of the building a full-scale battle developed, with casualties on both sides staggering to the rear, but neither gaining an advantage.

After fifteen minutes, Commander Wong, who had been pacing impatiently up and down along the line of his men, urging them on, lost patience and called out for the tear gas. A row of six constables fired a round of canisters at the windows and attempted to get them through the narrow gap in the doors.

This caused panic as some of the canisters flew inside, clattered to the ground and released their caustic contents. As it swirled around, the gas, emanating its toxic mix of scented chemicals, caused further tears of pain and anguish. Some bolder students picked up the canisters and flung them back out or kicked them into side rooms, while others tried to smother them with blankets. Everyone held onto soaked neckerchiefs and cloths around their faces. Many fled back towards the cafeteria — but the hard core hung on.

Finally, after repeated battering, the doors were prised open enough for two of the stronger officers to barge their way through. On entering, however, they found themselves facing a six- foot- high barricade of solid furniture. What's more, a rain of missiles descended on them — stones, bottles, and assorted objects. One of the officers fell, knocked down by a brick. The other hauled him back outside, to the cheers and jeers of the defenders.

As more officers moved up, a breakthrough seemed inevitable, for after almost half an hour's bruising confrontation, the students' resolve was wilting.

Then, quite suddenly, and shockingly to attackers and defenders alike, there were a series of dull thuds and explosive bursts of flame among the police just in front of the building. They lit up the darkness of the square in a ghostly fashion, illuminating the pale and shocked faces of the officers, who scurried back in panic, a number beating out flames from their uniforms or those of their comrades. More bursts of fire followed. And more. Molotov cocktails were being hurled from the upstairs windows.

Watching transfixed, Doug, who had recovered some of his resolve, saw the group he knew as "the militants", including Rocky, flinging the fiery bombs through the open sash windows. My God, Doug thought, they had quietly prepared themselves for a full-scale battle. This is like a medieval castle siege. They'll be throwing boiling oil on them next.

A great cheer of relief erupted within the building as those inside realised their attackers had retreated back across the square, and that, for a time at least, they had held their ground. They were still masters of the university building.

While some stayed at the front, to repair defences and keep a watch, most trudged wearily back to the cafeteria, where they slumped limply, tending to minor wounds and dealing with the effects of the gas.

When Doug returned, he was confronted with a chaotic scene. The place was littered with food containers plastic bottles, discarded clothing, sleeping bags, banners and flags. Protesters sat and lay about in a kind of stupor. Exhausted and elated, anxious yet buoyed by their success, they talked in hushed tones, waiting for further news and instruction.

Outside the gates of the university square, Commander Wong finished his call and switched off his radio phone. He waved away his sergeant and walked to one side, where he sat alone on a grass verge. He removed his cap, wiped his heavily perspiring brow, leaned forward with his elbows on his knees, and wiped the tears and sweat from his eyes with his forefingers.

Chapter Eleven
Unprofitable Desire

By two o'clock in the morning even this frenetic city was quietening. Some bars closed their doors around this time, gently ushering their rowdy customers out into the street, while others would continue to entertain their increasingly voluble and self-opinionated clientele until three or four. The night air was cooling, but still hung heavy with oppressive humidity. Daylight odours of petrol fumes, fast food fat and burnt soy had been replaced by a mixture of stale beer, cheap perfume and incense sticks, which wafted out from many doorways in this crowded entertainment area.

Drunken shouts of dispute or shallow joy punctuated the growing stillness. Glass tinkled and sometimes shattered in the distance. Doors slammed shut, as weary staff cleared up and closed down for the night. Streets, colourfully outlandish in their daytime finery of neon and self-promoting commercialism, began to look tawdry and grey under the thin yellow lamp light of the early hours. Stripped of their superficial glamour, they began to reveal their naked selves, like an elegant elderly woman, who removes her fine clothes and make-up at the end of the day and yields to reality again. Now and then a rat, disturbed by footsteps, scuttled nervously among the rubbish in the dark recesses, while the first human competitors for the leftovers of the evening lurked in the shadows.

Nursing his cut eyebrow with a bloodied handkerchief, and feeling heavy-headed from drink, Jack laboriously considered his next move, his thoughts tumbling over one another in a swirling fog of consciousness.

Need to go home... sleep. Drunk... again... enough now. Am I drunk? Must go home. Call home tomorrow. Check on Mum. Mum's birthday. She's got problems with Dad. Poor Mum. Where'd that girl go? Pretty. What's her name? Cherry? Nice girl. Anyway. Marion. See Marion next week. Lovely Marion. Why did she leave? Shame. Bastard. Let her down. Poor Marion. Seemed upset. Maybe we can work it out. Must remember Gaynor. Is that real? Poser. Money would be nice though. Lots of money.

Jack laughed out loud. Justin Gaynor — what a bullshitter! What a joke! Me... head of PR for KFIG! KFIG...! Awful. Awful people. Crooks! He laughed again, so that a couple walking past turned to look at him, as he sat on the pavement with his back against a shop door.

"You all right, mate?" the man asked.

"Yes! Oh yes! Wonderful!" replied Jack. "Wonderful. Absolutely spiffing. Going up... up in the world." He pointed skywards and giggled foolishly again.

"Looks like it!" said the man. Smiling at his partner, he tapped his temple with his forefinger, and the two strode on.

Struggling, Jack pulled himself upright, still leaning against the door for support. He looked from side to side, to see if there were any taxis around. But none were to be seen.

Deciding to head for the main junction, where he had more chance of finding a ride, he began to walk unsteadily along the road, stopping every ten yards or so to rest by leaning against the wall or shop front.

After a few minutes he saw, in front of him, a purple and orange light emanating from a doorway and illuminating the pavement with its garish glow. Standing in the light was a young, heavily made up Chinese woman, wearing extravagant layers of mascara and thick bright red lipstick. She wore a tight tank top, revealing her slim midriff, and bright green hot pants, which clung to her slender buttocks and thighs like an extra layer of skin. Tottering on high platform shoes, she moved out to block Jack's path.

"Hi, honey, where you going? Come inside. Have some fun. Nice place. Beers only thirty dollars. Nice girls. Come in."

"Hello," replied Jack, thinking that she was very sexy. "I'm going home," he added, gesturing with one arm into the distance. "Home... wherever that is."

"No," purred the girl, "too early for home. Time for some fun. I show you some fun. You like me?"

"Yes, yes," slurred Jack, trying hard to focus his gaze on her face. "You are very gorgeous, very gorgeous. But, must go home."

"Oh, honey, don't go," persisted the girl. She sidled up to Jack, taking his arm and steering him towards the door without difficulty. She leaned towards him, her strong perfume almost overpowering, and whispered in his ear.

"Come on, honey. Lilly show you a good time. Come inside."

Feeling her hot breath on his ear, Jack's sex drive was reawakening in equal measure to the weakening of his resolve.

"OK. OK. I'll come, but only for one beer."

"Of course, honey." They went inside.

Dazzled at first by the bright purple and orange lights that highlighted a central stage area, Jack's eyes took a few moments to adapt to the otherwise dingy interior. It was a deceptively large establishment, with many low round tables, surrounded by circular upholstered sofas. On the stage, in the centre of the room, a solitary dancer, wearing only bikini bottoms, swayed listlessly to the repetitive music, holding onto a pole with one hand, her expressionless face betraying her boredom and detachment from the whole scene. Only a few male customers were scattered around a largely empty place. They sat with one or sometimes two or three girls, apparently enjoying the attention they were getting.

Lilly pulled Jack to a seat at the edge of the room and sat him down. She joined him, clinging on to his arm and putting one hand on the inside of his thigh.

"See, honey. Nice place. I take care of you. What you want to drink. Brandy? Whisky?"

"Oh God, no," said Jack, suddenly a little more lucid. "A beer will do."

"You buy me a drink?

"Yeah, suppose so. What you having?"

"Ladies drink, please."

"OK, what's that then?"

"Special drink for ladies. Just small drink with vodka. You know. To make me feel horny for you." She fondled the inside of his thigh.

Jack wasn't quite drunk enough, and was familiar with the culture of these bars sufficiently not to be entirely taken in. He was aware this might be expensive. But he was drunk enough to think — what the hell! It's only one drink and it might lead to something interesting.

"How much is it?" he asked.

"For you, darling, special price. Only two hundred dollars."

"Wow, I dunno. That's very pricy. I dunno."

"No problem, honey, one drink for poor Lilly."

She leaned over and whispered in his ear.

"I get commission see. Good for Lilly."

"Oh, OK then," Jack conceded.

The girl raised her arm and within seconds an older woman appeared at the tableside. They spoke rapidly in Chinese. Looking at Jack quizzically, as if to say — he doesn't look fit for much — she disappeared, returning just a few minutes later with a beer and a drink, the colour of brandy, in a sherry glass.

She also carried a hot wet flannel, a towel and a plaster.

Handing them to Jack, she said, "You better clean up. You look a mess. No fighting here. You understand. This is decent club."

"Absolutely! Fine club," Jack replied, intending to sound ironic.

Nevertheless, he took the cloth gratefully and, with Lilly's help, wiped the drying blood from his face. When he was washed clean, Lilly carefully applied the plaster to the cut.

"That's sweet of you," he said and kissed her on the cheek. Now he was enjoying flirting again.

"Cheers, honey!" said Lilly, and took a large sip from her small drink.

"Cheers," said Jack, sinking back comfortably into the soft furniture.

"What's your name, honey?" asked the girl, kicking off her shoes, curling up her legs onto the sofa and sliding one arm through his.

"Jack," he answered, wearily, recognising a familiar routine, but playing along.

"And where are you from, Lilly?"

"From the north, but come here five years ago."

"Why?"

"Of course, money. Money to live. No work at home."

Usual story, thought Jack. Probably true too. Many girls working these bars came from the poorer regions and states neighbouring the territory. Most were illegal, living a twilight existence, out of sight of the authorities. Easy prey to the gangsters who ruled over most of these clubs.

"Well, be careful, Lilly," Jack advised, genuinely believing he was being helpful.

"There are some bad people around here."

"Mama looks after us," explained Lilly.

I bet she does, thought Jack.

For the next minutes — Jack couldn't say how long — they sat and talked idly. She, trying to get him interested in her; he, hovering between tiredness, boredom and lust.

Without him objecting, or really being aware of it, she ordered more drinks, and then suddenly, a second girl appeared, who sat down beside him.

"Honey, this is my friend Gloria. She got no customer, no drink. Buy her one drink, honey. She's very nice girl."

"I don't need two girlfriends," Jack said, trying to refuse without being impolite.

"Why not, honey, threesome good fun," countered Gloria without hesitation.

But before he could say any more, Gloria was cuddling up to him, unbuttoning his shirt and stroking his bare chest. Mama had arrived with another round of drinks for him and the two girls, which she plonked on the table.

"Don't worry. Have some fun. This beer on the house," she said reassuringly.

By now, Jack was befuddled enough to have lost count of the rounds of drinks, and took the gift of the free beer at face value. He was enjoying the attention. But a small corner of his consciousness, still glowing like a dying ember in the gloom, made him concerned about the possible cost of this generosity.

While the two women chatted on, flattering him and sipping their drinks, Jack began to lose concentration. Their words floated past him, dreamlike, meaningless, like conversations in a foreign language on a crowded bus. Looking around the bar, he felt the room sway slightly, as though he were on a boat, being rocked gently by a friendly sea. Seeing everything through a soft lens, at low speed, the pulsating colours of the disco floor and patterns of the soft furnishings merged together and then flared up before his eyes. He felt extremely tired and closed his eyes, leaning his head against the back of the sofa. A vision of Marion came to mind. She was crying, and he was comforting her. It was a good feeling. Marion was relying on him. She needed his care and protection. He also thought of his mother. She was drifting away. Where was his father? He had to get home to take care of them.

He dozed for some minutes, before being woken suddenly by Lilly shaking him. "You very tired now. Want to go home. Want to take me home?"

"That would be nice," he replied, yawning. "But… you know… how much would that be?"

"For you, special price. Just three thousand," she offered, completely sincere as to the reasonableness of the offer. "That includes bar fine… and me," she added, pouting.

"How about me too," chipped in the other woman, optimistically. "I come too."

"Oh wow, no way. I mean, sorry, I don't have that kind of money," he said definitively, sobering up a degree. "No, no, too much. Sorry, girls. No way."

Then he looked around conspiratorially, leaned towards Lilly and said in a hushed tone,

"How about I leave, and we meet later outside. Then no bar fine. I pay you taxi money, yeah?"

The girl's demeanour changed in a second. She frowned, stood up and put her hands on her hips.

"Bullshit. You bullshit. Cheapskate. I work in the bar. You know the way. You don't want me? OK… go wank yourself. I find another customer. Come on, Gloria… he's big cheapskate."

And with that, the two strode off, leaving him surprised and actually feeling slightly offended that she had dismissed his offer.

Oh shit, he thought, and struggled to stand up.

At that moment Mama appeared with the bill.

"Hey, mister, you don't like the girls, OK. If you leaving, then settle bill."

She handed him a scruffy piece of paper, ludicrously, he thought, on a small silver dish.

There was nothing ludicrous about the amount, however, and he blinked hard to focus on the figure.

"Are you kidding? Two thousand, six hundred? Are you joking?" He looked the Mama in the eye, who gazed at him coldly.

"No joking, ladies' drinks, ladies' company… you pay the bill."

"Hold on a minute." Jack tried to gather his thoughts and articulate clearly. "Hold on. Just had two or three drinks with that girl. Where is she? She'll tell you. Two or three drinks. That's all. This is a total rip-off."

"You pay bill. Or trouble."

"Oh, trouble?" he repeated sardonically. "No, no trouble. I'll give you one thousand. Here. That's all my cash. One thousand. Then… I'm leaving."

Pulling his wallet awkwardly from his back pocket, he fished out his last two notes and threw them onto the small tray.

"There!" he said, irritated, and he turned to go.

Only then did he see the three men blocking his way out towards the exit. They all wore dark glasses and were looking at Jack intently... threateningly. Probably triads, he thought, and experienced a tremor of fear down his back. But seconds later he relaxed, resigned to the fact he had lost this particular confrontation.

"Well, fuck you, then," he said to the Mama, as he picked up the notes and drew his credit card out of his wallet.

"No, fuck you to Mama," responded the woman, spitting her words out with unexpected venom. "I give you big trouble. You see, I—"

At this point a rich bass voice came booming from the entrance.

"Hi there, anyone at home in this rat shit hole of a bar?" It was Schmidt, the lawyer, poking his head through the doorway. He entered with a male friend, whom Jack didn't recognise.

Mama turned, and within a split second her expression changed from spiteful indignation to flirtatious delight. She broke into a broad smile.

"Schmidt," she called out, moving towards him.

"Come in, Schmidt, old friend. Long-time no see.

Welcome. Come in! Come in!"

She moved to greet him and the two had words, with the Mama speaking animatedly and pointing frequently at Jack. They approached him.

Schmidt held out his hand in greeting.

"Well, well. Mr Wilson, fancy seeing you here, in my favourite salubrious establishment. Way past your bedtime, isn't it? What have you done to your face, my boy, been scrapping? I thought civil servants were good boys, in bed by midnight. Mama tells me you've been a naughty boy and didn't want to pay your bill. Seeing you're a friend of mine, she'll knock twenty percent off, she says."

Relieved to have some support, Jack sighed and reluctantly handed over his credit card. Mama snatched it from his hand with a contemptuous look and marched off, while the three men settled back onto the sofa Jack was in the process of vacating.

"Friends of yours here, then?" Jack asked, not surprised at Schmidt's familiarity with the place.

"Shall we say... professional acquaintances?" Schmidt explained with a wave of his hand.

"Their business — as you can imagine — has its grey areas, and, on occasions, they are grateful for some legal expertise to get them out of, shall we say, complicated relationship problems, with the territory's fine law enforcement officers."

"Naturally," Schmidt continued, with a serious expression on his face, "I am happy to provide such expertise, to ensure the rigorous application of our beloved common law system. That is, of course, as long as they are able to meet my very reasonable fee schedule. And, in addition, their well-honed practice in the fine arts of hospitality lends itself to meeting my other sensory needs when required."

"Well said, Schmidt!" said his companion, clapping and laughing. He introduced himself as Matthis from Durban. Matthis, it transpired, was a gold dealer from Johannesburg, who had some complex transactional disputes in the territory. Schmidt, a friend from army days, was helping out.

Although Jack was too exhausted and drunk to fully enjoy Schmidt and Matthis's loud company, he soon found himself staring at another large beer and parrying the attention of one of the three bar girls who enthusiastically joined them. They had been attracted like moths round a flame, now that a well-known patron with a generous wallet was on hand.

Much of the conversation between the other two men and the women was swirling around Jack with little real engagement or comprehension on his part, until Schmidt paused and turned to Jack.

"By the way, I hope you got your leftie brother out of that university protest caper, 'cos rumour has it, it is turning very ugly."

Pulling himself out of his semi-stupor, Jack sat up, alarmed by Schmidt's revelation.

"What do you mean? What's happened?" he enquired urgently.

"Don't know for sure, but I heard there was a major punch-up and that a lot of protesters and police were hurt. It was on the TV in the last bar we were in half an hour ago. Looked pretty nasty. Quite a few police bust up. Seems like the protesters held 'em off though."

Standing up awkwardly and pulling his phone from his jacket pocket, Jack stared at its dull screen. He made out a couple of missed calls from Doug. Anxiously, he dialled Doug's number and raised the phone to his ear.

Come on, boy, come on, he said repeatedly to himself. Pick up, Doug. Pick up. Come on.

But it was no use. The call went to voicemail.

"I should be there," he blurted out to the others. "I was supposed to join him. I better go."

"Don't be a pillock," Schmidt said. "For a start, you'll get nowhere near the campus. It's all sealed off apparently. Second, you're pissed as a parrot and would be as useful as a pork sausage at a Jewish wedding. Sit down and finish your beer. Look here, this beautiful lady's in love with you," he said, yanking Jack back down by the shoulder onto the sofa. Schmidt and Matthis roared with laughter. Jack looked blankly at the girl.

"You like me?" she said. "Buy me drink?"

Jack hadn't the slightest interest in the girl, but felt embarrassed in front of Schmidt if he didn't join in the general camaraderie. He assumed it was going on Schmidt's tab anyway.

Potential embarrassment motivated Jack for the next half an hour. He didn't want to appear ungrateful after Schmidt's timely intervention, nor as a party spoiler. Attempting to join in the general banter of

Schmidt, Matthis and the girls they were flirting with, he exposed himself as too drunk to contribute with any kind of wit or much sense. Such interventions he made were greeted with sympathetic laughter by the other two, mainly because he was making a fool of himself.

At the same time, the thought of Doug and the news from Schmidt gnawed at the back of Jack's mind. He was unable to grasp the full import of the news of violence, but knew that his brother was probably in danger. Coupled with his sense of confusion was an underlying feeling of guilt. He had promised Doug for several weeks to join him in the political meeting and support the moderates. Doug will be all right, he thought reassuringly. He can look after himself.

"Buy me another drink, honey?" asked the girl again.

He had not spoken to her, but now looked at her. With her heavily made up face and fringe, she suddenly appeared to him as quite ridiculous.

"Um, no, no, sorry. I've got to go," he replied, slurring his words as he stood up, and swaying slightly.

"You leaving, Wilson?" barked Schmidt. "Can't take the pace, eh? Can't take their booze, these Brits, eh, Mattie?"

"Yeah, better get going. Thanks for the drinks."

"You OK to get home? Get yourself a cab, eh?" Schmidt turned away to his friend.

Changing the tone of her voice from seductively coy to fish market brusqueness, the girl shouted, "Mama, he's going."

Mama appeared in seconds, still glowering at Jack. She handed him the bill and the slip to sign. He looked at it but saw only a yellow blur with indistinct figures. Past arguing, certainly in front of the others, he meekly signed the chit and, with a weak wave, stumbled towards the door. It was now well past three o'clock.

Going out of the door of the air-conditioned club, he was immediately smothered by the embrace of the warm night air, which, still laden with moisture, made him breathe heavily and caused him to perspire.

Apart from a couple of black trouser-clad old lady street cleaners, who collected the detritus of a Friday night with mechanical efficiency, there were few people around. Only a couple of late-night revellers like Jack, the worse for drink, waited hopefully for taxis on street corners.

Once again, he made his way down the gloomy street, heading for the main junction. Walking unsteadily, he stopped every few moments to rest, breathing deeply in a vain attempt to sober up and straining to focus on the way ahead.

At one point, as he paused, he felt a tap on his shoulder.

"Hi there, you OK?" asked a female voice.

He turned to see a middle-aged Chinese woman, dressed in track suit bottoms and a shabby denim jacket.

She was full-figured and her unkempt hair fell over her face in an untidy fringe. She smiled.

"Yeah, yeah, fine. Just fine," he managed to reply.

"You want good time? I give you good time," she continued, leaning into him and holding his arm.

"Oh no, no. Thanks. Just going home," he answered.

But she kissed him on the cheek and began stroking his crotch.

Despite his weariness, his inebriation and the disorderly state of his seductress, he felt his sex drive rise again.

"Ah, see. You are horny. Come back to my place. Very close."

"No, really," he tried to protest and fight against his urge.

"Why not? Come on. I give you blowjob or hand job. Only two hundred dollars. Very cheap," she bargained, continuing to massage his privates.

Before he could answer, she led him, gripping him by the arm, twenty yards further on, before they turned off the pavement into one of the dark alleyways that ran between the tenements in this district. They moved down the alley into the darkest recess.

By this time Jack was compliant. The idea of sex, any sexual relief, would do. After all, the whole night had been miserable, with no positive gain. A kind of empty, pointless charade. He had been pretending to enjoy himself. The darkness of the alley was comforting. No need to pretend here. No one could see him or witness the action. Anonymity was good. Entirely personal. Contained within his own perceptions. This woman would gratify him, then disappear. Unlikely to see her again. No one would know. His parents, Doug, Marion, his colleagues — none would ever be aware of this harmless act of hedonism. Why not?

"You pay me first, OK? Two hundred dollars, OK?" urged the woman.

Fumbling, Jack extricated his wallet from his inside pocket. Feeling his way in the darkness, he opened it, pulled out a note and handed it over. She snatched it eagerly, thrust it into her pocket and then leaned him gently back against the wall.

"Just relax," she said, "I give you nice blowjob. No problem."

Looking upwards, he saw, through the narrow gap between the tall buildings enclosing them, the night sky — a dark purple strip. As he stared, the stars began to blink, swirl around and then streak away. He closed his eyes and put his head back against the hard brick, feeling nauseous, but with a strange sense of euphoria, as though he was floating away.

Kneeling down, the woman opened his fly zip.

Chapter Twelve
Deepening Darkness

In and around the university square, all was eerily silent. Empty, but littered with the debris of disorder, it lay abandoned and sorrowful in the night. The humid air hung heavy in the darkness, imposing an oppressive and foreboding atmosphere. Even the police were quiet, attending to their bruised bodies and punctured pride.

With the flush of initial success dissipating, the mood within the university building changed into one of sombre reflection and anxiety. Whilst the police advance had been repelled and a victory of sorts achieved, through stubborn resistance and the opportunity to attract media attention from outside, the majority of protesters were exhausted, many sore, cut and suffering from the searing effects of teargas. They lay in huddled groups, filling the main cafeteria, and in the corridors and lecture rooms, trying to rest, comforting each other, ever tense in expectation of the next call to action. In the air lingered the sour taste of the gas, along with the odour of sweating, crowded humanity and the remains of stale food.

Reunited with Dick Brandon, Doug sat in one corner of the room, along with several others of their group. Brandon was quietly but persistently arguing for continued resistance, at least until well into the daylight hours. In that way, he argued, the world would wake up to the news of their heroic action and bring their support to bear.

"It's a matter of time," he proclaimed. "If we can transform this from a localised student protest into a genuine revolutionary spark for democracy and independence, the people of the territory will sit up and applaud us. They will join us," he said, emphasising the word "join" and waving his index finger like an admonishing school teacher. "And when they do, the international community cannot sit by idly."

"But it's a matter of time," he repeated. "We need time to repeat and publicise our demands — which must be clear and bold. We must sit tight. I can't see the police doing any more till morning. And they can't hide their actions in daylight."

Although murmuring their agreement, the others were unenthusiastic. Even the more militant members, like Jo Chan and Alice, Doug noticed, were avoiding Brandon's gaze.

"Jo, you with me on this? Doug?" Brandon asked.

"Not sure," Jo responded hesitantly. "We've won so far. Maybe we should be marching out of here. Heads held high. Let the public see us. Get their support that way."

"If we try to go now," Brandon persisted, "the police will block us. We don't gain anything. Everyone will just say — oh, those pesky students again, causing trouble and trashing the place. If we march out of here, we do it in broad daylight, tomorrow at midday, with our banners waving for the cameras, when everyone in this city knows about it and when we'll have the people marching with us. Then the police will be overwhelmed. And you know what — the only place we'll march to is the House of Delegates, to the heart of the city. To the heart of power. For this is a political protest."

"I don't know," chimed in Doug, feeling he had to say something. "But I think everyone's exhausted and escalating this into a major march and challenging the government direct is a step too far right now. Our message demanding more democracy has gone out to the people and the media through a hundred phone messages and videos. We've shown we can stand up to the police, but we weren't the aggressors. Opinion will be on our side. Do we want to provoke more violence?"

At this moment their conversation was interrupted by a loud voice booming over the general melee. Jonathon Yu, surrounded by his cohort of Action Group faithful was standing on a table at the end of the room.

Rallying the students, who sat up and stood to listen, gathering round him, he spoke emotionally about the night's events and encouraged them to hold on. It had been a victory, he said, speaking in Cantonese, but the time for battling the police should stop, because too many people on both sides had been injured.

He proposed that they move out of the building and occupy the expansive university square. When the police tried to move them on, he proposed only passive resistance this time. Quoting Gandhi's civil disobedience methods, he suggested everyone should just lie down and refuse to move. If the police dragged them away, so be it. There were still two thousand protesters there. It would be a long night for the police and a golden opportunity to show the territory and the world how determined, yet how disciplined they were. "We've shown we can fight," he finished up, "but no need to shed any more blood."

Doug found himself nodding in agreement and noted that Yu's ideas seemed to please most of the audience. There was warm, if not enthusiastic, applause. One or two shouted angrily "sell out" and "shame." Dick Brandon looked distinctly displeased, shaking his head and muttering, "That's mad. What a waste." But Yu was the one with authority.

Within minutes, some of the bolder students were tentatively exiting the front doors of the block, to check out the situation. They were quickly reporting back that there was no sign of the police in the square. In fact, they found that the police units and their vehicles had even withdrawn from the road immediately outside the main gates, retreating at least a hundred metres in both directions.

Cries of "They've gone! They've had enough!" and, "It's all clear!" echoed around the building.

As a result, more students, relieved but still wary, filed out of the building. It was true — there were no police to be seen.

Many collected blankets and sleeping bags or whatever clothes they could find and settled down on the portico and its surroundings. After twenty minutes and still no sign of police response, they began to relax, to sing songs of resistance to embolden themselves.

Brandon, meanwhile, still flanked by Doug and the others, found his way over to Jonathon Yu.

"Jon, what's going on?"

"Brandon," said the charismatic leader, "are you happy with our success? Are you still with us?"

"You know, Jon," Brandon replied, "a lot's been achieved, but why are you throwing the success away by giving up now? You could launch a thunderbolt into the political establishment here if you went on the offensive. You should be marching on the city. The people would be with you. Don't chicken out now."

Yu was stung by the criticism.

"Ah, Brandon. Mr Political Theory. Mr Professor. Mr Englishman," he reacted with sarcasm in his voice. "It's not really your fight, is it? You don't fight for your future like us. You have your fancy ideas from your books. But you haven't been on the front line, have you? You have no cuts or bruises. I don't see your eyes are swollen from gas or pepper. Our soldiers are tired. A good general knows when to halt and regroup. The democrats and the moderates in the government are moved by this and have called a halt too. Why do you think the police have stepped back? Tomorrow we negotiate from strength and set a time for talks."

"You're missing a great chance, Jon," persisted the older man. "As for the police retreat, maybe they are just drawing you out in the open."

"Perhaps. But that is why we are changing our tactics," insisted Yu, and he pointedly turned his back on Brandon and began to talk with others.

"I don't like it," Brandon muttered to Doug. "The authorities will simply claim the sit-in has ended and the students have given up and will return to their studies. There's no negotiating strength to be had."

Doug tried to straighten out his thinking. As they returned to their group, he pondered Yu's words. He was, of course, right that this was a fight for the local students and people of the territory. Not for Brandon, nor himself. He was also right, thought Doug, that Brandon was all theory. Who was he to overlay his Marxist theories of protest and uprising on the down-to-earth concerns of these passionate students, whose very futures and homes were at stake in the power struggle with the federation? And, anyway, how could they 'march on the city' as Brandon proposed? The police would easily block the way in the narrow streets around the university. How would they know that that the local people would support them? They had shown immense bravery, and their resistance to police violence would be a news story around the world. Sympathy would surely come their way, from here and abroad, especially if they now adopted a non-violent approach.

He suddenly felt very tired. Glancing at his watch, he noticed it was after half past two. Jack's probably in bed by now, he thought. No point in disturbing him. He would have liked his brother by his side right now. He lay down on some bedding next to Jo Chan and Alice, who smiled at him, and closed his eyes.

After twenty minutes or more, but what seemed like only a few moments, he was rudely awoken by frantic shouting and the urgent jostling of everyone around leaping up to their feet and grabbing equipment.

"They're coming! They're coming again! Get up! Get to the front! The police are coming again!" He heard the alarm spread in panic and struggled to his feet. Those heading to the front of the building were hastily donning their now-familiar battle gear — helmets, face masks, goggles and gloves — and seizing whatever could help as a shield or club.

Doug felt frightened. This was shaping up like a war zone. Brandon had already disappeared, but Jo and Alice encouraged Doug to join them.

"Come on," said Alice. "Let's go upstairs. We can see everything. And it's safer."

"Sounds good to me," said Doug, wiping the perspiration from his brow, and obediently following them.

As before, large crowds were packing into the first-floor corridors and rooms with the windows fronting the square. It was difficult to see what was going on outside.

There was a great deal of commotion and uncertainty as to what was happening, so Jo tried to find out from those at the front.

"Many trucks approaching the main gate from both directions," they shouted back. It was the deep-throated rumbling of these vehicles as they progressed down the road that had triggered the strident warnings.

Down in the square, there was tension and alarm. Protesters who had been camping in the square gathered up their bedding and retreated back to the comfort zone of the portico, from where they could at least dash into the building if another assault came.

There was a screech of breaks as the column of trucks came to a halt, and an uneasy silence descended on the square and building, broken only by the sound of boots clattering on the road.

Then, a pause, followed by barked orders and whistles. Without warning, a column of officers came crashing through the wrought-iron gates. They jogged in unison, fanning out on the edge of the square opposite the building to form two rows.

Their appearance was greeted with howls of anguish and anger from the students.

"What's up? What's happening?" Doug asked, fearful of the reaction around him.

Alice, looking pale, turned to him.

"They are not police. They are soldiers," she said in a whisper. "They are federation soldiers! My God, how could our people do this to us? I didn't believe they would do this."

Holding Alice's hand, Doug muscled his way towards the front to try to catch a glimpse of what was happening. He stood on tiptoe to gain a view through the window. Squads of soldiers, dressed in green army fatigues, and green helmets, were lining up. They were armed, not only with batons, but with automatic rifles.

"Jesus Christ," said Doug, "I hope Jonathon's got enough sense to reign in the hotheads and stop this now. We can't deal with this lot."

Jonathon Yu was doing just that. Calling his group to pull back to the portico, he told them to quieten down and relax. There was no battle to win here. It was time to talk. Waving a makeshift white flag, put together from a table cloth and a curtain rail, he advanced slowly, along with two of his followers, towards the troops. Speaking in Chinese, he called for calm and wanted to discuss terms for leaving. There was no apparent response.

What happened next no one could have imagined. A single gunshot rang out. No one knew where it came from, or who it was aimed at.

After a sickening second's pause, as protesters and soldiers alike looked up and around for the source of the threat, Jonathon and his partners hurled themselves to the ground. The soldiers in the front row, however, dropped onto one knee or lay prone. They fired a devastating volley indiscriminately into the crowd before the building.

Dozens of students in the front row fell, dead or wounded, their blood spattering the pale grey stone paving of the square and portico, as well as those standing behind. The screams of the wounded, and howls of all, enveloped the square like the cry of some primeval beast.

Mayhem ensued as the living fought with each other, trampling on the wounded, grappling and tearing at each other to escape the carnage back through the main door. Some, who couldn't reach the door, dived to the floor, their hands behind their heads in a futile gesture of defence or abject surrender. A few, who tried to escape to the side of the building, were shot down as they ran.

Advancing now at a jog, some troops drew long batons and charged at the student body, clubbing viciously at anyone in the way. They surged over Jonathon and his colleagues, who disappeared under the boots of the charging mass of attackers.

"Get down," they shouted. "Or we shoot. Surrender, or we shoot."

Traumatised, the defenders had no answer to this level of lethal violence. Most lay down as ordered, and were swiftly and roughly handcuffed with plastic cuffs and hauled away.

Those few, who knew no fear and resisted, were summarily shot. Rocky "Jesus" Ocampo, shouting

"Murderers! Killers", charged at one of the leading soldiers and knocked him sideways with a blow from his club, only to receive a bullet in the heart the next instant. He died instantly.

Upstairs, terror took hold. None could believe the full horror of what they were witnessing from above. Some were in such a state of shock they couldn't move, but stood paralysed, waiting for the troops to find the stairways and reach them. There was no way out. The rear entrances had been left open, to allow students to flee, but they were narrow and few.

Doug shook himself from his torpor and recovered the icy perception which comes from the need to survive mortal danger. He grabbed Alice by the arm and wrenched her away.

"Come on," he bellowed. "We've got to get out of here."

Too frightened to think, she allowed herself to be dragged out of the room.

Downstairs, the federation soldiers were doing their job with ruthless efficiency. Rampaging through the ground floor rooms, they dealt harshly with all they encountered, dispatching those who dared stand up and roughly binding those who followed their orders to submit. Many were dragged out to the square and ordered to sit in rows, their heads bowed and their hands bound behind them.

When they reached the cafeteria, a sorrowful scene awaited them. Even the most battle-hardened would have felt some pity for those near death, the many injured and those simply cowering and sobbing with fear. Many had made it back to what had been their safe haven and rallying point earlier, but now resembled a casualty station in a war zone.

By this time, after the onslaught had lasted barely fifteen minutes, the shooting was less frequent and the troops were limiting their deadly attention to those who protested, or were trying to film their operation.

Their attempts to conceal their brutal assault on unarmed students came too late. Despite the panic, some had managed to capture fleeting shots of the troops' advance, their shooting, the resulting carnage, the spilling of blood and the panic of the flight on their mobile phones. Before those witnesses could be recognised or seized, many had already sent their critical evidence of their government's actions beyond the boundaries of the university and the killing ground. Throughout the city, media offices were picking up the shocking images, with their discordant sound tracks, and trying to make sense of them. Like unstoppable truth itself, the reality of the disaster was being spread in the city's consciousness and beyond into the darkness of the night.

By this time, in a belated gesture of humanity or callous public relations, army medics were making their way to the cafeteria, where the wounded were being assembled. They worked to save lives, and patch up the wounds of the injured, as if in an attempt to mitigate the awfulness of the action. Lines of medics were stretchering out the worst cases, so that they could be transferred to ambulances and rushed off to hospital through the city streets, their sirens muted to prevent their screaming public notification of the disaster to a gradually awakening population.

Others were being held in detention in the university square, where they sat, heads bowed and fearful, as officers moved among them, picking out the ringleaders they could identify, whose names they knew, and roughly questioning everyone about those who had led the protest. Those selected were led away to the trucks parked beyond the gates.

In an attempt to isolate the disaster from the general population, the authorities had pushed back the barriers at the ends of the avenue, which led up the university gates. Barricades, heavily manned by local police, were stationed there to prevent the growing crowds from accessing the scene. But news of the attack was filtering through the city, causing dismay and disbelief. Friends and relatives receiving frightened messages from the scene were switching on radios and TVs at that early hour, only to have their worst fears realised.

Anxious parents, unable to contact their sons and daughters, rushed towards the university, only to be held back at a distance. In the absence of credible news, gossip and rumour crackled among the crowds. "There

was shooting, wasn't there? People have been killed...
is that so? Who did the firing? How many are dead? My
God, they've been shooting the students! They've been
killing our kids!"

In face of the rising tension, the director of the
university and senior security ministers were meeting
with members of the government, some hastily
summoned from their beds.

The security minister was lambasted by his more
temperate colleagues.

"What the hell were you thinking by inviting the
federation in to deal with this? Are you mad? This could
cause a major uprising in our streets. Who gave
permission for this act of folly? What happens now?"

Self-consciously aware of his vulnerable position,
the pale-faced minister blustered his response.

"Look, the situation was out of control. Our local
guys were under serious attack from extremists and
anarchists in the student ranks. They could not cope.
Many officers were hurt. We simply could not allow
these revolutionaries to prevail. It would have led to
chaos. They had to be suppressed. In cases of threats to
the civil order, we have the constitutional right to ask
for protection from the federation. And that's what we
did."

"Of course, we didn't expect them to use lethal
force, but the troops were fired on first. They were
responding to gunfire. Any casualty is regrettable, but

at least the situation is now under control… we can manage this."

Responding icily to these words, one of the ministers noted that the situation was far from under control and that the options were bleak. The security minister, he said, seemed to fail to grasp the gravity of the deaths of students and the resulting public fury. Either the government imposes martial law and maintains the federal troops there to contain matters, or there will be serious social unrest. Alternatively, the federal action is condemned and the troops immediately withdrawn. In that case, he added, we have handed the independence movement a major strategic victory.

Government announcements began to flow out from the official news centre. They recognised the seriousness of the "incident" at the university, which had unfortunately been provoked by hostile forces, which had infiltrated the student protesters. Police forces, called in to end the illegal occupation, had been attacked with dangerous weapons and Molotov cocktails. Federal troops had been invited in to provide support but shots had been fired at them. In the resulting confusion, a number of fatalities had regrettably occurred and injuries suffered on both sides. Those hurt were being cared for and everything was now calm. The public were urged to go about their business as normal and not pay attention to rumours and false information being peddled by enemies of the territory and the federation.

Half an hour after the soldiers' attack had started, Doug crouched uncomfortably, with a trembling Alice by his side, at the back of a stationery cupboard on the first floor of the building. Having led Alice away from the front area, they had together tried to flee to the rear to find an escape route out of the back. They ran, in fear of their lives, along a dark, bare corridor, which linked many of the lecture and study rooms. They met others, confused and disoriented, on the way. Some ran with them, others in the opposite direction.

"Out the back way!" screamed Doug. "Go that way!" pointing ahead. But when they came to one of the staircases, which would take them to the exits at the back, they heard the soldiers below.

Instead, he grabbed Alice by the hand again, and guided her upwards to the third floor. Frantically, he looked right and left, looking for an escape route, but the clatter of army boots on the stone steps was getting louder, so he took her into the nearest side room. This was a seminar room he had used himself and he still had a key. They rushed in, and he locked the door behind them. He then pulled Alice into the stationery room, and, using the same key, locked it from within. And so, they squatted behind the shelves, hoping that, somehow, they would be overlooked.

"It's OK. We're safe for the moment. If they find us, they've no need to shoot us," he said, trying to find words to comfort the quietly sobbing girl.

He knew his words were hollow. As he tried to come to terms with the full horror of what he had witnessed, he knew that everything was unpredictable. How had it come to this? He just wanted to support the students in their peaceable endeavours. He just wanted to support the ideas of democracy and fairness. How had this monstrous experience exploded into his life, threatening his very existence. What if he was killed? Not seeing his parents or Jack again. Not going home. Dying here in this miserable cupboard. He glanced at his watch. It was coming up to four a.m.

Just as he was contemplating the worst, both he and Alice leapt up in response to a loud crash. Soldiers had broken into the seminar room, shouting in Chinese.

Alice hid her face on Doug's shoulder.

"They are calling for anyone to surrender, or be shot," she translated in a quivering voice.

Without hesitation, Doug shouted back.

"OK! OK! We're coming out! Don't shoot! Don't shoot!"

He unlocked the door and threw it open. They stepped out to find themselves confronted by three fresh-faced young federation soldiers, none older than the students they had been violating. Each pointed their rifle at them.

Indicating with their rifles, they ordered them to raise their hands over their heads.

As they did so, two of them approached Alice, spun her around and bound her hands behind her back with plastic cord. She protested in Chinese, but one of the soldiers just slapped her and began to pull her roughly from the room.

Stepping forward, Doug tried to intervene, saying, "Stop, she's with me. I'm a teacher here!" but his words were pointless. Another soldier clubbed Doug round the side of the head with his rifle.

Momentarily stunned, Doug fell onto one knee, clutching the side of his head. Within seconds he too was bound with his hands behind him. While Alice was dragged away down the corridor, still protesting, the remaining soldiers looked at Doug with some curiosity. What was a foreigner doing here? What do we do with him? Let him go, or take him to our commander?

Deciding on the latter, they led the dazed teacher back along the corridor and down the stairs to the ground floor, before proceeding along through the cafeteria to the front doors.

As they passed through the cafeteria, tears came into Doug's eyes. It was a desolate, scene. Only a few soldiers remained, clearly ordered to start the process of cleaning up and concealment. Blood-stained clothing, sleeping bags and bandages gave a macabre taint to the atmosphere of hopelessness and crushed dreams.

Outside, the two troopers took Doug across the square and out through the gates. Everywhere, the federal troops were clearing up, but few students were to be seen. Doug was taken to face an officer, who took one, contemptuous look at Doug and then barked a peremptory order.

He was taken to what looked like a police van. They blindfolded him and then, half-lifting him, bundled him into the back of the van. He sat uncomfortably on a wooden bench that ran along the side.

After further mutterings, the soldiers slammed the van doors shut, condemning Doug to the pitch-black of the interior.

Chapter 13
Changing Fortunes

That morning, Bill prepared himself for work in the same way he always did. Having showered, cleaned his teeth and shaved, meticulously, with an old-fashioned razor, he dressed methodically. Grey slacks, a neatly pressed white shirt, and one of his three diagonally striped ties, were complemented with his regular blue blazer, decorated with folded white handkerchief in the top pocket. He brushed his thinning grey hair, checked that his shoes were polished and re-examined himself in the mirror, pulling faces to check that the lines were not obviously increasing.

Not bad for sixty, he told himself. Don't look my age.

After his customary breakfast of tea, cornflakes and poached egg on toast, he pecked Elizabeth on the cheek and made his way out to drive to work.

Arriving at approximately eight thirty a.m., half an hour before the office opened, as he always did, he made himself a coffee, from the drinks machine in the corridor, and settled down to read his emails. There weren't too many this day — not that he ever received vast numbers — and he answered those needing a response quickly, rapidly deleting those he instantly decided as irrelevant. Still time for a quick look at The Times he had bought on the way in, before the other staff arrived. A peremptory glance at the headlines resulted in him scowling and grumbling at the general incompetence and moral turpitude of politicians, a class for whom he had little respect, especially those on the left. Then he glanced at the sports pages, preferably cricket at this time of the year, before settling down to the business of the day.

Life wasn't too bad, he mused. It was summer and the new millennium had just begun without mishap. He had extricated himself from the affair with Marjorie, and although he regretted betraying Elizabeth, he felt she was getting over it. Jack's getting married to that nice-looking classy girl Pru later that same year had been a welcome distraction, and a fillip for everyone. Hard to think that almost two years had flown by already. At least he and Elizabeth were healthy and had a few good years left yet. The two of them were free to travel a bit now the boys were all sorted. Chance to see some of the world.

"Mornin', Mr Wilson!" The cheery greeting interrupted his reverie. "Let me know when you're ready for the financial report!" It was one of the admin team — Shareen — who normally helped him key in the monthly report for the board. Bill could of course do it himself, but his typing was slow and inaccurate. Shareen, on the other hand, was quick and precise, and she was also young and attractive. He enjoyed having her around.

"Thanks, sweetheart," answered Bill. "Should have it ready by ten."

He got down to work, checking line by line the draft reports his bookkeepers had given him. Although he could never say he enjoyed his work, he was proud of his professionalism and eye for detail. There was satisfaction in a complete and orderly set of monthly figures. Quick to spot any anomalies or inaccuracies, he could be scathing in his criticism of junior members of the finance team who had the misfortune to make any errors. In general, however, he was a considerate and respected, if not popular, boss, whom the others nicknamed the "Sergeant Major".

He was just about ready to call in Shareen to key in the report, when his desk phone rang. It was the chief executive, David Parkinson, one of the members of the family that had founded the company nearly a century earlier.

"Morning, Bill," Parkinson greeted him brusquely. "Step up to my office, will you. Need to go over something important."

"Right, Mr Parkinson, be right with you," answered Bill, feeling surprised by the request and irritated at having his routine interrupted. Normally, he had very little to do with David, the older of the two Parkinson brothers that ran the company. Usually he reported in to Graham, the younger sibling — the director who oversaw the finances. If David was involved, then there was usually a problem or some new initiative to deal with, both equally troublesome.

"Come in, Bill. Take a seat," said the chief executive, as Bill went into his spacious but gloomy wood-panelled office. David Parkinson was in his early fifties. A well-built former rugby player, he was now overweight. Dressed in his pin-striped suit, seated behind his heavy mahogany desk, he peered at Bill in a friendly manner over the top of his black-rimmed glasses. Graham, who was also present, introduced a third person — a stranger, who was called Marcus Reece.

"Well, what's up here then? Looks very important," teased Bill in a familiar tone. He had worked conscientiously for this family-owned company for more than twenty years, and the management held no fears for him, though he had never entirely trusted them, being, as they were, businessmen with the scruples of the business world.

Ignoring his finance officer's comment, David Parkinson, fidgeting with a silver fountain pen in both hands, got straight to the point.

"Bill, you know as well as anyone that Parkinson's Metal has in recent years, shall we say, drifted? Stagnated? Oh, we've got by, held our heads above water, made a living, survived. But the world's changing fast. There's much more competition, here and from abroad. Technologies changing apace.

Markets opening up. Environmental concerns. Demand in the marketplace evolving. It's hard to keep pace."

"Trouble is, Bill, we don't feel we're changing fast enough to keep up. We are, in fact, on a downhill slope and we've got to do something about it. Bill, how much profit did we make last year? It was barely fifty grand, right?"

Bill nodded in agreement, thinking 'where's this going?'

"And the year before?"

"A small loss," Bill confirmed. "Due to factors not entirely within our control," he added.

"And the underlying problem is," Parkinson continued, "our turnover has been declining over the last few years, hasn't it? We're now down to under twenty million a year."

Again, Bill nodded, feeling uncomfortable, as though these results were somehow his fault.

At this point, Graham took over from his older brother.

"The fact is, Bill, we've had an approach, which could turn the whole thing round, in a big way. An exciting opportunity, which could give Parkinson's Metal a new lease of life and a bright future. That's why Marcus is here. Marcus works for an investment bank representing an international investor interested in supporting us."

"What kind of investor?" Bill asked suspiciously. "Not one o' them asset stripping bunches, hopefully?

You need to be careful, you know." He glared at Marcus Reece, who smiled back defensively.

"No, no, no! Don't get all het up, Bill," countered David. "We're talking about an injection of substantial capital. An opportunity, for us and the investor. Look at our cutting and grinding machines. Look at our welding equipment. Look at the state of our factory floor, our canteen. Thirty years out of date. We should be modernising all this. Diversifying our production. Doing more steel and copper. Growing our product line. We can do a lot more than cabinets and window frames.

Modernisation, Bill, expansion, new ideas, that's what we're talking about."

It was undeniable, the company was in a rut.

"OK. I get your point, but what do you want me to do?" asked Bill cautiously.

"Well, as our finance man, you're crucial to this, Bill," said David.

"We need to put together a complete set of figures for the last four years — good figures — plus projected budgets for the next four years. We need all that for next week's board meeting, when we'll meet people from our potential partner. We need you to work with Marcus on this, Bill, to make sure we present the strongest case possible. See what I mean?"

"Well, fine, I get your meaning. Most of the figures are there already, and projections... well, they're projections, aren't they?" answered Bill.

At this point Marcus Reece opened his mouth for the first time.

"Well, I'll be pleased to help you, Mr Wilson," he said. "As investment bankers we specialise in this. We can help take a fresh look at things and present the company's prospects in the most positive light. It's just a matter of interpretation in many cases. We obviously want Parkinson's to look like an attractive as possible investment vehicle for our client."

Inwardly, Bill recoiled at the words of the smartly dressed young man, with his slick short haircut, expensive designer suit and gleaming teeth.

"Well, I'm not sure what you can add to what's there in black and white," he said pointedly. "But if that's what the boss wants, so be it."

"Great, well, we'll leave you two to get together and make the arrangements. But make sure we see drafts two days before the board meeting, OK?" added David, standing up and extending a hand to Bill.

"Thanks, Bill," he said, showing him to the door. "We appreciate your hard work and we will all benefit from this, I'm sure."

"Hope so," thought Bill, as he left.

The next few days and weeks were as difficult as any Bill had faced during his working life. It was not the overtime required to complete the task — he had never shied away from hard work — nor the complexity of the forward planning, but the challenges to his routine way of working, the subtle undermining of his authority, and the questioning of his long-held assumptions about the probity of accounting, that upset him the most.

He resented the interference of Marcus Reece and his slick colleagues, who continually questioned past figures, massaging and amending them in ways, which, though not illegal, were pushing the boundaries of professional norms. They sought ways to maximise revenue, recalculate accrued income, shift costs and adjust profit and loss with manipulation of the balance sheet. Similarly, Bill's carefully calibrated projections were brushed aside as "unnecessarily conservative" or "lacking positivity". Audited figures were to be complemented by a "parallel perspective" which invoked "the commercial potential behind conventional accounting" and projections were to reflect the diverse opportunities to be unleashed by the upgrading of capital stock.

It came as no surprise that he was not invited to the next board meeting. Convention had been that he accompanied Graham Parkinson to these monthly affairs, at least being called in when they discussed the accounts. He was there to support his line manager, whom he usually briefed, by providing supportive statistics, correcting any errors he made and answering any probing questions from the directors. But this time he was told that, because of certain legal conditions of confidentiality, his presence was not required (though his work was much appreciated). The newly tabulated past and future figures were to be presented by the investment bank to representatives of the mysterious investor, in attendance to receive and consider them.

Within three months a deal was struck, and the new majority shareholders, a US-based private equity company called Atlanta Holdings — took over.

According to the terms of the deal, the Parkinson brothers still ran the company, or, at least, they appeared to. All employees were summoned to a general meeting, where an enthusiastic David Parkinson outlined the visionary plans for the new entity. There would be no sweeping changes, he assured everyone, and restructuring only when absolutely necessary to take full advantage of the new resources available. Any questions about job security or closures were brushed aside, and doubters chided for their pessimism and lack of imagination.

Bill was one of the first to be laid off.

"I'm really sorry about this, Bill," explained a defensive Graham Parkinson a few weeks after the general meeting.

"We've been through some ups and downs over the years, haven't we? But we'll be reporting direct into the Atlanta people and they insist on their own finance team in place, so we really can't do anything. We'll give you a decent redundancy package, of course. You've deserved it, Bill. Anyway, you deserve a break and a chance to enjoy retirement, don't you?"

Bill didn't see it that way. His job was central to his life and he had no intention of retiring. Despite the signs, he thought he was secure and hadn't seen this coming.

"I think it's bloody outrageous!" was his initial response. "I know this company and its finances better than anyone, warts and all. And now you just want to kick me out like a piece of rubbish, after all these years. Well, let me tell you, Mr David Parkinson, I'm not going easily. Those yanks can't just throw me out like that. I've got my rights."

Parkinson was taken aback. This could be difficult.

"Calm down, Bill. Calm down," he said, shifting uneasily in his leather-padded office chair. "There's no need to get upset. Think about it. This is good for you. You're at retirement age and deserve to enjoy life. Most people would jump at this chance we're offering you. You wouldn't like the fancy ways of this new management lot anyway, would you?"

Once the initial shock and anger had worn off, though, Bill sullenly accepted defeat. He had always refused to join any union, so no help was forthcoming from that direction. After discussing the matter with Elizabeth, who was inwardly very concerned at the thought of Bill not being employed and spending his time at home, he reluctantly accepted that taking legal action would be too costly and stressful.

Although he was given three months' formal notice, he was required to clear his desk within three days. After enduring an embarrassing farewell event, at which he was subjected to Marjorie's sympathetic gaze, causing him intense discomfort, and collecting his gift of a Waterford cut-glass whisky decanter and six glasses, he drove home from the factory for the last time. Once there he slumped into his armchair in the living room and looked at the blank television set. Elizabeth was at work.

"Bugger me," he said to himself, "is that it then?"

For the next six months or more, he rallied and made determined efforts to find another job. He wasn't finished yet. No, he had a good, few years left and damned if he was going to sit around like some decrepit pensioner. He had professional skills that were needed out there. He had the experience and the drive to make a contribution.

He wrote more than forty applications. But the net result was only two interviews. At the first, he found himself embarrassed by his lack of knowledge of the IT systems and software packages in use at the company in question. At the second, being interviewed by two executives no older than his sons, he felt patronised and was told on feedback that he was overqualified for the position.

"Overaged more like," he said to Elizabeth later.

After six months the applications became far fewer and less ambitious. Despite his willingness to take a lower salary, to undertake a more junior role, even to volunteer, nothing seemed to work.

Elizabeth, taking on a more supportive role in their relationship, encouraged him to develop an interest or hobby. She saw the need to get him out of the house and engage with others.

Attempts to take up golf failed, however. Not only did he find himself lacking in skill, but he disliked the snobbery of the members he met at the local golf club. Efforts to get him to join a local walking club were also dismissed. He was sure he wasn't going to enjoy a bunch of aging hippies. Instead, he took increasing comfort in the company of two familiar and undemanding companions — the television and drink.

At first, it seemed harmless enough. He watched the sports channel, catching up on the cricket, following an entire five-day test match hour by hour. Over the summer there was Wimbledon and the golf open. As the autumn came on, there was football, and football repeats. But as the interest in searching for another job was blunted by repeated failure, lethargy enveloped him as a seasonal mist creeping down on a lonely vale. He began to gaze thoughtlessly, without paying attention, at vacuous quiz shows and superficial soap operas.

Worse still, he developed the habit of taking his first glass of Scotch at lunchtime. Rarely in his past had he drunk spirits, but now a midday shot was alluring as an opiate, quelling the ache of boredom and fear of worthlessness that lay deep in the pit of his stomach.

His wife, summoning the feelings of affection and loyalty she felt towards the man she had once loved and respected, did her best to support and encourage him. Ironically, the tables were turning in their relationship.

Increasingly, she was the one now making suggestions for activities and chores, the one initiating ideas for trips out, for meals, or even for shopping. Elizabeth, once the recipient of sympathy and comfort, was now the deliverer, in an ironic reversal of their roles.

Their sons visited occasionally — Doug being the more frequent and aware of the two. Their stays were usually brief, sometimes overnight, so their father's gradually changing behaviour was not generally remarked upon, beyond the casual observance that he was getting older and therefore needed more rest.

A year after his forced retirement, however, Bill's uncharacteristic reticence and apathy began to worry Doug.

One day, he asked his mother what she thought about it.

"What's going on, Mum? I know Dad's getting on an' all, but, for Christ's sake, he's only sixty-one. He mopes around like he's twenty years older than that. Shouldn't we be doing more? I mean, this looks like he needs some counselling or something. Do you think it's normal? What do you reckon?"

Elizabeth sipped at her tea, as they sat in the kitchen. She looked into her mug, cradling it in both hands, rather than at her son.

"Well, I don't know, Doug. He changed a lot since, you know, losing his job. I think it's a matter of self-respect. He's a very proud man, as you well know, and now he feels useless. He was always the breadwinner, while I ran the house. That's the way we grew up. Now he's lost his role and hasn't found anything to take its place. He's at a loss, but I'm guessing he'll come round in the long run."

"Yeah, I get all that," said Doug, unconvinced by his mother's fatalism. "But he can't just give up. I mean, something's wrong. He's a tough ol' bastard. He should be fighting this, not surrendering. Can't we get him involved with the British Legion or something? He'd find like-minded souls there, wouldn't he? Some old soldiers to talk to about the good old days. Something to get him off his arse and out the house. Sorry, Mum, but you know what I mean."

"I know, love. That's all very well, but, believe me, I've tried. Fact is, he was never one for clubs and things. I sometimes used to think he doesn't like people very much, apart from his family, like," mused his mother.

Not willing to let matters drift, Doug was determined to try and help his father. The very next day, when Elizabeth was at work, he was sitting with his father in the lounge at noon. As Bill was gazing at his newspaper, he took his chance.

"Dad," he began. "I know I don't get to see you as much as I'd like, but when I have done lately, I notice you're not really yourself. Is there anything I can do? You seem down in the dumps, and I hate to see you like this. You're not even as bloody-minded as you used to be. Do you reckon we should get you along to Doctor Martin to check you out?"

Bill Wilson lowered his paper onto his lap and turned to look at his son. It was a quizzical look, but the eyes betrayed a level of vacancy, which alarmed his son.

"Oh, Doug. That's nice of you, son. But I'm fine. I get tired lately, I must admit, but, hey, I'm getting on a bit, you know. Everyone has to slow down. I don't think I'd want to trouble Doctor... what's his name..."

"Don't you worry. I enjoy life. In fact..." he paused and looked over his shoulder conspiratorially, "I enjoy a nice, yer know, when your mother's not around. Fancy a tipple, come on."

Before Doug could even protest, he pulled himself up out of the chair and walked over to the cupboard holding the crockery and drinks. He took a bottle of Scotch out from the back of the cupboard and poured two shots, at least doubles. With a wink, he handed one to Doug. "Bottoms up!" And he downed the lot in one go.

Doug was appalled. This was not his father.

"Dad!" he exclaimed. "Dad, it's barely twelve o'clock. Why are you drinking this stuff so early?"

Bill giggled like an embarrassed child.

"I know. It's a bit naughty, but it helps the long afternoon pass. I'm retired now, you know. No one's, you know... Look here, Doug. Don't tell your mother. Right?"

Summoning Doug over to the cabinet, he opened a lower drawer. Beaming with pride, he pulled aside some tablecloths to reveal another bottle of whisky and one of vodka, which was half empty.

Putting a finger to his lips, he whispered, "My little secret, see. Don't tell her."

Following this exchange, which prompted Doug into action, Jack was consulted and the family persuaded Bill that daytime drinking was not a good idea, and that he should see Doctor Martin. He was reluctant to agree to the appointment, declaring himself in no need of doctors, but finally he gave way.

After comprehensively examining Bill, whom he'd known for a good number of years, the doctor spoke separately to Elizabeth and Doug.

"Well, I must say I'm quite surprised by his condition. Physically, he has deteriorated since I last saw him a couple of years ago. He seems older than his sixty years, and there are clear signs of chronic depression, almost certainly brought on by his retirement. He also shows some mild signs of early-onset dementia. Is he commonly forgetful, Elizabeth?"

She looked at Doug for support.

"I haven't really noticed anything beyond normal stuff," she replied. "Nothing more than how we all forget things as we get older."

"He has been drinking a bit too much, we think," added Doug. Elizabeth stared at him reproachfully for breaking what she saw as a family confidence.

"Ah, yes, well. Need to keep an eye on that. That won't help," said the doctor.

"Try to keep the drinking to a minimum and, meanwhile, I'm giving you some anti-depressants. Elizabeth, he needs to move as much as possible. Exercise is good. Even a fifteen-minute walk every day will be beneficial."

She did her best in the months that followed. The drugs helped Bill overcome his apathy to a degree, and she urged him to take short walks in the evenings. Doug visited more often, and, when he did, searched the usual hiding places for Bill's secret caches of booze. Any contraband he discovered he confiscated, much to his father's irritation. In this way, his state of mind was at least brightened and his condition stabilised.

But in 2002, the home situation was again subject to turbulence, when Jack announced that he and Pru were heading off to Asia. Elizabeth absorbed this with resignation and sadness. Of course, you couldn't stop your children from making their way in life, but the other side of the world? It was like losing another son.

For Bill, it was barely comprehensible. Why would anyone want to go somewhere like Asia, for God's sake? Jack had a good job in London, in the best country in the world, and a lovely wife. Why not just settle down? Why this restlessness and search for some elusive satisfaction? All his life, Bill had worked for the security and comfort that had been denied him in his youth. And now, this generation would risk it for the sake of some crazy adventure in an alien city thousands of miles away.

But that wasn't the worst of it. Jack's example inspired his younger brother, at the time dispirited through personal setbacks and professional frustration, to follow in his footsteps. A year later and Doug was packing his bags and following his brother to the Far East.

By this time Bill was simply confused by the disappearance of his youngest son, and didn't really grasp the implications of his relocation. Elizabeth's concern was more immediate. She would now be left to take care of Bill on her own. At least Doug had been within visiting range up till then, and could reach home within an hour. Now his support would be removed.

She made him promise to call at least once a week and return to the UK to see them at least once a year.

Doug made those promises and was determined to keep them. He was, he told his mother with all sincerity, only going for a two-year contract and would definitely come home after that.

Nevertheless, as he finally set out for the airport, he did so with a heavy heart, carrying a burden of guilt, far weightier than the packed rucksack he heaved onto his back. He hugged his parents tightly, not even being sure if he would see them again. At that moment they seemed so vulnerable, and he was deserting them.

"See you soon, then," said his father, as Doug walked down the front drive to the waiting taxi. "Don't be too long. We'll go for a beer, shall we? Like the old days, with Jack and Mat."

Chapter Fourteen
The Light of Day

He woke up in great discomfort, his head pounding from the night's alcohol, his back aching and his vision blurred. His father was gently shaking him by the shoulder. "Wake up, son. Time to get up. Wake up, Jack."

Except it wasn't his father bending over him, and encouraging him to wake up, but an elderly Chinese man, who was muttering incomprehensible but gentle words of concern.

Slowly, he opened his eyes, and, rubbing them with his knuckles, focused with greater clarity. Looking up into a kindly, heavily wrinkled oriental face, adorned with a wispy chalk-white moustache and capped with a glistening bald pate, he thought for a moment he was meeting face to face with a Chinese sage from an ancient legend.

"You OK?" said the sage, switching from Chinese to English with an American accent. "Were you robbed? You look damn awful. Can you get up?"

Groaning as he twisted himself into an upright seated position, Jack looked around him. It was daylight. Glancing at his watch, he noted it was just after six. Still in shadow, the wretched alleyway into which he had washed up, stretched away in both directions. To the left it ran fifty yards or more before disappearing into gloomy tenement yards. It was strewn with plastic rubbish and covered in pools of water, fed from leaking pipes overhead. Ten yards to the right, it offered a shaft of burnishing morning sun, as it collided with the street.

"Shit! Oh fuck! You fucking idiot!" he said under his breath with vehemence.

"Sorry, my friend. Just trying to help," said the old man, recoiling at the words.

"No, no, no. Not you. Not you. I mean me. It's so awful. I'm so embarrassed. Sorry, you're very kind. I'm just so bloody stupid," Jack moaned, by way of explanation.

"We all make mistakes," said the Good Samaritan. "Teach you not to booze too much. You need to get home. Get a shower. Change your filthy clothes. Take care of your eye. What happened to you?"

Gingerly, Jack put two fingers to his left eyebrow. The wound ached and was sensitive to the touch. It was swollen and the plaster and surrounding area caked in dried blood.

"I... I can't remember exactly. Like you say — drank too much."

Taking advantage of the old man's outstretched hand, Jack slowly pulled himself up the wall, straightening his weary legs until he stood upright. Only then he realised that his helper was short and frail, no more than five feet in height.

"Thanks. So good of you. I could have been robbed!" Jack said, perspiring profusely. His entire body ached, as though he had just finished running a marathon.

"Well, I think you probably were. See here." The old man bent down and picked up an open wallet lying a few feet away. Jack's wallet. He handed it over. As if random flashes of torchlight were illuminating the dark corners of a room, Jack suddenly recalled fleeting images of his time in the night club and the woman afterwards in the street. He examined the wallet. It was empty. All his money had been taken. His credit card was missing too.

Instinctively, he reached down to check his trousers and found his fly zip still fully open, partially exposing himself. Flushing hot with embarrassment in the gloom, he quickly snatched at the zip and recovered his modesty. The old man diplomatically pretended not to notice, which compounded the humiliation.

"Look, I'd better get going. Thanks again for the help," he said, offering a handshake to his rescuer.

"OK. You all right now. Don't drink so much, eh?" he replied, turning, and, without looking back, ambled his way deliberately down into the shadowy depths of the tenement complex.

Jesus, what a mess; you're just pathetic, thought Jack as he headed for the street.

As he made his way out, his limbs still aching, the harsh glare of the morning sun caught him unawares. Shielding his eyes with one hand, he looked down and began brushing some of the grime of the alleyway from his trousers. He took off his jacket to give it the same treatment. One or two passers-by looked at him sympathetically, probably assuming, he thought, he was a typical drunken Westerner who had overdone it.

It dawned on him that as he was penniless and couldn't draw any cash without his bank card, he would have to walk home. That meant covering a distance of some four miles. In normal circumstances it would present no problem, but in his current hung over and exhausted state it represented a challenge.

He was wearily walking along the street, heading in the direction of home, when he had the idea of at least refreshing himself in a nearby hotel he knew. His throat was parched and his head still throbbed, so the thought of a drink of cold water was compelling.

Having made his way there, he mustered all the dignity he could summon and marched confidently through the front doors of the establishment, striding past the reception desk, where the staff were fortunately busy, and straight up the stairs to the mezzanine floor, where he knew the gents' toilet was located.

Looking around to see if anyone else was behind him, he pushed open the door to the toilet to check if it was busy. Someone brushed past him on the way out — a business man probably, who looked back curiously at the dishevelled figure entering. But otherwise all was quiet at that early hour.

Jack hurried to the sink and turned on the cold tap. Bending over, he doused his face and head, scooping up the cool water in cupped hands and drinking greedily. It was a great relief.

Taking a sharp intake of breath and exhaling noisily, he brushed the excess drops from his face and lifted his head to confront himself in the mirror. What he saw shocked him. There was a sad-looking middle-aged man peering back, with a badly bruised eye, discoloured yellow and purple above and below, adorned with a ragged plaster, bloodied and half hanging off. His hair was disordered and sprinkled with grey dust. Unshaven and engraved with the evidence of a sleepless night, the face was grey and haunted, like a man who has endured solitary confinement in a dark cell. His tie was missing, his shirt collar askew and stained red.

He stared at himself for a full minute, as if he had seen an apparition.

"Jesus Christ. What a mess. What have I come to?" he said softly. His disappointment sprang not only from his immediate embarrassment, that of a man socially ashamed, but from a much deeper source, which judged him for his failure to meet his own ideals and ambitions.

"That's it," he muttered. "That's it!" as he carefully peeled off the plaster over his left eye, to expose a vivid half-inch long cut just above the eyebrow. Washing his face again, gently, with soap, he cleaned away the remains of congealed blood and, with his fingers, brushed and straightened his hair as best he could. Taking off his jacket, he held it up in one hand and dusted it down with the other, removing as much evidence of his makeshift sleeping quarters as he could, though it remained stained in places, as did his trousers.

Feeling nauseous, from the combined excesses of the night before and his self-disgust, he left the toilet and made his way down the staircase, heading for the hotel's front door.

Before exiting, however, he was distracted by a small but agitated crowd, which was huddled around a TV screen, set on the wall above the lobby bar. There were European businessmen and Chinese and Indian men and women, looking like guests, as well as a number of uniformed staff. All of them were transfixed on the screen and talking among themselves in an agitated manner, jabbing their fingers at the screen. It was clearly an upsetting programme, and Jack moved towards the TV to get a better look.

He saw anguished scenes of distraught, weeping adults being interviewed, and of thousands of people gathering before a police barrier. Remembering Schmidt's comments earlier about the university protest turning into a "major punch up", and thinking of Doug, he became alarmed.

"What's happening?" he enquired of the nearest spectators, not understanding the rapid-fire Chinese TV commentary.

"You don't know?" replied a woman standing next to him, turning and looking at him with some disdain. "Where've you been? They've been slaughtering our kids. They've been shooting them! Those murderers!"

"What?" Jack exclaimed. "Who's been slaughtering our kids? Is this the university? It was just a sit-in!"

As the awful truth was revealed to him, the full extent of the horror dawned upon Jack. Violent, deadly clashes between students and police. Federation troops using live fire. Over fifty — maybe more — students killed. Hundreds injured. Many arrested. It was chaos. No one knew exactly what was happening. The territory was in uproar. Hundreds of thousands of people were heading towards the university, in search of loved ones, to demonstrate their outrage or out of morbid curiosity.

Doug! Jack panicked and fumbled for his phone. It was missing.

At first, he considered heading to the university to look for Doug. But he had no money and felt too wretched to travel across to the other side of the city. Besides, he reasoned, it sounded like the whole area was cordoned off, which would make the journey pointless. Assuming he wasn't a victim, or had been injured, Doug could be anywhere. If safe, he would surely head for his flat at the university. No, better to get home, Jack reasoned, clean up and get some rest. Then he would find Doug.

Slinking out of the hotel, though no one took any notice of him, Jack began to trudge along the side street towards the main road. From there it was a two-mile slog away from the business district on the long straight avenue, which was lined with modern shops and office blocks. Then a climb up, following the curves of the hill for a mile, where at least the lines of broad-leafed banyan trees would offer some relief from the uncompromising sun as it began its morning ascent. Finally, he would turn off to the right into his road, which followed the contour of the hillside, until he came to his block of flats.

Reaching the junction, he was made instantly aware of the air of menace permeating the city. Two armed policemen stood at the junction, keeping uneasy watch for any unusual activity, which they could neither anticipate or identify, given the nebulous nature of their orders.

Stopping Jack, they demanded to see his I.D. card and asked him where he had come from and where he was going. He complied, and then found himself explaining why he had a split brow and black eye, but no I.D. card. Unsmiling and uninterested in his story, they waved him on. A hung over and scruffy European, who stank of beer, was not under suspicion of playing any part in the grave events of the hours before.

Usually beginning to fill at this time of the morning with rush-hour traffic, the carriageways were only sparsely occupied that morning. A mile further down his route, Jack came across another police checkpoint.

This time, after further explanations, Jack ventured to ask the police sergeant what was going on.

"The people are very angry," he responded. "They want the soldiers out and they want justice. We just keep the peace. No more bloodshed. Go home and stay there. We don't know what's happening. The politicians are talking. They are always talking," he added fatalistically.

Needing no further encouragement, Jack hurried on his way, feeling weak and increasingly uncomfortable under the hot sun. Trudging up the hill, where he encountered few passers-by, he found he had to stop every so often to rest and catch his breath. Veering between irritation and confusion about his lack of energy, Jack's thoughts tumbled over one another — a vortex sucking him into a slew of depression and despair.

Here I am, he thought, after another pointless, drunken night, going back to an empty place I can't even call home. I'm just drifting and it's not leading anywhere. I should go back home to England. I don't like my job. I don't have a partner. I'm lonely. I'm not even sure I have any ambition left. I'm tired. I can't go on like this. Something's got to change.

At the top of the hill, he paused to collect his strength. Before him stood a small, whitewashed Catholic church, which he had passed by on innumerable occasions, but never entered. With a history stretching back to well over a hundred and fifty years, this building was a legacy of the territory's colonial and religious past. Lasting evidence of the European invaders and their internecine theological wars, it had survived the years. Not many of the indigenous peoples of this place were seduced by the spiritual offerings of their new masters. The commercial opportunities provided were more convincing. But a minority found solace in the pragmatic and undemanding rituals of the Anglican Church. And even fewer succumbed to the teachings of the Church of St. Peter, whose evangelists had first arrived on these distant shores.

In need of a drink and a place to sit down, and seeing the door was open, he decided to go inside to take a short rest. Although not religious — in fact, a committed atheist — he also recognised in the church a place where he might, for a few minutes, gather his thoughts undisturbed by the world. Pushing aside the large wooden door, which creaked loudly, as if to affirm its ancient pedigree, he poked his head inside.

Surprisingly spacious, the high gable-roofed nave was dark and cool, silent and still. Jack walked slowly down the central aisle, listening to the echo of his own footsteps on the stone flags, looking around at the paintings and statues, and gazing up at the wooden beams supporting the roof. Halfway down he slid into a pew, and feeling cooler and more relaxed, he leaned forward onto the back of the row in front, resting his head on his hands, hoping to ease the throbbing in his head.

That's the last time, he ordered himself. This is the turning point. Meet Gaynor next week. At least check it out. Meet Marion. See what's happening there. Quit this job. Maybe time to leave Asia. Always an outsider here anyway.

"Are you all right? Can I help?" A softly spoken voice jerked Jack from his reverie, causing him to sit up suddenly.

"Oh! Well, no. I'm fine, thanks. Well, that is… if you know the place, I could do with some water." He stumbled over his words, addressing the clean-shaven young Chinese man who stood by him, examining him sympathetically. Dressed simply in grey flannels and a neatly pressed white shirt, he was tall and gangly, with close-cropped dark hair.

"Dear God, what happened to you? Run into a train? Were you at the university? So bad, isn't it?" he said.

"No, no. Nothing so serious. In fact, a bar room brawl," Jack admitted, instinctively touching his wound.

"Wait a minute," said his interlocutor, as he turned and disappeared into one of the transepts.

He returned bearing a large glass of water, a wet cloth and a fresh plaster, which he passed over to Jack, before sitting beside him. Jack gratefully gulped down most of the water, wiped his face and attempted to put the plaster over his eye.

"Here, let me," said his comforter, who deftly applied the dressing.

"Thanks, appreciate it," said Jack, conscious it was the second time that morning a stranger had bothered to assist him.

"No problem, all part of the service," replied the young man with a smile. Jack noticed his perfect white teeth and fresh complexion. Probably in the choir, he guessed. Looks like a choirboy.

"In fact, in the job description, you could say, helping those in need," added the choirboy, grinning at his own joke.

"Don't tell me you're a priest," Jack said with genuine surprise. "I mean, you hardly look old enough... no offence intended. And no... you know," Jack pulled his index finger along his throat.

"I am. And none taken," said the young man. "Well, to be precise, I'm going to be a priest. So, no collar right now. I'm on a sort of work placement here. Lovely place to work, don't you think?" He waved a hand in the air acknowledging the lofty dimensions of the church. "I've not long finished a theology degree at Oxford. Only been here a month. Fascinating place, isn't it? Politics seem terrible, though. Awful news this morning. Did you hear? All those students killed. So shocking. Do you think the territory can get away from the federation?"

"Don't know," said Jack with a shrug. "Depends how people react to this morning. I hope to God they do make it."

"You trust in God, then?" queried the aspiring priest in a teasing tone.

"No. Sorry to disappoint you. Just a figure of speech. I'm an atheist. A heathen, as a priest once called me. A pagan." Jack smiled back at the expectant questioner.

"Fair enough," he said. "What turned you off? Or were you ever on? Oh, and, by the way, I'm just curious, not on a mission to convert you." The smile was returned.

"Well, I just can't accept the basic idea that we have to personalise the great mystery of life. Why can't we just enjoy the unexplained beauties of the world, without inventing — and mankind did, after all, invent gods — without needing the fairy tale of the old man in the sky? And all the claptrap surrounding him. Heaven and angels and saints. It's a contrived universe, devised by men, to sustain their influence through religion. Sorry, I'm beginning to rant," apologised Jack.

"That's OK, I can understand your doubts. Even us wannabe priests have our doubts about God. But the thing is, people find it hard to decipher the meaning of their lives in philosophical ideas. And religion, the

Christian religion, provides a story — to be sure largely symbolic — but a story, with recognisable heroes and villains, that helps interpret the "Mystery of Life" as you call it. It explains profound metaphysical concepts in human terms."

"Well, of course, I get that," said Jack, warming to the conversation. "But it's a kind of deceit, based on faith, instead of reason. For example, I just couldn't believe, even from a young age, that Jesus was the son of God. I mean, can you honestly say you believe explicitly in the immaculate conception?"

"I believe that Jesus was imbued with divine inspiration, yes. I believe his teachings to be so pure and good, so original, as to come from a higher intelligence, something above and beyond our normal, poor human experience," replied the young man.

"But you see," he continued. "You, the man supposedly without God. Where do you come when you look for peace and some sympathy when you are down and weary? To a church. To God. You don't call him God. But who were you talking to when I came across you?"

"No, no. You won't get me with that one," Jack chuckled. "I came here because it's quiet and cool and good for thinking. I came to think about my state and what I need to do about it. I don't need God for that. I'll make do with family and friends — and people like you — to do my talking to."

"What's your name?" asked the young man.

"Jack," he said.

"Well, Jack, what is your state? Why are you so miserable? Just a bit hung over after a bender last night? Not as miserable as most people in this territory today."

"Sure, of course," Jack agreed. "But all these things are relative, aren't they? I guess my life hasn't been going to plan lately. I behaved like an idiot last night. Not the first time. Reached the bottom of the pit. Don't feel in control. The important thing, though, is to get a grip on our own lives and change matters, rather than moaning about them or feeling sorry for ourselves. I'll do that. I'll do that without your God."

"And you are?" he added.

"Seb," he answered. "Actually... Sebastian Chow. Yes, afraid so. Doomed by my very name. Mum was Catholic, and her favourite saint was... yes... the one with all the arrows."

"So, Jack," he continued. "You sinned last night, and now you've made your confession. I'm sure our Lord will forgive you and you will be redeemed."

"Not the way I would put it, but I appreciate your interest," countered Jack.

"I would put my guilt down more to stupidity and wastefulness than sin. At least the guilt will motivate me to make better use of my time. Now, I'm shattered and better get home. Thanks for the water and the patching up and I enjoyed our talk." He stood up and offered his hand.

The trainee priest reciprocated.

277

"Well," he said, "if you have a Damascene conversion in the near future, come and see us. And if you don't… come and see us anyway… for a beer and a chat."

"Sounds more like my kind of religion," Jack shot back. He turned and waved as he left the church and was instantly dazzled by the bright sunshine outside.

Though refreshed by the drink and the rest, he continued to feel the effects of the night's excesses and there was still a full mile to trek before reaching his flat. By now it was almost nine and the sun was already testing. He shuffled rather than strode along the pavement. There was little traffic, much less than a normal Saturday, and fewer people around. Many were indoors, mesmerised by the appalling but patchy news being relayed by TV and radio.

His road home was straight and narrow, one of the lateral arteries on this hillside. On either side stood a mixture of buildings — an unplanned row of the old and the new. Along with a few former elegant colonial blocks of only three to four storeys stood soaring, brutish towers, tributes to the frenzied property booms of former years, when land was scarce and developers ran roughshod over any sense of heritage or aesthetic consideration. But at least this road had some character, retaining traces of the past and that's why he had chosen it. He didn't want to live in one of the so-called "expat ghettoes" and opted for a modest flat in a mainly Chinese and Indian-occupied block. It was a choice he had never regretted, enjoying both the sounds and aromas of the two cultures that embraced him there.

As he trudged along wearily, Jack looked down at the dusty pavement, thinking that he really had reached a turning point in his life. It was time for decisions. As soon as he got home, he would first call Doug — find his brother, make sure he was safe. Second, he would call home to check on his mother and father. Wish his mother happy birthday. The call was overdue, but depending on their condition, he would make a decision about returning home to support them. Then there was Marion. He would meet her, and though his reason told him not to hope for much from her, his heart beat with optimism. Yes, things were going to get better now. He would change his lifestyle.

Perspiring uncomfortably, he finally reached his block of flats and unlocked the main door. Nodding to the expressionless caretaker, who looked at him curiously, probably thinking he had been involved in the "riot" at the university, Jack entered the lift and went up the third floor.

Once inside, he slammed the door shut and leaned back on it, closing his eyes and feeling dizzy. At last, he thought. That was a slog.

His flat, which he had occupied for a year, was modest but comfortable. Looking spartan since Marion had left and removed her things, it was at least clean and tidy. Right now, it seemed to him devoid of warmth and full of melancholy. There had been moments, when he and Marion had hosted friends and colleagues, it had resonated with laughter and companionship. Now, looking around, he felt like a stranger within its walls.

Going straight to the fridge, he pulled out a carton of juice and drank greedily from it. Although he was hungry, he found little to eat and slammed the door shut in irritation, cursing under his breath. Then he picked up his house phone and dialled Doug's mobile number. No response.

Flicking on the TV, he was bombarded with scenes from around the university and from outside hospitals, of worried and furious relatives trying to find out if their loved ones were safe. Local politicians were also being interviewed, condemning the killings and demanding independence from the federation.

After ten minutes Jack switched it off, too exhausted to bear the enormity of what was passing. Throwing off his suit jacket and shoes, he flung himself onto his bed, and, lying prone with his arms spread, fell into a deep and troubled sleep.

Chapter Fifteen
Alone

Soon after the van carrying Doug started moving away, he became aware, in the black void of his situation, that he was not alone. He could hear someone shifting position to maintain balance as the vehicle swayed along the road, as well as the muffled groans of fellow captives.

"Who's there?" he ventured in a whisper.

"Ashok," came the reply. "Who are you?"

"Doug. Doug Wilson," he affirmed. "Ashok— of the student committee?"

"Yes, Ashok Sharma, they picked me up trying to get out the back way," came the reply.

"Doug Wilson, is that you?" came a second voice, instantly recognisable as that of Jonathon Yu.

"Jon. Christ, you made it. I thought they'd shot you. They trampled all over you. How are you doing?"

"Not good," answered Yu, in a hoarse voice. "Shot in the shoulder. They patched it up, but hurts like hell. Beat the crap out of me."

"Where do you think they're taking us," asked Doug, articulating a visceral fear they were all feeling.

"Don't know," said Sharma. "Let's hope it's not over the border, or we're in real shit."

"They wouldn't dare, would they?" countered Doug. "Kidnapping citizens of another state? There would be an international outcry."

A cynical laugh from Yu.

"Wilson. You see what they do. We just disappear. Missing persons. These dogs don't play by the rules."

The unthinkable entered Doug's head. Was he to become a "disappeared"? Has it really come to this? That he could be incarcerated without trace... or even shot and his body disposed of... like trash. The thought made him shiver. He sucked in a deep breath and exhaled noisily. He began to compose himself, with the strength of the survivor.

Right. Stay calm. It'll be OK. You just took part in a political discussion group. You are only a junior lecturer. You never instigated or led the protest. You were only there to show solidarity with a peaceful sit-in. You never took part in any violence. You are not interesting to the federation forces. Anyway, you're British. A foreigner. That's trouble for them. People will be looking for you. Jack will be looking for you right now. The consulate will be informed. You can't just disappear. It'll be OK. We'll get through this.

But the worst imaginings flared up again.

Jo's right though. No rules here. If they shoot us in a rage of retribution, diplomatic niceties will mean nothing. God! My life evaporated in a second. And I've done nothing. Achieved nothing. I'm too young. Mum and Dad and Jack. They won't even know what happened. He was shot resisting arrest, or attacking our military, they'll say, or some other excuse. What a waste! He felt a surge of resentment force tears into his eyes.

"Don't worry," came the comforting words from Ashok Sharma, in answer to Jo Yu's menacing warning. "I don't think it will come to that. They've gone too far already. There will be massive backlash in the territory. Our student committee has some powerful relatives and friends in government. Even the federation will tread carefully. I think the worst is a show trial of some kind, just to browbeat the democrats and independence supporters. It's just a tragedy — that you radicals had to push it to the brink," he added, pointing his remark at Jo Yu.

"There was no choice but to fight back, can't you see!" hissed Jon Yu in response to the criticism. "They were looking to murder us. We had to defend ourselves, and fight back!"

"Not much point in arguing over that now. It's happened and one way or another we have to live with it," said Doug.

"Let's hope it is to live," shot back Yu.

There was silence for a while as the three helpless prisoners pondered their fate, their thoughts gloomy, like black clouds hovering on the horizon before the tempest.

The police van rumbled on, giving no indication to Doug and the others about the direction it was taking, or the final destination.

Finally, after some thirty minutes driving, it slowed down, made a sharp turn and jerked to a halt.

"Still in the territory, I think," said Sharma in a hushed tone. "Can't have reached the border yet." That was at least small consolation.

This is it, then, thought Doug and tried to regulate his breathing and subdue his trembling.

They heard gruff voices outside. Orders being rapped out and responded to. Then the rear doors of the van were flung open, the streetlights suddenly easing the darkness of the blindfold.

Doug was roughly grabbed by the arms and hauled out headfirst. He feared he would crash to the ground headlong, but was supported by his captors tightly gripping both arms. They dragged him away, his feet barely touching the floor.

Sensing he was being taken indoors, he was hit by a smell of disinfectant mingled with urine, and wondered if it was a hospital. But the creaking and metal clanging of doors being opened and shut, and echoing shouts, suggested a prison, police station or barracks. The cries of anguish and anger grew louder on both sides as they moved on. At one point he heard a shrill female voice over the din.

"Doug! Doug! We're here! Help us! Don't leave us here!" It was Alice. Doug could barely get his words out. "I won't, Alice... I won't," before he was smacked on the back of the head. "No talk. No talk," came the command.

Finally, with the discordant sounds beginning to fade behind them, came the rattle of a key in a heavy door, followed by a mournful groan as it opened. Doug was pushed in. His blindfold was removed. Dazzled by the unaccustomed light, he blinked, adjusting himself to the glare. He was in a small, spartan cell, no more than ten feet square. There was no window, the only light being a naked bulb in the middle of the ceiling, protected behind a wire grill.

His jailers released his hand ties. Rubbing his wrists to restore circulation, he instinctively turned to face them, but they shouted at him, and shoved him against the wall. Glimpsing the young, brutish faces of the soldiers, who wore the green camouflage uniform of the federation army, his heart and his hopes sank. But then, Ashok Sharma was surely right. We didn't travel far enough to cross the border, he thought. This glimmer of comfort sustained him.

After they had slammed the door and locked it, Doug was consumed with an overwhelming sense of despair. Exhausted after having barely slept all night, thirsty and hungry, his head throbbing from the blow he had received earlier, he sat down wearily on the narrow iron bed. The featureless concrete walls and ceiling offered no relief and the only other furniture was a squat brick toilet, which stank.

Putting his hand beneath his head, Doug lay down on his side. He soon drifted into a fitful sleep.

Frightful images from the events of the night swirled before his closed eyes, like some kaleidoscope of horror, accompanied by the screams and howls of the wounded and dying. He saw again the rampaging troops of the federation overwhelm the young protesters — individuals he had taught and supported. He heard again the sharp crack of the gunshots and the pitiful cries for help. As his fatigue dragged him into a deeper slumber, his mind resurrected random memories from home, as if to give him a last confirmation of his existence before the final moment of death. He imagined sitting at the breakfast table at home, with his father reading the daily paper and his mother repeatedly getting up and down to provide him and the three boys with their toast or eggs. He saw himself, occupying the sofa with Jack and Matthew, as they watched some vacuous soap opera on TV with their parents. How the complacency and lack of ambition of it all had frustrated him at times. How he yearned now for the banal safety it represented.

Then more threatening visions intruded, until he looked down on himself, from above, kneeling, blindfolded and tied, while a soldier stood behind him, holding a revolver to the back of his head. Even in his sleep, every muscle contracted as he braced himself for oblivion.

He saw the finger on the trigger, and… a deafening crash! The cell door flew open, and he was suddenly sucked from the black hole of death. Before he could even wake fully or stand, the two soldiers seized him, dragged him upright, pinned his arms behind his back, bound his hands and put a black hood over his head. Defenceless again, he was half-marched, half-carried out.

A few minutes later, he was pushed into a chair and the hood removed. Giddy from his disturbed sleep, he tried to gather his thoughts and anxiously looked around. He now sat in what appeared to be a shabby office. It had a window, which was covered with a dark blind. Facing him, across an expansive, plain wooden desk, sat a large man with a bullish neck, bulbous nose, close-cropped hair and stubbled beard. Next to him, a thin-faced bespectacled person, whose narrow eyes and insubstantial lips gave the immediate impression of insouciant cruelty. Behind Jack, two junior officers stood to attention, their hands behind their backs.

No one spoke for a while. Then the officer sitting opposite, without lifting his gaze, but continuing to write on a form, muttered something in Chinese. The interpreter, for that was clearly his role, coldly asked Doug for his full name and nationality. Doug complied. He was then asked about his job and his reason for being in the territory. Feeling that this questioning was innocent enough and just harmless detail, Doug answered.

Then came questions about his relationship to his political group, its purpose and his relationship to

Brandon. This was trickier, but Doug didn't feel threatened, and to buy time he asked for some water. Glancing at his superior, the interpreter tentatively relayed the request. For the first time the officer looked up. At first, he smiled, as if amused, but the expression quickly turned to a scowl. Suddenly, he leaned forward and bellowed at Doug, who instinctively leaned back in his chair.

"The captain," relayed the interpreter, sitting bolt upright and betraying not a trace of emotion, "says that you will get no water or anything else, until you admit to your crimes."

Feeling the blood drain from his face, Doug replied meekly, "What do you mean? What crimes?"

At a command from the officer in charge, one of the soldiers released Doug's hands and a piece of paper and a pen were pushed in front of him.

"You must sign this," ordered the interpreter.

With panic rising in his chest, Doug bent forward and methodically read the statement on the paper. It was a crudely written confession, declaring that the undersigned had been a spy in the pay of "foreign agencies", that he had taken part in illegal political activities aimed at the subversion of the government of the territory and the undermining of the bonds of unity between the territory and the federation, that he had participated in planning a violent student protest that had caused the deaths of officers of the law and threatened law and order."

I'm done for if I sign this, he thought. Better try and hold out. What will they do to me? He lifted his head and looked the interpreter in the eye, finding a scrap of courage.

"Sorry. I can't sign this. I'm not a spy. Not a political agitator. Just a language teacher. I didn't plan anything."

Having heard Doug's reply from the interpreter, the officer lolled back in his chair, sucking his pen. He stared at his captive and let out an impatient sigh. By raising his eyebrows and slightly tilting his head up, he conveyed an order to his men and without warning, Doug received a forceful blow from behind to the side of his head. The force of it knocked him sideways off his chair. The soldiers heaved him up and sat him down again. He felt faint and there was a ringing in his ear. His throat was so dry he could hardly speak.

The captain muttered further words, which the interpreter translated.

"My captain says he is running out of patience and has no time for games. He says if you don't sign the confession it will be very painful for you."

His vision now blurred from the blow and sweat pouring from his brow, Doug slumped forward and pretended to read the document again. I can't take this, he said to himself, I'm no hero. He picked up the pen, ready to sign. But as it touched the paper, he put it down again, resigned to more beating.

"No," he croaked. "No, I won't sign. I'm not a spy. Please believe me."

Without waiting for any translation, the captain leapt to his feet and raged at Doug. He gestured to his men, who clubbed Doug to the ground again and then forced him back to his feet. He felt he was going to throw up and any strength he had left was draining from him. The room swung around him and he felt he would pass out.

At that critical moment, quite suddenly and without warning, an icy chill entered the office, as though some malign incubus was taking occupancy. Doug was unceremoniously dumped back on the chair, as the officers, the interpreter and the captain jumped to attention and saluted. The object of their deference was a slim, middle-aged Asian man, of indeterminate origin. Dressed in a well-cut dark suit, shiny black shoes and an open-necked white shirt, he was clean-shaven, even handsome, with fulsome black hair immaculately slicked back and oiled in the fashion of the film stars of the 1930s.

Doug's saviour strolled in nonchalantly, casually drawing on a cigarette. He rasped a few barely audible orders in Chinese, and the captain frantically collected his papers and scuttled out, with the interpreter and soldiers trailing him. They were clearly unnerved.

Seating himself behind the desk, the stylish newcomer leaned back and crossed his legs. Still puffing on his cigarette, he observed Doug for a few moments, before saying, in drawn-out, perfect English,

"Well, Mr Douglas Wilson. You have got yourself into a... what do you English say... a pretty pickle? You really must take more care in choosing your company. You'll have to excuse the crudity of our military men. They are uneducated peasants and scum for the most part, but they are prepared to lay down their lives in defence of the motherland, so they have their value."

Stretching his arm, he stubbed out the remains of the cigarette and clapped his hands. An orderly came in carrying a metal tray, which was put in front of Doug. On it was a bottle of water, a cup of Chinese tea and a white-bread sandwich with a filling of unrecognisable substance.

"Please, help yourself. Have something to eat and drink. You've had a distressful time, and I want you feeling better. Because, you know..." he paused as if choosing his words carefully, "we do need to have a civilised talk about the unfortunate situation in which you find yourself."

Trying to control himself so as not to seem too desperate, though by now parched and aching with hunger, Doug gratefully drank much of the water and bit greedily into the tasteless sandwich.

Observing Doug with interest, but without speaking, the stranger lit another cigarette. When the food was finished, however, he broke the silence.

"You're probably wondering who I am," he began. Doug didn't react.

"Well, my name's Alexander Lee and I work for the federation's home security department. Basically, just keeping an eye out for the federation's enemies and making sure they cause us no harm."

"I know your country well. I studied PPE at Oxford. A happy and illuminating time. I found out much about British views and prejudices. Some impressive... and some less admirable. Behind the sophistication? Ruthlessness and arrogance. I also know quite a lot about you, Douglas. May I call you Douglas?"

Doug shrugged, not really knowing how to respond, and not wanting to let his guard down.

"I know, for example, that you worked for the radical wing of the Labour Party back home and that you came here with good intentions, to teach our ambitious youngsters English. But, tell me," he rested his elbows on the desk and smiled with considered sympathy, "how on earth did you get yourself involved with the planning and leadership of this morning's bloody uprising?"

Doug wiped his mouth on the back of his shirt sleeve. His head still pounded from his earlier treatment.

"Seriously, I had nothing to do with planning... nothing. Certainly not leading it. It was a peaceful sit-in, and I wanted to show solidarity with my students. I had no idea it would escalate into such a... such a bloodbath," he said, screwing up his eyes.

"Come now, Douglas," persisted his interrogator, "you are being a little disingenuous, aren't you? I mean, this so-called political discussion group — didn't it hold workshops on democracy and freedom and didn't it actively campaign for the break-up of our cherished federation?" He emphasised the word "cherished" with a hint of satire.

Unsettled by his questioner's reservoir of accurate information, Doug shifted uncomfortably in his chair.

"Whatever we did... that was theoretical and academic. It was about educating our students. The sit-in resulted from the students' own legitimate complaints about their conditions, their curriculum and the behaviour of the director. Our group didn't organise or even suggest it," he explained with forced sincerity.

"I see," replied Lee. "But who, then, persuaded the student body to defy the time limit quite reasonably proposed by the police to leave the establishment they were illegally occupying? And who, precisely, organised and encouraged the arming of the students with weapons such as Molotov cocktails and pistols. I really would like some names just to have a clear picture of events."

"I really can't say," Doug stammered. "It was very confusing. There were heated debates and many people spoke. I didn't see any students with guns. And any violence that occurred, I must say, started with the police. They beat unarmed protesters without mercy."

"Yes, I thought you might say that." Lee looked at the ceiling as if bored, and then continued. "Police brutality is a good excuse for using force. Anyway, we know a great deal about your little discussion group. You see, our people infiltrated it months ago. Tell me about Mr Dick Brandon. Interesting character, no? Of course, very left wing. Hard line Marxist, one could say. He saw the sit-in as an opportunity to provoke a revolutionary moment, did he not?"

Shaken by the revelation, Doug tried to imagine who were the spies among his fellow group members. He also wondered about Brandon's fate. Did he survive? Was he taken? Or did he manage to get away in the chaos?

"Well?" repeated Lee. "Mr Brandon?"

"He was very theoretical, with his head in the clouds," Doug blustered. "I don't think the students took him very seriously from a practical point of view."

"Mmmm. A very loyal response," mused Lee. "Actually, we think Mr Brandon has a lot to answer for, and is not quite so innocently bookish as you pretend. As a foreign agent working against the unity of our federation, he will pay his dues."

The mood darkened.

"And you, Douglas. Who do you really work for?" continued Lee.

"Oh no. No, no, no. I'm just a humble language tutor. Too much of a coward for anything like that," Doug protested.

"I really don't get it," said Lee, his tone less intimate and hardening. "Why you Western academics and idealists still come here interfering, trying to teach us how to run our politics. Can't you see? Your time is long over. Colonialism is dead. Your time in the ascendant is over. We are evolving our own systems without your flabby Western democracy."

Deciding Lee was inviting a response, Doug was emboldened.

"I didn't come here to preach about politics, but to teach students and that means freedom of thought and open debate. You can't carry on with suppression. People get better educated. They get more information in today's world. There's the internet. They travel. It's not a dangerous political idea but human nature to want to be heard and not dictated to. It's a matter of human rights. Your strong government is nothing but a dictatorship. Dictatorships fail in long run, corrupted by their own power. You can't succeed in imprisoning or killing all dissent. Societies evolve. You can't hold the lid on a simmering pot for ever."

"Very impassioned," noted Lee. "Lord Acton would approve." Placing his latest cigarette in the ashtray, he raised his eyebrows and clasped his hands together.

"But fatally flawed. You see, you forget one essential fact. Our people here have no experience of your democracy, or human rights. They don't know what these concepts mean. They only know two things in our long history. They know peace, under wise and strong leadership. And they know chaos — destruction, civil war and famine. There is nothing in between. Look at this morning. You offer your ideals. You encourage dissent. And you get bloodshed. Your offer results in destruction."

"Times change," persisted Doug, forgetting the fragility of his position. "Societies change. How do you know your people cannot deal with democracy? Many other nations, around the world, have embraced it for the first time. And democracy itself evolves. Depriving people of their basic freedoms in itself will lead to frustration, resistance, anger and violence. Better to introduce these freedoms and allow communities the hope establishing them. Don't you see? Your troops' brutality this morning has done more than anything to fire up political awareness here and energise the independence movement."

"Perhaps," Lee sighed. "But remember we were invited in by the leadership to help maintain law and order. Meanwhile, my own humble role is to suppress sedition and enable General Khan to proceed with the building of the power and prosperity of the federation."

"As for you, Mr Wilson, your days as political agitator are numbered. Oh, don't worry, you're not going to be a guest in one of our labour camps this time. You're small fry, and we are more interested in the bigger fish. Anyway, it seems your friends have managed to rouse your consulate into unaccustomed activity. We're letting you go. Pity, I was rather enjoying our little talk."

"However," he stared at Doug with narrowed eyes, "we expect you to leave this territory within the next forty-eight hours. If not, I really can't take responsibility for the actions of some of my more uncivilised colleagues."

"Oh! And by the way, might be a good idea to take that wastrel brother of yours with you. Yes, we know all about him. Goodbye, Mr Wilson. Go home. Grow some roses. Read some Shakespeare and Hobbes. Deliver leaflets for the Labour Party. I hope we can meet in more pleasant surroundings one day, perhaps in London, for tea."

With that, he stood up, barked an order, and walked out, leaving Doug white-faced, not knowing whether to rejoice at the news or despair at the stark warning.

Two soldiers marched in. They bound Doug's hands again and hooded him.

"Hey, what's going on?" he pleaded, but his words were wasted.

This time he was not taken back to his cell, but back along the corridor and outside. For the second time that morning, he was pushed into the back of a vehicle.

"What's happening?" he called in alarm. "Where are you taking me? He said I could go!" Fear tautened the muscles in his limbs and made him sweat profusely.

He was driven for some twenty minutes, but being completely disoriented, exhausted near to the point of collapse, he had no idea of his location or the direction of travel. Just not over the border, he kept saying to himself. Just not over the border.

Finally, the van pulled to a stop. The doors opened and he was unceremoniously bundled from his seat into the open air. To his relief, his hands were released and the hood taken from his head. At first, he was blinded by the strong sunshine of a morning and shielded his eyes with his forearm.

A voice, with a clipped English accent, was speaking.

"Douglas Wilson? Are you all right? You are free now, and quite safe. Do you need any medical help? We have your things here."

He raised his head and saw a young man, about mid-twenties in age, wearing grey flannels and a white short-sleeved shirt. He brushed his generous shock of dark hair from his brow as he spoke. Public school, thought Doug.

"I'm Peter Barrington. From the consulate. Glad to see you safe. We got a bit worried. Brandon roused us first thing. We got straight on the case. They owed us though, and after their overreaction this morning, we were able to press for your release," he explained breathlessly, like a schoolboy eager to please.

"It wasn't an 'overreaction'. It was a fucking massacre," croaked Doug.

"Yes, quite," said the young official, handing over a plastic bag. Doug found his wallet, watch and mobile phone, which had been confiscated at the time of his arrival at the prison site. Nine fifteen, he noted. Much earlier than he could have guessed.

Turning his head, he took in the surroundings and guessed he was in one of the territory's outlying suburbs, unfamiliar to him. They stood outside a metro station. He also became aware of two policemen — from the territory's force — standing nearby.

Aware Doug was eyeing them up suspiciously, Barrington explained they were here to make sure his handover from the federation troops was smooth and they were to drive them to the consulate, or hospital first, as Doug required.

"I don't need the hospital and I certainly don't want to go to the consulate. Not now anyway. I just want to go home and rest."

But having looked at his phone, and seen several missed calls, he dialled Jack. When the call went to voice mail, he became concerned and asked to be taken to his brother's flat. He needed to make sure Jack was safe, and he wanted to tell him about everything that had happened.

Barrington explained that much of the territory was in lock down, but that massive demonstrations were being planned for midday. Handing over his name card, he requested that Doug contact him once he had rested, to "diarise" a debriefing meeting.

Doug climbed wearily into the back of the police car, exhilarated to be free and lightheaded from fatigue.

He could hardly believe what he had been through in the past hours. It was as though he had experienced a nightmare, from which he was just emerging, like someone half-waking from a fearful dream in the grey light of dawn, unaware of his state of consciousness.

As the car drew away, he sat back, reclining against the head rest and closing his eyes. He saw the dead and wounded, and Brandon's austere face, and Alice's softness, and the captain, and Alexander Lee. He choked back a sob of relief. He was safe. He was alive.

Chapter Sixteen
The Search for Redemption

A shaft of golden sunlight shone through the window of the flat. Within it floated a myriad of dust particles, creating a universe in their own right, and highlighting the silence and stillness of the room with their floating presence. It was a sparsely furnished place devoid of care. But the shabbiness of the scene was at least gilded at that moment by the bright sunshine. A worn three-seater leather sofa and a small TV perched on a small side table constituted the main evidence of habitation, while pushed against the wall was an unvarnished wooden dining table and four matching chairs, which, by the precision of their positioning, suggested to the observer that they had not been in recent use.

On the bottom shelf of a cheap rattan bookshelf nearby was a CD player, along with an untidy pile of music CDs, in no particular order and favouring no particular genre. On the shelves above, an eclectic range of books leaned — mostly well-thumbed paperbacks — indicating an owner of wide but non-discriminating taste. Graham Greene sat side by side with Tolstoy, Tolkien, Rankin, Agatha Christie and a biography of George Best, among others.

An open door led through to the adjacent kitchen. There, the lack of equipment and largely vacant shelves, along with the casual order of things, pointed to an occupant irregular in the habit of cooking. The flat clearly belonged to someone who used the place as a refuge from the demands of a working life, but who was uninterested in investing time in grafting their personality onto it.

A second door led from the living room into a bedroom, furnished with a plain white framed double bed, which occupied most of the area of the floor, and a fitted wardrobe, which covered one entire wall. On a bed side table stood a metallic adjustable lamp, which was still switched on, and two books, lying open face down. The upper one was a book, translated into English, about the harsh, self-denying creed of the samurai, written by the Japanese writer Mishima.

Lying prone on top of the covers on the bed, fully dressed apart from shoes and jacket, which had been flung onto the floor, his arms spread wide, was Jack. He slept the deep sleep of the exhausted, breathing softly and evenly, his cheek pressed directly against the sheet. His dreams swung from scenes of fear and discomfort, lust and humiliation to downright absurdity, but he would not remember any of the details when he woke up.

This happened when he was disturbed by an insistent buzzing sound. Thinking at first it was a mosquito circling his head, he attempted to swat it away. But when this failed and the noise persisted enough to bring him to consciousness, he sat up suddenly, rubbing his eyes and cursing. For a second, he assumed it was the sound of construction — a stone saw or drill — until he reached clarity of mind enough to recognise the sound of his own flat intercom, signalling someone was at the entrance of his block.

Swinging his legs round to the edge of the bed, he stood up and, yawning continuously, reluctantly made his way to the device on the wall next to his front door.

Snatching the receiver from its holder, he asked in an irritated voice, "Yes, flat 6A. Who is it? What do you want?"

"Jack, it's me, Doug. For Christ's sake, let me in, will you?"

In an instant, the realities of the night before and the present crashed in upon Jack with the effect of an electric shock, jolting him into action and making him feel quite sober with sudden stress.

"Doug. You're OK. Thank God. Come up!" he replied, clearing his throat.

Pressing the access button, and replacing the receiver, he went back hurriedly into his bedroom and quickly tidied up, throwing his jacket and shoes into the wardrobe and hastily straightening the bedclothes. Rushing to the bathroom, he cupped his hands and scooped up handfuls of water to wash his face and gargled, spitting out into the sink. Looking into the mirror, he was shocked by the sight of his own bruised face. But there was nothing to be done.

The doorbell rang and Jack opened it to face his brother.

For a few moments they looked at each other in disbelief.

Then they hugged each other tightly. Doug sobbed with relief, before Jack led him to the table where they pulled out two chairs.

"I was so worried when I heard about the massacre," said Jack, his arm around his brother's shoulder. "You could've been killed. What happened to you? Are you hurt?"

"Apart from a thick head thanks to a few clouts around the ear, no," replied Doug. "Jack, it was horrendous. Just a nightmare. They shot those kids down like they were animals. Mass murder. I was lucky to get out alive. Have you got something to drink? I'm parched."

"Oh yeah, sorry, I'll make some tea. Hold on," and he went to the kitchen. Doug went to the sofa and lay down. Then he got up and turned on the TV. On the local channel a rolling news programme ran, covering the disaster. He sat on the edge of the sofa, with his elbows on his knees and his chin cupped in his hands, absorbed in the report.

Jack returned with two mugs of tea and sat next to him. "What's the latest?" he asked, nodding towards the TV.

"Can't really see yet. They're reporting more than fifty dead and dozens wounded. Those bastards. I can't believe it. Look! There are massive demonstrations in the streets against the federation. Seems like their barbarity might have backfired."

He sipped his tea gratefully. "Say, Jack, got anything stronger? Need something to settle my nerves." For the first time, Jack noticed that his brother was shivering.

"Sure, I think I've got some Scotch left." He got up and pulled out a bottle from the bookshelf. It was about a half full. He was looking for a glass when Doug indicated he wanted the bottle. Grabbing it, he took a large swig direct and then poured more into his tea.

"What happened to you?" asked Jack. "Where have you been?"

"We were hiding. Me and Alice. In the main union building, when they caught us. I was arrested. They took us… I don't know where… and I really thought I was a goner. Feared for my life. Then I had the weirdest interrogation. Surreal. First a crude guy. Some army thug. They roughed me up a bit. I was shitting myself. Then, someone else came in. Like the guy was some kind of spook. Like an intelligence agent. Said he was an Oxford graduate — wanting a friendly chat. They seemed to know all about me. Even you. They knew about you too. Asked me if I was a spy. And asked for names. I didn't say much. Didn't have to. Then just as suddenly, they let me go. And they handed me over to the territory police, who brought me here."

"Jack." He looked seriously at his brother. "Do you think it's partly our fault? I mean, me, Brandon, and the others. Did we encourage the students to go too far? Should we have stayed out of it?"

"Well, no," his brother reassured him. "The movement was there before you. You didn't organise anything. You didn't plan it. You didn't incite violence… did you? You aren't responsible for the federation's murderers, are you."

"No, no, of course not. But we might have given them the idea they shouldn't compromise," worried Doug.

"But what about you?" he asked, turning to his brother and pointing to his black eye and cut above it. "You look absolute shit. Did you get mixed up in something on the fringes? Did you try to find me? You said you would come, you know."

"No, no, I got caught up in a business meeting, which went on all evening," Jack explained, feeling himself blush and hoping Doug wouldn't notice.

"You got thumped in a business meeting? Some business!" said Doug incredulously.

"No, well, I got socked by some drunk yobbo in one of the bars, getting caught up in their scrap. It's nothing really. I came home after that," he said, not knowing why he needed to make it up.

"I tried a good few times to call you," Doug added.

"I know, I mislaid my phone during the evening," Jack replied.

"Pissed, I suppose," said Doug, in an accusing tone.

"No, not really. Had a few... you know, while talking shop," answered Jack, staring at the TV.

They both turned their attention to the news reports.

They learned that the federal troops had withdrawn rapidly from the territory after the massacre, in face of overwhelming popular and political pressure. Millions of citizens — no one knew exactly how many — had surged onto the streets, surrounding the university area and venting their anger and disgust at the action of the federation troops and politicians who had summoned them. They watched transfixed as the news broke that several of the territory's leading Prosperity Party pro-federation politicians had resigned, including the Secretary for Security, who spoke live, tearfully offering his apologies and denying his role in the disaster.

"The lying bastard," spat out Doug contemptuously. "I hope they string him up."

Although no official reaction was coming from the federation, it was being speculated that even General Khan was under pressure, as internal critics pointed to the outcome of the intervention as a sign of his weakness.

Internally, democratic leaders were calling for a war crimes response and punishment to all ministers who had collaborated with the federal involvement.

They were in the ascendancy. A shocked international community was also responding. Already a UN emergency meeting had been called. The USA was talking about manoeuvring its Pacific fleet closer to the scene to "warn against further human rights abuses" in the territory.

"You see," said Jack after a long pause. "Something good might come out of the evil yet."

"I hope so!" said Doug, who now lay back on the sofa and closed his eyes. "I really do hope so."

Just as he seemed to be drifting into sleep, his phone rang. He snatched it up quickly and answered breathlessly.

"Dick, is it you? Where are you? What happened to you? Are the others OK?"

Jack could hear Brandon's voice as a muffled murmur, while Doug, now wide-eyed, listened and nodded frequently.

"Yes, I'm OK now. I'm with my brother. I'm safe. No, not really hurt. They smacked me around a bit, and threatened a lot, but, in the end, wanted me to confirm information they already had. They reckon you work for intelligence, Dick. Do you?"

Jack heard a dull laugh from the phone.

Doug listened attentively for a few minutes more, then abruptly ended the call.

"Seems most people arrested have been released," he informed Jack, "but we're still missing a couple from our group. We don't know if they've been killed or in hospital or are still being held."

"Sorry, that's awful for you," said his brother.

"Yeah," replied Doug, who fell into silence. Rocky dead, Jonathon Yu and Jo Chan still unaccounted for, he thought, but at least Alice was out and safe, according to Brandon.

He picked up his phone again and dialled Alice's number. To his relief, she picked up. She was at home with her parents, she told him. She had been held for a couple of hours and then interrogated. Although frightening, the questioning had been superficial and when it finished, they threatened her with severe consequences if she ever involved herself again in any political action. Then, without further explanation, released her. She had no news of those missing.

"I'll call you tomorrow, when you've rested. Take care and stay at home," said Doug, concluding the call.

"Well, thank God she's OK," he said. "I was with her when they took us. Impressive, gutsy young woman."

"Girlfriend?" asked Jack.

"That would be nice," responded Doug, with a half-smile.

"What about you?" he continued. "What were you up to last night? Another bender, I suppose."

"Just a catch up with Les and Val, then I bumped into Marion of all people," related Jack.

"Marion! What the hell is she doing back here? I thought she had dumped you and headed for London with a better prospect," Doug said.

"Yeah, thanks for your sensitivity. Actually, she was back for the trade fair. And she's not having a great time with lover boy. In fact… well, she seems to have split up for the time being. We're having lunch on Monday," Jack explained with some reluctance.

Doug's reaction was predictable.

"Oh! Jack! You're fucking hopeless, you know. Leave her alone. You'll just get disappointed again. She's a nice kid, but all over the place. She's not right for you. She's a party animal. A good-time girl. Give yourself a break and just let go."

"No, no, that's really not fair," replied Jack. "There's a lot more to her than that. She's a good person. But, maybe you're right. I shouldn't get my hopes up."

But inwardly he thought differently.

"Anyway, I've got to make some major decisions. I mean, about me, and what I do now. A business partner — you remember Justin Gaynor? — has offered me a plum job. A chance to escape the ministry. A chance to get away from this routine. I know I'm in a rut and boozing too much. I'm thinking about it, or even of going back home. I'm not enjoying my job and don't like what I'm becoming here. I've really decided it's time to make a break. A new start," he said quietly.

"What's the job about," Doug asked. "Where is it… here?"

"Yeah," answered Jack, not wanting to go into details. "It's local, but I don't think it's for me anyway."

"Well, for what it's worth, advice from a younger brother, I reckon you should go back home," Doug said.

"You haven't been yourself since you broke up with Marion. You obviously hate your job. And you are drinking too much. Go home and chill for a few months. Get away from this hothouse and put things in perspective. Spend time with Mum and Dad. God knows, Mum needs all the help she can get right now, and we've been no use at all, being so far away. Go back and help Mum. Get some peace of mind."

"Anyhow," he added in a serious tone, "our federation friend who interrogated me left a nasty warning if either of us hang around in the territory, basically threatening us with violence."

He went on to explain to Jack that the federation officer seemed to have detailed knowledge of both of them and their activities, and that he had given both of them forty-eight hours to leave the territory or face the consequences.

Jack visibly paled and sat down.

"The consequences being?" he said.

"Well, violence against us, arrest, harassment, who knows for sure," Doug replied. "But it might be a good idea for you to leave… to be on the safe side."

"Sounds a bit melodramatic, doesn't it?" Jack said. "Forty-eight hours? That's a bit ridiculous. Sounds like a Le Carré spy novel. What do you think?"

"I think it's designed to scare us off. But, anyway, I'm not leaving," asserted Doug firmly.

"What do you mean, you're not leaving? Your life's in danger. You can't play around with these people. Doug, this is deadly serious stuff. I think the both of us should get the hell out of here as soon as possible," Jack said with some agitation.

"You don't have to talk to me about how deadly this is," Doug replied with annoyance.

"I was there last night. I saw those students being killed. I feared for my life. While you were on the piss!"

He grabbed the whisky bottle and poured a large slug into his empty tea cup. He took a swig and blinked fiercely.

"OK. OK," said his older brother, "you're the big hero. But you've done your bit. This whole situation here is getting out of control. There could be serious violence. What are you going to do here? It's not your fight."

"But it is now. It is," said Doug. "I can help. I want to help. The more foreigners here involved, the more international the interest, and the more pressure on the federation to back off. Anyway, I'm staying. I feel an obligation. I feel responsible."

"But you, Jack," he continued. "You got nothing here. Go home and sort yourself out. Go home and help

Mum. You know Dad's getting steadily worse, and she really can't cope much longer. I'm seriously worried. Last summer the dementia was bad enough, but he needs a proper diagnosis. Mum's too passive to get anything done. Too nervous of 'the authorities'. You need to get back there and help. Get him into a doctor and insist on a full examination and diagnosis, then at least she'll get some social welfare back up. Jack, you can do that."

"Well, I guess you're right. Of course, I'll help. Don't like the sound of prospects here, that's for sure," Jack said, resigned.

The two sat together on the sofa for a while, without talking, sipping tea and whisky and watching the running TV news.

By midday the two of them were half asleep, lounging on the sofa, with the TV still blaring away, though not being paid attention to. Jack stirred himself.

"Why don't you lie down and sleep? Use the bed," he said. "I've had a few hours already, so I'll just kip here."

"Maybe you're right. I feel crap now," answered Doug and got up to make his way to the bedroom.

But before he had taken more than a few steps, his phone rang again.

It was Brandon.

"Dick! What's up? Not bad news, I hope?" he asked.

Matters were moving fast, Brandon explained. The Democrats were holding a major press conference at four p.m. that day, in response to a deluge of enquiries from around the world about what was going on. The world's press would be there. It was a golden opportunity for the democratic movement to make its mark and there were rumours that they might declare for unilateral independence from the federation.

It was imperative the students were represented and that witnesses of the massacre were there in person to present first-hand accounts of what had happened. Brandon was going and he urged Doug to attend too. Their presence as foreign witnesses and teachers added strength to the case, he argued.

"Yes, OK, OK, I got it," Doug agreed. "Don't worry, I'll be there."

Telling Jack about the call, Doug made ready to go.

"I need to go home and get cleaned up and change into some clean clothes," he said. "You coming?"

"No," said his brother. "I look too much of a mess. And I need some rest. You do too."

"I know, but, Jack, you know, this is history in the making!" Doug said.

"Fine," Jack shrugged his shoulders," but for Christ's sake take care and stay out of trouble."

They embraced.

"Call Mum, today, Jack," said Doug. "She'll be upset if you don't call her on her birthday. Call her and tell her you will be coming home. Do it, Jack. Make a commitment. It'll be good for her and good for you," he urged his brother, hands on his shoulders and looking him straight in the eye.

"I know. I will," Jack promised, as Doug turned and left the flat. Jack watched him enter the lift and, with a last wave, closed the door.

Turning round, he suddenly felt very tired, alone and vulnerable. His flat seemed bereft of comfort and alien, like a third-rate hotel room on a business trip might feel. He switched off the TV and, downing the last drop of whisky from the bottle, took it and the cups to the kitchen.

Looking at his watch, he saw it was just after midday, and he decided to call home at four p.m. His parents would be awake by then.

After throwing off his clothes, he took a long, hot shower, systematically soaping and washing, as if to purify himself after the night's events. He shaved and put a fresh plaster on the cut over his eye.

Pulling on some clean pants and a T-shirt, he then lay down again on his bed. He set his alarm for a quarter to four. Although dizzy from tiredness, he found it hard to sleep.

Picking up the book by his bedside, he tried to read, hoping it would hasten sleep. The words, about the samurai's code of honour and bravery, intrigued him. How he would like to be so selfless and brave, to the point of self-sacrifice. Even if this bore little relevance to his life, he could at least try to be more decisive and determined in his choices, he thought, and not just drift through life. The true warrior, he read, faces adversity and danger unflinching. He grits the teeth and juts out the jaw, in defiance of his fate.

After a few pages he replaced the book, put his hands behind his head and closed his eyes. He pictured his mother and father, when they were younger and family life had seemed so content and uncomplicated. He thought of Doug, energetic and obstinate, engaged in his causes and Matthew, reserved and enigmatic, whom he never really knew.

Then he saw Pru, and he felt sorry and wanted to apologise to her. What a lousy husband, he thought. I was so self-centred. I knew what I wanted but didn't think of her needs. She just wanted a decent home and a family somewhere in the home counties. I suppose she got that. I hope she's happy.

Then he thought of Marion and the happiness he had experienced in the few months they had spent together. Perhaps there was a chance to replicate that, if the situation was different. Here, in this place, he was too unsettled, too distracted, too mesmerised by the sensory riches of the surroundings. Perhaps, in London, in calmer circumstances… perhaps? She said she'd call. He wanted the phone to ring. He wanted it to be Marion, saying how much she was looking forward to seeing him on Monday. How much she had missed him and that she was sorry she had made a hasty decision in leaving. Should he call her? No, that would pressure her too much. Must give her time.

But he would leave now, he thought. Time to go. Would he miss the territory? He had so much relished the professional and personal experience it gave him. But, unlike Doug, he felt no political affinity to the place. He felt like a stranger — a foreigner — who could not share the emotion and sacrifice for the cause. Although he felt pity and sorrow for the students and those fighting for the independence of the place, his solidarity was detached, considered, unlike the visceral passion with which Doug supported the movement.

With such ideas swirling around in his mind, Jack finally fell asleep. The only sound in the bedroom was now the low hum of the air-conditioning unit.

He was oblivious to the political storm clouds gathering outside. The city streets still heaved with masses of angry and distraught citizens, demanding retribution and justice for their young people so senselessly slaughtered. They gathered around the federation offices and pelted them with rocks and bottles, while the officials inside cowered, in fear of their lives. Elsewhere, leading Democrat politicians were honing their speeches for the most decisive press conference of their lives. Brandon was also busy among them, briefing officials and journalists, and prompting students as to the way forward.

Doug sat in a taxi, on the way back to his flat, the vehicle stuck in a sea of protesters. He was exhilarated but overwhelmed by the scale of the events unfolding around him — carrying him along like an irresistible ocean current.

Back in Jack's flat, the silence was broken by the phone ringing.

He sat up, shaken from his sleep. Who's that now, he thought, then remembered Marion.

Rushing to the phone, he picked it up.

"Hello, Jack Wilson."

"Jack. Jack. Is that you?"

"Yes, Mum. What's up? Happy Birthday! You're calling early."

"It's your father, Jack. He's had a stroke. He's dead. Your father's dead."